P9-CLS-820

RANDOM
HOUSE
LARGE
PRINT

The Dark Side

Also by Danielle Steel
Available from Random House Large Print

Blessing in Disguise
Silent Night
Turning Point
Beauchamp Hall
In His Father's Footsteps
The Good Fight
The Cast
Accidental Heroes
Fall from Grace
Past Perfect
Fairytale
The Right Time
The Duchess
Against All Odds
Dangerous Games
The Mistress
The Award
Rushing Waters
Magic
The Apartment
Property of a Noblewoman
Blue
Precious Gifts
Undercover
Country
Prodigal Son
Pegasus
A Perfect Life
Power Play
Winners
First Sight
Until the End of Time
Friends Forever
Hotel Vendome
Happy Birthday
One Day At a Time
A Good Woman

Danielle Steel

The Dark Side

A Novel

Published in the United States of America by Random House Large Print in association with Delacorte Press, an imprint of Random House, a division of Penguin Random House LLC, New York.

Cover design: Eileen Carey
Cover photograph: © Irene Lamprakou/Arcangel

The Library of Congress has established a Cataloging-in-Publication record for this title.

ISBN: 978-0-593-16816-5

www.penguinrandomhouse.com/large-print-format-books

FIRST LARGE PRINT EDITION

Printed in the United States of America

10 9 8 7 6 5 4 3 2 1

This Large Print edition published in accord with the standards of the N.A.V.H.

To my darling beloved children,
Beatie, Trevor, Todd, Nick,
Sam, Victoria, Vanessa,
Maxx, and Zara,

May darkness never touch you,
May you live in light
and be ever safe and loved.

I love you with all my heart,
forever and always.

Mommy / ds

The Dark Side

Chapter 1

Zoe and Rose Morgan were the perfect complement to each other as sisters. Zoe had straight, dark, shining hair. Rose had a halo of white-blond curls, which sat like a cap on her head. Zoe's features were beautiful, though sharp and well defined for a child so young. Rose looked like a cherub, everything about her was round, including her small, smiling face. Zoe was long and angular, all legs and arms, like a young colt. There were no sharp edges to Rose. She was loving and soft. She had learned to blow kisses before she could say hello. Rose was an irresistible child. Zoe had always been shy, although having the irrepressible, fearless Rose as her little sister made Zoe bolder and stronger. Rose loved following her around. It annoyed Zoe at times, particularly if Rose ran off with one of Zoe's toys, and Zoe gave her a sound scolding for it when she did. Zoe was three when Rose was born and had stared in wonderment at her in the bassinet. Rose had bonded with her immediately. Her face lit up whenever Zoe walked into the room.

Zoe was six when Rose was diagnosed with leukemia at three. Zoe didn't know what it meant. Her mother had explained it to her, that it was a sickness Rose had in her blood. She would have "treatments," and have to go to the hospital and stay there sometimes. She was going to have "chemotherapy." When they were alone, Zoe had asked her mother if it would hurt, and she said it might, and it would make Rose sick for a little while, but in the end, it would make her well. She would be fine again. Zoe saw something in her mother's eyes then that she had never seen there before: fear. She could see that both her parents were afraid. Her father said he was going to take care of her whenever Rose had to go to the hospital, so their mother could stay there with Rose. And when Rose got well again, everything would go back to normal. He promised her that it would, and she believed him. She could tell that he believed it too.

Three days later, Rose left for the hospital, with Beth, their mother. Zoe remembered that she had a little pink suitcase and took her favorite teddy bear, Pinkie, with her. She was gone for four weeks, and their mother stayed with her, and came home for an hour or two every few days, to get more clothes and give Zoe a hug. When Rose came home the white-blond curls were gone. Rose slept a lot, and she lay on the couch, but she wanted to play when Zoe came home from school. And Zoe was happy to have Rose and their mom home again.

Rose stayed at the hospital a lot in that first year, and she had something called a bone marrow transplant. Their mom gave her some of her bone marrow, and it helped. Rose got better after that, just like Brad, their father, had said. Her curls grew back, although they were a darker blond, and her eyebrows and eyelashes came back too. Zoe didn't yell at her anymore when Rose took her toys. She was just happy Rose was home, and so were their mom and dad. Zoe was used to spending most of her time with her father by then. It wasn't quite as good as being with her mom, who always had everything perfectly organized and in control, but he was almost as good at it as her mom was by the end of that first year. Zoe told him what he didn't know, like how she liked her toast, and which cereal was Rose's. He did the laundry, made the beds, picked her up at school, cooked the meals. He let Zoe help him make s'mores for dessert every night if she wanted them. He read her bedtime stories, and they always called Rose before Zoe went to sleep, if she was at the hospital that week. They had a party for just the four of them every time Rose came home. They made cupcakes for her, or baked a cake. They put candles on them, and Rose got to blow them out. It was like her birthday every other week.

Zoe knew she was lucky that her father could stay with her because he worked at home, and had a studio upstairs. He had been an animation artist at Disney studios, until he wrote a book about the adventures of Ollie the Mouse, who loved to travel and went everywhere. He did the illustrations himself. The first Ollie book was an instant success. After the second one, a TV show was produced, which led to merchandising and Ollie dolls. Brad left Disney then, and moved to San Francisco with Beth, right before Zoe was born. They had never expected the book to be such a huge success. It was sold all over the world in sixteen languages. Zoe loved it when he read the Ollie books to her, and a new one came out every year. Eventually, Ollie married a little white mouse named Marina, who was a ballerina, and they had twin baby mice named Charlie and Seraphina. Their family was complete and their adventures continued. From the time Beth and Brad moved to San Francisco and Zoe was born, Brad continued to work at home in his studio. When she was old enough, Zoe loved going upstairs to visit him. She had a little table in a corner, with her own drawing pad and colored pencils and crayons, and later paints. She loved drawing Ollie and Marina and the twins too.

Zoe's mother didn't work. She had worked in a hospital in L.A. as a surgical nurse before they'd moved, but once Zoe was born in San Francisco, Beth became a full-time mom. They went to the park every day, baked cookies, went to swimming lessons and play groups, and took a music class for moms and little kids. They were busy all the time. Zoe had just started preschool when Rose was born. She kept everyone busy, and Zoe felt like their family was complete, just like Ollie and Marina and their twins in their dad's books. Zoe's mother even let Zoe take Rose to show-and-tell at school, so everyone could see her, when she was four months old. Rose smiled at everyone while Zoe held her, and then she fell asleep. Her visit was a big success, and everyone agreed that she looked like an angel. The children commented that Zoe and her baby sister looked very different, except that they both had big blue eyes like their mom.

Zoe loved living in San Francisco. It was the only home she had ever known, and she loved their rambling old house with a view of the bay and the Golden Gate Bridge. She and Rose shared a room, and there was lots of space to play. At first, Rose slept in a basket in their parents' room, next to their parents' bed, and when she was too big to sleep in the basket anymore, Rose slept in a crib across from Zoe's bed. Zoe would tiptoe over to peek at her, sound asleep in her crib, and then go back to her own bed. By the time Rose got sick, they were both sleeping in beds. Their father had painted a magical garden on the wall, with fairies flying over it. Zoe loved it. They had the best room in the world. When Rose was in the hospital, Zoe would look at her empty bed at night and miss her. The room seemed sad when she was gone. She counted the days until Rose came home.

Zoe loved her status as big sister. Even if Rose was a pest at times, Zoe loved her. Later on, her memories of her first six years, until Rose got sick, were as close to perfect as you could get, with adoring parents, happy days, and a little sister who was fun to play with. She couldn't wait for Rose to start school with her, but she started a year late, since she'd been sick.

Rose had a year after the bone marrow transplant, and then the leukemia came back with a vengeance, and made her even sicker than she'd been before. Her hair fell out again, she had to have something called a port, because she got chemotherapy so often and they couldn't use the veins in her arms anymore. From the time she was diagnosed again, and was no longer in remission, her deterioration was slow but steady over the next two years. Her life was a living hell. At nine, Zoe understood that now.

She saw her parents crying lots of times, and their mom was almost always gone. She never left Rose alone at the hospital, and Zoe hardly saw her. There was too much going on, too many decisions to make, too many doctors they had to see and call, or meet at the hospital. Her father went a lot too, and Zoe stayed with the neighbors when he had to be at meetings with the doctors, or went to visit Rose. Rose usually came home between rounds of chemotherapy, but she cried a lot, and slept most of the time. Zoe watched her slip away inch by inch. Their mother said Rose was going to get well, but their father didn't make promises anymore. When Zoe asked him what was going to happen, he said he didn't know. She could always tell from their eyes when bad things were happening, which was most of the time during the last year. Zoe was nine then, and Rose was six. She still looked like a little girl, but her eyes were very old. Sometimes when she was home, Zoe would sit next to her bed on the floor and hold her hand. She asked Zoe once if she thought the fairies would come down from Heaven to get her, as tears rolled down Zoe's cheeks, and Zoe told her sternly she wasn't going anywhere.

Zoe had heard her parents say that Rose had a rare form of particularly virulent leukemia. Other children had recovered from different kinds of the disease, but the one Rose had was harder to beat. The doctors tried everything. Zoe could no longer remember a time when her parents laughed at anything, smiled, or relaxed. They looked terrified all the time, and in the end, no matter how hard they tried, or how lovingly Beth nursed her, Rose slipped away in her sleep at the hospital one night. She had told their mother that Pinkie, the pink teddy bear she had slept with all her life, wanted to sleep with Zoe when she went to Heaven. When their mother handed it to Zoe the next morning, Zoe knew what had happened. She felt like someone had ripped her heart out of her chest. Rose would never come home again.

Zoe was ten when her sister died, and Rose was seven. She had fought the battle for four years, and the moment she died, their parents turned into people Zoe didn't know. Her mother lost all hope and turned into a zombie. After the funeral, which was unbearable for all three of them, Beth no longer got out of bed. Brad wanted her to see a doctor but she wouldn't. She said nothing would bring Rose back, so what did it matter now. He wandered around the house day and night like a ghost. Zoe tried to reach out to both of them, but nothing she said or did helped. There had been so many happy times in their lives before Rose died, and none that Zoe could remember after that. Their home became a ghost town, as Zoe lay in bed at night, clutching Pinkie to her chest, trying to picture Rose's angelic face before she got sick. All she could remember now was how she'd looked without hair, ravaged by the disease. Old photographs of her no longer looked like the Rose she knew.

For the four years of Rose's illness, their parents' lives had focused entirely on her needs. Zoe's had to take a backseat, and her father had promised again and again that one day their life would get back to normal, but that time had never come, even once

Rose was gone. They were too stunned and broken to deal with Zoe after it happened. All they could think of was their own grief, which filled the house like a numbing gas and rendered them unable to relate to anyone else. They could barely function or speak, even to each other, and didn't want to. Zoe was always just beyond their ability to focus on too. Brad tried a little harder to reach out to her, with no success. Beth just couldn't. She had been a beacon of hope for all of them for four years, but her light had finally gone out when Rose's did. Her emotional tanks were dry, for everyone, even herself. She had given all she had to give to her youngest daughter, and Zoe seemed to be beyond her horizon. Beth slept almost all the time. Brad saw to it that Zoe got to and from school, and then signed her up for a carpool. He ordered in meals at night, mostly fast food.

Zoe always had the feeling that in their heart of hearts they believed that the best of their children had died, and they had been left with the "other one." Their disappointment seemed total. Rose had been the little angel among them, and now she was gone. It never occurred to Zoe that if she had died and not Rose, they might have felt the same way about her. Zoe didn't believe that. In their unrelenting grief, they made it clear that she was second best. They talked of Rose's absence when they talked at all, and never of Zoe's presence, as though she had become invisible. For two years after Rose's death, her parents were emotionally inaccessible. She had to learn to take care of herself, to meet her own needs and expect nothing from them, which was all she was getting.

Her father was the first to awaken from the nightmare that had engulfed them. Zoe had just turned twelve, her parents waited for her in the kitchen when she came home from school, and told her they were separating. The pain had just deepened for her. She had clung to a wisp of hope that things would get back to normal again one day, but now even that hope was dashed. Her father told her the bad news as they sat at the kitchen table. Her mother said nothing, as though she had become mute. He explained that he'd wanted to go into therapy with her, and Beth had refused. He gentled it by saying she wasn't ready. She looked dead as she sat staring at the dishwasher and not her daughter and didn't speak, or try to explain what she was feeling. They all knew. She had given everything of herself to her daughter and lost her anyway, and now she was losing her husband too. She didn't have the strength to resist. She was drowning, or already had.

"Can't you two try to work it out?" Zoe asked in a pleading tone, as Brad slowly shook his head and Beth said nothing.

"I don't think so," he said softly, glancing at the woman who was still his wife, but was now unrecognizable as the woman he had loved. He couldn't imagine her becoming that person again, and she refused to try. She had been turning down his pleas for marriage counseling since grief had overwhelmed them, with devastating results. "We'll see what happens," Brad said vaguely. He told Zoe they weren't getting divorced yet, but he felt he needed counseling to help him get over Rose's death. He thought they all did, but Beth insisted Zoe was fine. She was getting good grades in school, wasn't on drugs or acting out. She was a child, she would survive it. Beth wasn't sure that she herself would. She thought probably not. And she felt Brad's wanting to get past it was a form of betrayal. His wanting to get over their crippling grief felt to her like an abandonment of their daughter, and his wife. She was intending to mourn forever, to honor Rose, while once again overlooking Zoe in the process. Zoe was used to it by now, from both of them. They only thought of themselves and what they were feeling. After all they had done for Rose, she had never before realized how selfish they were.

Brad moved out that weekend. He'd found a studio apartment on Broadway in a building that people referred to as the Heartbreak Hotel. It was usually the first step in a divorce, while people got their bearings. There was nowhere for Zoe to stay in the apartment. He took her to dinner once a week, which meant that her main caretaker for all four years of her sister's illness, and the two years since, had jumped ship and become an occasional visitor. Her mother was even more withdrawn after he left. She hardly came out of her room anymore. Zoe cooked her own meals in the kitchen, cans of ravioli or spaghetti, frozen dinners her mother bought and left in the freezer for her to prepare. Beth hardly ate and had lost a shocking amount of weight. Zoe had gotten much thinner too. They all had.

Six months after he had moved out, Brad told Zoe over dinner that he had filed for divorce. Beth was still refusing any form of therapy, and would barely speak to him. There was no malice in the separation, or even in the divorce, but there was a total absence of communication. They were completely out of step with each other, and Brad explained to Zoe, at the tender age of twelve and a half, that their marriage had died with Rose. Beth didn't deny it. It was a relief for Beth in a way that he expected nothing more from her. All he wanted was out after two and a half years of intense mourning. He wanted to heal and move on. Beth simply couldn't do it, at least not yet, and she wouldn't even try.

Zoe knew her father was in therapy, and he mentioned vaguely that he had changed therapists around the time he filed for divorce. He didn't explain why, until Zoe turned thirteen and the divorce was final. He had begun dating his therapist, and ethically, she had insisted that he find another therapist, and had helped him do it, a man. His original therapist, whom he had seen for six months, was a woman named Pam, which was all Zoe knew about her. Brad had just turned forty when the divorce became final, Pam was thirty-five, had never been married and had no children, and both of them wanted a fresh start in life. Her lover of several years had died, and Brad had lost his youngest child. They married within months of the divorce, and moved to Santa Barbara, where Brad bought a house and Pam joined another practice.

Zoe met Pam shortly before they got married, and felt disloyal to her mother when she did. Pam was a nice woman, and they both insisted that they wanted Zoe to visit whenever she wanted to, their home would be open to her at all times. But Beth managed to convey that whenever Zoe went to stay with them, she committed an act of treason. She didn't have to say it, the message came through her pores, in her days of even heavier silence when Zoe got back. There was a stone wall between Zoe and her mother that she couldn't scale, and hadn't been able to for three years since Rose's death. She still slept with Rose's teddy bear, Pinkie, who felt like her only friend.

She started high school at fourteen, the same month that Brad and Pam's first child was born, ten months after the wedding Zoe hadn't attended, out of loyalty to her mother. Her new half-sibling was a baby boy named Christopher. Her father was over the moon about him. He had always wanted a son, and now he had one. Zoe felt left out of the circle of their love, and couldn't bring herself to feel anything for the baby. Her sense of isolation was complete a year later, when their second child was born, a baby girl they named Ashley, who added insult to injury by looking shockingly like Rose, with white-blond hair that framed her face in the same way. Zoe couldn't bear looking at her. She was fifteen when Ashley was born, five years after Rose's death. Coincidentally, Beth went back to work then, as a nurse, after taking a refresher class. Her mother working changed very little in Zoe's life, except that instead of sleeping all day as she had for five years, she was at work. She had been absent from Zoe's life for what seemed like an eternity by then.

Beth began dating a doctor a year later, when Zoe was sixteen. He had children older than Zoe, whom she decided not to meet, and Beth didn't insist. They weren't getting married, they were only dating. Zoe went to Santa Barbara as seldom as possible. She had excluded herself from both her parents' lives, just as they had excluded her for years. She was used to taking care of herself by then, and had been since she was ten. She was remarkably self-sufficient.

Zoe plunged herself into her studies all through high school, and had few friends. She didn't want to explain to anyone the reasons for the strangeness of her home life, and her lack of engagement with her parents. Both of them had moved on, and accidentally left her behind, like a piece of luggage they had overlooked.

Neither of them was surprised when she was valedictorian of her class. They had come to expect nothing less of her, and didn't seem to realize how remarkable it was that she had outstanding grades despite her lonely home life and lack of emotional support from her parents. She had gotten in to almost every college she applied to, and accepted a place at Yale, as a pre-med student. Her goal was to become a pediatrician in underdeveloped countries and save the lives of children who might die otherwise.

Both her parents had come to her high school graduation and said they were proud of her, which she found hard to believe. They barely knew her or anything about her. She felt as though they had divorced her before they even dissolved their marriage. The family she had grown up in for six happy years had disappeared. They were strangers to each other now. Zoe found every excuse she could not to go home to either of them for holidays when she was in college. Seeing her half-sister had remained acutely painful. Ashley was three when Zoe started college, and continued to remind everyone of Rose. She was the image of her.

Zoe graduated from Yale with honors. She hadn't enjoyed her years in college, but had done well.

She had dated very little, and remained closed with everyone she met.

She was accepted into medical school at Duke, and excelled for two years, when a summer of soul-searching made her realize that she didn't want to spend the next seven years in medical school, and as an intern and resident. She wanted more instant gratification, and to do some good in the world.

She took a leave of absence from medical school and went to work for a non-profit, a shelter for abused children on the Upper West Side in New York. She was direly needed there and could relate to the children, who were in deep physical and emotional pain. The reasons for their grief were different from hers. Most of them had been physically abandoned by their parents. She had been emotionally abandoned, but the agony was similar, and she related to them immediately. The children and her superiors could see Zoe's empathy.

Her medical training was helpful to her, and she eventually got a master's at NYU in the administration of non-profits.

She was twenty-four when she left medical school, and made rapid advances in the hierarchy of the non-profit. She loved the anonymity of living in New York, in a studio apartment she found in the West Village. Her father and Pam visited her whenever he went to see his publisher. Her mother never traveled. She had sold the house in San Francisco by then, and moved into an apartment with the doctor she had dated for almost ten years. Beth told her there was a room for her, but Zoe never used it. She had no desire to stay with either of her parents and they didn't insist. They were both a powerful reminder of a painful past that each of them had managed to survive differently, either by forging new lives or running away, which was Zoe's way of dealing with the past. Whenever they saw her, Pam expressed her concern about her, and told Brad she wished that Zoe would seek therapy. Pam thought she was too removed, too disengaged. There seemed to be a part of her that never really connected with people, even with the children at the shelter, whom she claimed she cared about so much. Pam didn't believe her. But Brad insisted she was doing fine. He always reminded Pam that she'd had remarkable academic success, and was now in a job that satisfied her deeply. He thought she was happy, which wasn't a word Pam would have used to describe her. Both professionally and personally, Pam could sense how abandoned Zoe had felt by all of them, and how scarred she was as a result. Zoe's lack of serious attachment to any man, or even her parents, concerned Pam. Some part of her was missing, had died within her or was too damaged to engage. Outwardly, Zoe appeared to be fully functional, to a high degree, but Pam was afraid it was more of an act than real.

Brad had done well emotionally thanks to Pam, and the love of their children, which had healed him. He cared about Zoe too but no longer knew how to reach her. Beth was happy with the man she lived with, but deeply affected by the loss of her youngest child. She was a quiet woman whose pain was etched on her face.

At twenty-eight, Zoe was assistant administrator of the non-profit in New York, where she still worked. She was considered gifted with abused children and supremely competent. And she met Austin Roberts, handsome, Harvard educated, a well-known child advocacy attorney who took pro bono cases for some of the children at the shelter, and had recently joined the board. He was mesmerized by Zoe, bowled over by her beauty, and enormously impressed by how knowledgeable, dedicated, and talented she was. She was a dazzling combination of beauty and brains, and she was cool and aloof enough with him to provide a challenge he couldn't resist. She turned him down several times before agreeing to have dinner, which felt like a victory.

Zoe was intrigued by his family history. His father was an attorney, his mother had a doctorate in psychology. They were both engaged in philanthropic pursuits. He had two older brothers, both married with children. He was thirty-six, had gone to Harvard undergrad and law school, and had an intensely busy practice. He spoke warmly of his family, and his youth, and she could tell that they were close, unlike her own family which had been shattered by Rose's death. He was also strikingly good-looking, tall, athletic, with dark hair and dark eyes. The evening flew by as they got to know each other, and they saw each other frequently after that. After three months of serious dating, they admitted that they were in love. For Zoe, it was a first. Professionally, they were a perfect match, with common interests in the well-being of disadvantaged children. Personally, they came from opposite poles. He was from a close family and enjoyed spending time with them. He loved his brothers, and their wives and children. Zoe told him of her childhood, her sister's illness, their disrupted home life during her deterioration, and the total collapse of their family after her death. His heart ached as he listened to her. He was touched by how warm and kind she was with his five nephews. They were a family of boys. She was good with children, which he liked. His parents and brothers and their families welcomed her warmly as they got to know her. His mother was particularly touched by the history Austin shared with her and marveled at how whole and well-balanced Zoe was in spite of it.

"She's perfect," Austin said to his mother, beaming.

"It's a wonder she's as sane, warm, and normal as she is," Constance Roberts said, pleased to see her son so happy. "It sounds like she had a very tough time."

"She was basically on her own growing up while they grieved for her sister."

"It happens that way sometimes," Constance responded. "Grief can be incredibly isolating. People mourn at different rates. A lot of marriages don't survive it." Constance liked her immensely, and had enormous compassion for what she'd been through as a young girl. Zoe admitted that she wasn't close to either of her parents as a result. She had kind words for her father's wife, whom she said was a nice woman and a wonderful partner for her father, but she had come into Zoe's life at the wrong time. She'd been in her teens and in pain herself and had never let her in. And it seemed too late to her now. There was too much water under the bridge for all of them, although her father was faithful in his efforts to stay in touch and see her when he came to New York. He had given up trying to convince her to visit them in California. He suspected that his daughter Ashley's striking resemblance to Rose might be part of the problem. Zoe could see it in the family photos her father sent. She had grown to look as they guessed Rose would have if she'd survived.

Austin and Zoe dated for two years before they moved in together, in a small one-bedroom apartment they found in the West Village, near where Zoe had been living. They loved the neighborhood, and furnished the new apartment. They got on famously. When they began living together, she was thirty, and he was thirty-eight, and he wanted to get married sooner rather than later. They wanted to start a family, but neither of them was in a rush, and both of them had demanding careers. His family had accepted her warmly by then, but were discreet and didn't want to push. Austin's mother, Constance, was sure that her parents' divorce made Zoe fearful of making a mistake.

After a year of living together, they finally decided to get married, which they did in the garden of Austin's parents' weekend home in Sag Harbor on Long Island. It was a very small wedding, which was what they wanted. Both of Zoe's parents came, with Pam and Hank, Beth's partner. It was a beautiful summer day, and everyone enjoyed it and felt close, sharing Austin and Zoe's special day. The couple honeymooned in Wyoming, hiking and fishing and riding, which Zoe had learned to like while dating Austin. He loved the peace of the outdoors to balance his often stressful work life, and she had come to appreciate it too. They were in perfect harmony, with common interests.

They came back to New York relaxed and happy. They had agreed to start trying to get pregnant on their honeymoon. It was a romantic adventure trying to do so, which brought them closer. At thirty-one and thirty-nine, after three years together, they both felt ready for parenthood. But Zoe was disappointed month by month, and so was Austin, when nothing happened. It added some tension to their marriage. They'd been married for a year with no results, and went to a fertility specialist at

Zoe's suggestion. The doctor agreed to start an aggressive treatment program with hormone shots for Zoe, which Austin administered. The fertility plan gave them hope that their dreams of a baby would come true.

They went through four attempts at in vitro fertilization, until the final one succeeded fifteen months after they had begun. With real excitement, they were cautiously victorious, and waited three months before they told their families, although Constance suspected it before, but didn't want to be intrusive and ask them, knowing it was a sensitive subject.

Zoe had an easy pregnancy, read every book she could lay her hands on, and was very intense about child rearing theories and the importance of a wholesome pregnancy. She was diligent about her health and the baby's, and she and Austin were both excited. They decided not to find out the baby's sex and be surprised at the birth. She planned to take a four-month maternity leave from the non-profit she was running by then, and Austin was taking three weeks off to help her after the baby came. Zoe insisted she didn't want a nanny or a baby nurse, she wanted to do it all herself, bond with the baby, and emulate her own mother, who had taken care of them without help, and said she had loved it. Zoe's mother was pleased for them when Zoe told her she was pregnant, but she made no plans to come to New York before or after the delivery, and said she couldn't leave work. Zoe could tell it was an excuse, and suspected that bonding with the baby would bring back painful memories for her.

Jaime Rose Roberts made her appearance four hours after Zoe left work on a busy Wednesday. Her water broke as soon as she got to the apartment, and she called Austin immediately. He rushed home from the office where he was working late. The delivery was fast and easy, and everything about it was normal and went smoothly. Jaime lay in her mother's arms afterward. Austin looked at them adoringly. He had never been happier in his life. Jaime was a beautiful baby, and looked just like Zoe, with dark hair and blue eyes. They had chosen the name from one of a dozen books they had. They loved it because **j'aime** meant "I love" in French, and she was certainly one of the most loved infants in the world.

As Zoe held her, she felt something that she hadn't felt since Rose had died. There had been something missing from her life for all those years, the little girl she had loved with all her heart, and had lost so tragically when she was ten. Zoe was thirty-four years old now, and Austin forty-two. For twenty-four years, there had been an aching void in her life without Rose. And now Jaime had arrived to fill it. As she looked from her husband to her daughter, Zoe finally felt complete.

Chapter 2

Before Jaime was born, Zoe felt thoroughly ready to embrace motherhood. She had read so many books, she felt prepared and had many theories of her own. She and Austin were confident, and Zoe had everything organized and under control. Since Jaime was a healthy baby, and the delivery had been natural and without complications, they only spent one night in the hospital, and were then told they could leave. They were both excited at the prospect of bringing their daughter home.

Both sets of grandparents were elated at the news of Jaime's arrival. Jaime was the first grandchild on Zoe's side, and the first girl on Austin's, so she was a star on both sides of the coin. They emailed photographs of her to everyone, and the entire family agreed that she was exquisite. She weighed over eight pounds and looked like a healthy, robust baby.

She was sleeping peacefully in a bassinet in Zoe's room at the hospital the day after she was born, when Zoe moved into high gear, and asked to see the attending pediatrician. He had to sign the baby out anyway for them to leave, and looked startled when Zoe asked in detail about the various tests that had been administered as part of the routine after a birth. Zoe had read about all of them, knew how they were scored, and assured the doctor she knew what the results meant, which impressed Austin. She was thorough about everything she touched and took her responsibilities seriously, motherhood being the most important one of all, as far as she was concerned. She was satisfied with the test results the doctor shared with them. He gave them a few helpful tips for their first few days at home, how to manage the nursing, how long to nurse, what to do if she got cracked nipples, and what not to be alarmed by, since they were brand new parents and this was their first child. He assured them that they could get the baby on a schedule in the first few weeks, and Zoe looked at him in disapproval.

"Putting them on a nursing schedule can cause serious psychological damage later on. It amounts to withholding nourishment from them, and will make them feel as though you're starving them. I'm not going to do that to my daughter," Zoe said firmly. She was very intense about it, and definite in her ideas, as Austin and the doctor exchanged a look. Austin hadn't realized until then that Zoe was opposed to schedules.

"If you don't try to work out some kind of routine, your milk supply could become erratic and she might not get enough to eat, and you and your husband won't get much sleep," the doctor said gently, realizing how inexperienced they were. So far, Zoe had done all the reading, and she had all the theories and information. Austin was planning to leave that up to her. She had had stacks of baby books on her night table for months, and was annoyed when he didn't have time to read them. She wanted them to be informed modern parents, on the cutting edge about the baby's upbringing and health. She had gotten increasingly intense about it as the birth approached.

"I'm sure we'll figure it out," Austin said calmly. "And my mother and sisters-in-law can help with advice." Austin was eager to leave the hospital, take the baby home, and begin their life as parents of a beautiful baby girl.

"Good luck," the doctor said warmly, after he signed the release form. Their own pediatrician had been in to check Jaime early that morning and she had stopped in to see Zoe. They were going to her office in five days. Zoe had already met her and interviewed her at length, when she was six months pregnant. Cathy Clark was a competent, well-recommended pediatrician, and Zoe liked the mix of serious, warm, modern, relaxed, but thorough medicine that she espoused. She was three years older than Zoe, had gone to medical school at Duke too, and was intrigued to hear that Zoe had completed two years of medical school, along with her master's degree. She was very impressed with them as prospective parents, and also by the intelligent, meticulous questions Zoe had asked before and after the birth.

Zoe had shared with Dr. Clark some of the theories and methods she planned to use with Jaime, and also the fact that she was going to care for Jaime herself for four months until she went back to work. She didn't want to miss a moment with her, and Cathy Clark could sense a super-mom in the making and was in favor of it. She enjoyed working with moms who were responsible, informed, and intelligent, and Zoe was all of those.

Cathy Clark wasn't married and had no children of her own, but was a very dedicated physician, who loved children. She liked Zoe's energy, thirst to learn, and enthusiasm.

"She's a very lucky little girl, and you're going to be great parents," she said confidently before she left Zoe's hospital room to visit another patient, who had given birth to twins. Zoe had liked Cathy immediately when she'd met her, and appreciated the fact that she hadn't dismissed any of Zoe's theories, which she had yet to put into practice.

Dr. Clark's only warning was not to go overboard about the demand feedings, and to be sure to give herself time between feeds to produce enough milk, or they'd have a hungry baby on their hands. So far it all sounded simple to Zoe and Austin, and more than manageable, although he looked a little daunted by all the equipment Zoe said they needed for the baby. The ultra-sophisticated car seat Zoe had bought was tricky, and Austin struggled with it when he had to figure it out for the first time leaving the hospital. Zoe put Jaime into it, and she woke up looking startled and started to cry.

"I'm afraid to pinch something like one of her tiny fingers," he said, looking anxious, as he did up all the buckles and straps. Because she was so young, she had to face backward in case they got into an accident. Zoe looked calm as she got into the front seat, and the baby went back to sleep. It was a short distance from NYU hospital to their apartment, and ten minutes later, they were home, to the apartment they had longed to bring their baby to. Now it felt like a proving ground for all her theories and how adequate they would be as parents. Zoe became instantly tense from the moment they arrived.

Zoe carried the baby, wrapped in a blanket, while Austin managed the car seat, two suitcases, and an enormous pink teddy bear Zoe's father had had delivered by the hospital gift shop. He and Pam were planning to come to see the baby soon.

While Zoe was pregnant, they had moved into a duplex apartment with a second bedroom, in the same building. Zoe looked proud and confident again as they put Jaime in a Moses basket with pink ribbons on a rolling stand when they got upstairs, and she carried it up a short flight of stairs to their bedroom, placed it next to the bed, and lay down. She was more tired than she'd expected to be, but it was less than twenty-four hours since she'd given birth. She was having hot flashes which the nurses had told her were from the change of hormones, and her milk hadn't come in yet. She was staring at the beautiful baby in the basket, as Jaime screwed up her face and let out a howl. Zoe started to look nervous then, uncertain about what had made Jaime cry.

Austin came into the room, helped Zoe change the baby, which turned into a two-person operation, and then watched in wonder as Zoe unbuttoned her blouse and put the baby to her breast, as she had done in the hospital. She made it look so natural and simple, and then winced as the infant latched on. They had warned her it might hurt at first, but each time the pain was sharper than she expected, and Jaime sucked hard. She was only getting colostrum, the substance Zoe provided for the first day or two, until the milk came in. She smiled as she looked down at her after a few minutes. Jaime was the most beautiful sight she had ever seen. She only drank for a moment and then fell asleep, and Zoe left her at her breast, while Austin went to make them lunch. He came back in a few minutes with sandwiches, and Jaime woke up and tried to nurse again. She clearly wanted more than Zoe had to give, which made Zoe anxious and look worried, as Austin tried to reassure her. Zoe was less confident now that they were home on their own, without the nurses she'd been able to call on at the hospital.

Jaime spent the entire day nursing, which was the theory Zoe had adopted and seemed the right one to her, but by the end of the afternoon, her nipples were raw and red, and the baby was crying constantly, which sounded like cries of anguish to Zoe, just as the pediatrician at the hospital had warned. It was too soon for her to get any milk, and Zoe's breasts were already sore. She went to take a shower while Austin held Jaime, and the baby cried the whole time Zoe was in the shower. Austin was looking frazzled when she came back to bed.

"I think she's hungry, Zoe," he said, looking worried. "Are you sure she's getting enough of the other stuff to hold her over till your milk comes in?" He felt helpless and inept.

"No, she's not, my milk isn't in yet, this is just the practice round," and her nipples were already burning and cracked. The baby finally went back to sleep, and Zoe's milk came in with a rush two hours later and poured all over the bed. Her breasts were pounding, and she picked up the baby and woke her to nurse, which made Jaime howl until she settled at the breast, and then choked at how fast the milk was coming, and couldn't drink fast enough or seem to get the hang of it. All three of them were novices, and Zoe and Austin were both looking stressed as he tried to suggest how to do it, and Zoe snapped at him that she knew the correct position of the breast, she'd read all the books on breast-feeding, but she couldn't seem to make it work. The baby was getting drenched, and Zoe's nightgown was soaking wet. The books hadn't mentioned that.

"My mother said it's easiest to nurse," he said, looking frustrated, as the baby cried and Zoe looked as though she might too.

"Your mother had her last baby forty-two years ago," Zoe snapped at him. "Maybe she doesn't remember this part. I've got the name of a lactation specialist if we need one," Zoe said, trying to settle the baby against her wet nightgown, and guide her pouring breast into Jaime's mouth, as she choked again.

"What's a lactation specialist?" Austin looked confused.

"They teach you how to nurse," Zoe said, visibly unnerved. This was not going as she'd planned. At least not yet. She had thought the baby would know what to do instinctively, but she didn't. She was as inexperienced as her parents.

"Can't you figure it out for yourself? Women have been doing this for thousands of years. It can't be that complicated," Austin said casually, as Zoe bristled.

"Why don't you try it, then?" she said, annoyed. Nursing was proving to be stressful and harder than she thought, and one of her breasts was bleeding.

"I'd love to, but I don't have what she wants. Do you want a glass of wine?" he offered innocently, and Zoe looked shocked.

"Of course not. I'm not going to drink while I'm nursing." She had been diligent about not doing so while she was pregnant, and was terrified of fetal alcohol syndrome, but there was no risk of that now, so it seemed harmless to him. Zoe treated him like a criminal at the suggestion.

"Maybe she'll sleep better between feedings if you drink some wine." He was half serious and she could see it. She changed the baby then, took off her own wet nightgown, put on a fresh one, and a few minutes later, the baby was crying again. Zoe put her to the breast. Jaime started to choke on the fast flow of milk and then figured out how to do it, and fell asleep two minutes later, before she'd had a full feeding, which was supposed to last forty minutes, twenty on each side. No one had explained the timing issue to Jaime, who kept falling asleep after two minutes at the breast, so every time she woke up she was starving and then passed out again at the first breast and never got to the second one, which felt to Zoe like it was going to explode.

"They ought to come with an owner's manual," Austin said, joking, trying to lighten the moment. The nursing had been difficult since they got home, and the baby was fussy, hungry, frustrated, and tired, and so were they. Zoe hated feeling so incompetent, and Austin had never seen her that way. Normally she controlled every situation. Her ineptitude at nursing made her seem so vulnerable, which touched him. He drank the wine that Zoe had refused, just as she started to cry.

"What kind of mother am I? I can't even figure out how to nurse. I'm calling the lactation specialist tomorrow." She looked like a little girl and he leaned over and kissed her. Their first hours at home had been anxiety inducing and confusing, which neither of them had expected. They were both people who usually did everything right on the first try.

"Why don't you just relax. The baby doesn't know how to do it either. We all need to get used to each other. You'll figure it out eventually. It can't be that complicated, Zoe. Just take it easy. Why don't we watch TV for a while?" The baby howled as he said it, and continued to cry for the next ten minutes, until Zoe put the breast in her mouth, which quieted the baby, and then Zoe let out a scream.

"She really hurts." There were tears in her eyes from the pain.

"She's been chomping on you all day. If I did that, you'd kill me," he teased her and turned on the TV, which added more noise and chaos to the scene, as the baby continued crying, and Zoe joined her. She picked up her cellphone and called the lactation expert a few minutes later, and left a message to call first thing the next morning. She said that she had a serious problem with a one-day-old baby who wasn't nursing. She made it sound urgent and alarming.

By ten o'clock that night, Austin and Zoe were exhausted, the baby was asleep in the Moses basket and had been on the breast for most of the day and evening, and Zoe's breasts were so tender she cried every time the baby latched on to nurse. When Austin's mother called and he told her about it, she reassured him that the baby would settle in during the next few weeks, and Zoe would get used to nursing. Austin hoped so. The first day had not been the peaceful idyllic scene he'd imagined, and Zoe either cried or snapped at him every time he spoke to her. This was not the calm, confident woman he knew. He could see that she was genuinely in pain every time she tried to feed the baby, who acted like she was starving, but either choked and wouldn't nurse or fell asleep before she had a full feed. It was beginning to seem like a heroically difficult project, and not the simple, natural process it was supposed to be.

The baby slept for about an hour, and Austin and Zoe dozed off until the baby started crying again and woke them both. Zoe tried all the techniques she'd read about so diligently, but the baby was too frantic to cooperate and just screamed. The piercing sound of her baby crying cut through Zoe like a knife, and she looked at Austin in despair.

"I could pump, and we could give her breast milk in a bottle," she said, remembering the suggestion from a book.

"That sounds convoluted to me." It would be so much simpler if the baby would just nurse.

Zoe handed the baby to him then, still screaming, went to get a large cumbersome box out of her closet, and pulled out a machine that resembled something from Dr. Frankenstein's laboratory. It looked torturous to him.

"What's that?"

"A breast pump," she said, reading the instructions carefully. "I got it for when I go back to work. I can freeze the milk and leave it at home. And I bought a smaller pump to take to work."

"Won't that thing hurt more than she does?" He looked worried. He had seen how red and raw her nipples were when she changed her nightgown. "Why don't you try nursing her again?" he suggested gently over the baby's desperate screams. They had to find a way to feed her, whatever it took, and he didn't want to seem critical of Zoe. He had no idea what to do either, and was silently wishing they'd hired a baby nurse to teach them, at least for the first few weeks. He had no idea why Zoe was so opposed to it. For their first baby, they clearly needed help. They were intelligent, highly educated, sensible people, but this was all new to them. The baby hadn't had a decent feeding since they got home from the hospital that morning, and he and Zoe looked beaten up. He was exhausted, and was hoping they'd get some sleep that night. It was beginning to seem unlikely that they'd sleep at all.

Zoe tried again then, and this time Jaime took the breast more peacefully, and managed ten whole minutes on one side before she fell asleep. Zoe stroked her cheek to try to wake her for the other side, but Jaime was already in a deep sleep, and no longer hungry, which left Zoe with one breast drained and the other feeling like it was going to burst, as the milk poured onto the sheets again, and she was lying in a pool of milk.

Bottle feeding was beginning to sound like a great idea to Austin, but he wouldn't have dared say it to Zoe, even in jest, not to mention the aggressive-looking machine that was still sitting on the floor next to the bed. Zoe had already figured out that she was going to be in pain until Jaime nursed from the other breast, but she showed no sign of waking up. In one day, the baby had turned their life upside down. When he said it, Zoe burst into tears and took it as criticism of her.

She put the baby back in the Moses basket, and they managed to doze off for half an hour, Zoe with her breast throbbing, and half an hour later Jaime woke up, hungry again, since she had taken less than half a feed before. Zoe picked her up, and put her at the full breast, with tears running down her cheeks as Jaime latched on fiercely. It hurt like hell, but less than an overfull breast that needed the baby to nurse.

Zoe changed Jaime's diaper after she finished nursing, swaddled her tightly in a little pink blanket, as they had shown her in the hospital, and put the baby back in the basket. She and Austin managed to sleep for an entire hour, before the baby woke up again. She was alternating breasts now, and couldn't stay awake long enough to nurse from both, so Zoe constantly had one breast or the other throbbing, and she was getting less than an hour to rest and produce milk between feeds. She seemed to be producing too much, more than the baby wanted. Her mother had told her that her milk supply would adjust to the baby's needs, but that would take several weeks. Zoe couldn't imagine going through this until then. Childbirth had been easy compared to nursing, but she was worn out by both.

By morning, both parents looked like they'd been shipwrecked, and Jaime had cried for most of the night. Zoe called their pediatrician and told her what was happening. She told Zoe that they needed to get more time between feeds, even if Austin had to take the baby in another room to hold her and distract her, or rock her to sleep, and keep her away from Zoe. It sounded easier than it was, dealing with a howling infant. She assured Zoe that it would settle down as the baby adjusted, and when the lactation specialist came at noon, she told her the same things. She told Zoe not to use the pump, or she would produce even more milk, for the moment she had more than the baby wanted, and they had to get in sync. The whole process seemed exhausting and overwhelming, and the second night was harder than the first. Zoe had never felt so inept in her life. She was failing the most basic element of motherhood, Nursing 101.

By the time they went to Cathy Clark's office for their scheduled visit when Jaime was five days old, Zoe had been in tears for several days, she and Austin were snapping at each other, which they normally never did. Their relationship had been smooth and easy until then. But neither of them had had a decent night's sleep all week. Zoe told the doctor that Jaime had colic. She had read about it, and she showed all the signs. She was worried that Jaime might have a stomach obstruction of some kind which kept her from nursing, and she said that she had had projectile vomiting that morning. Dr. Clark gave Zoe a pamphlet with helpful hints about nursing, calmly reassured them both, and said there was no indication or symptom of an obstruction. Babies vomit, she told them, and real projectile vomiting could go six or eight feet, which wasn't the case here. She wasn't colicky, they didn't have the nursing in sync with the baby's needs yet, and they needed to be patient, and try to relax. She suggested that they hire a night nurse, to help get them on a schedule, and some kind of routine. She said an experienced nurse could have them on the right path in a week or two, and they could get some sleep, all of which would relieve the stress for them. She could see how tense they were, and the baby could feel it too.

"I'm not putting my five-day-old baby on a schedule. That's abusive," Zoe said with a look of steely determination in response to the doctor's suggestion. Austin had never seen Zoe as obsessive about anything as she was about the nursing. "And I don't want anyone handling her except the two of us. We need to bond with her. We don't want a nurse." She spoke for Austin too, although he wanted one desperately. He wanted his wife back, not the stressed anxious wreck she was becoming ever since the baby was born. The gentle woman he loved had turned into a shrew.

"You already are on a schedule, just not a good one," Dr. Clark said smoothly, "and I can give you a list of reliable nurses if you want to try one. We've used them all before. It might put some semblance of order back into your life," she offered helpfully. Austin looked pleadingly at Zoe, and she shook her head.

"I can't do this every night when I go back to work," he warned her, and Zoe looked daggers at him. They were suddenly becoming adversaries instead of allies.

"She'll be fine in three weeks," Zoe tried to sound convincing. The books had told her that healthy babies adjust after the first month.

"Not if we don't train her, and you and I don't know how to do it. We've demonstrated that amply in the last five days." He sounded annoyed too. She was being unreasonable and it seemed ridiculous to him.

"She's not a dog, for heaven's sake, or a trained seal," Zoe shot at him.

"No," Cathy Clark said quietly, trying to calm them, "but babies can be stubborn, and they're clever little beings even at this age. They know when they've got you on the run, and they take advantage of it. They can feel it when someone is confident and experienced. It's comforting for them. I don't think it's abusive to put a baby on a schedule." Cathy sounded calm to reassure them.

"And a good baby nurse could teach you a few tricks of the trade too. Our parents are usually very pleased with them." She was all in favor of it.

"I don't need tricks, I'm her mother. I don't want her to get confused about who is," Zoe said desperately, feeling ganged up on.

"She won't." Cathy smiled at them. "You're the milk producer. A nurse might help you get some sleep, which would be good for you." She looked at Zoe when she said it, but she wasn't convinced. They thanked the doctor and left a few minutes later. Zoe was quiet when they got in the car, and Jaime fell asleep as soon as they started moving. She was exhausted from the doctor's visit, and so were they, after five nights of almost no sleep.

"Why are you so against at least having a night nurse?" Austin asked her, it seemed irrational to him. His mother thought they should have one too. "My mom had baby nurses for us, and I'm not hopelessly screwed up, or confused about who my mother is. And none of us are axe murderers." Zoe was being rigid and inflexible, which was new to him.

"We don't need a baby nurse," Zoe said stubbornly. "She has us. I don't want a stranger handling our baby."

"She'd probably be safer with a nurse than with us, if we don't know what we're doing, and neither of us does." Instinct had not kicked in for either of them, or the baby yet.

"We just have to get used to nursing, **without** putting her on a schedule. On demand is better for her, even if it's hard on us. Every book I read said so."

"I haven't slept since the day before you gave birth," he grumbled. He normally wasn't a complainer, but sleep deprivation was affecting both of them. They had been arguing all week, about everything, and feeding times were fraught with tension, which he was sure the baby could feel too. His mother had dropped by to visit, and she felt sorry for both of them. They were nervous, stressed, exhausted, and confused. And Zoe didn't want advice from anyone. She had her own ideas, and intended to stick to them.

They drove home in silence, and Austin carried the car seat upstairs with the baby sleeping in it, and as soon as they walked into the apartment, Jaime woke up and started to scream. It was time to feed her, but Zoe's breasts were aching, and the doctor had warned her of the danger of getting a breast infection with cracked nipples. It wasn't dangerous, but would be even more painful than what she was dealing with now. She had given her a cream to provide some relief.

Zoe picked Jaime up and took her to bed with her. She settled back against the pillows the way the lactation specialist had told her to do, with one arm propped up on a stack of pillows. She opened her blouse and put Jaime on her breast, and let out a short scream when Jaime latched on, but she was so hungry she emptied both breasts for the first time and went back to sleep while Zoe held her. She looked up and saw Austin watching them with a worried look.

"How was that? Any better?" he asked hopefully. He felt sorry for Zoe, she wanted to do everything perfectly, as she always did, and this was hard for her. She was determined to be the consummate mother. She hated feeling so incompetent, and she always measured herself against her own mother, who had seemed like the perfect mother to her when she and Rose were children. Everything had fallen apart when Rose died, but before that, Beth had always known what to do. It made Zoe miss her now, she needed her wise advice, but her mother couldn't come. She couldn't get the time off from her job in the pediatric ICU at UCSF. And Zoe didn't want to admit to her mother how inadequate she felt. Her mother had taken care of her child with cancer for four years, and Zoe couldn't figure out how to nurse her baby after a week.

Things started to get better in the second week. Jaime was going almost two hours between feedings, although the goal was three. They weren't forcing a schedule on her, and Jaime was regulating herself, which was Zoe's goal. She wanted to meet the baby's needs, not force theirs on her. The theory was good but the reality didn't work so well. At the end of two weeks, the nursing was still just as painful for Zoe, but at least the baby wasn't screaming all the time, although she got fussier at night. She had day and night reversed, which Zoe's sister-in-law said was normal. She'd had the same problem with their twins, one had been fussy in the daytime, the other at night, and they'd been up around the clock with them, but they had hired a nurse. She said she would have lost her mind if she hadn't, and Eric would have divorced her.

The one thing Zoe and Austin agreed on was that they could no longer imagine how they could manage a newborn and a toddler, if they had another child. They had always said they wanted three children, but after a year of hormone shots, four rounds of in vitro fertilization, and now a rough beginning with what Zoe still insisted was a colicky baby, whatever the doctor said, the idea of doing it again was overwhelming, and inconceivable to both of them. Austin said it to her one night when the baby was finally asleep after screaming for three hours for no apparent reason, which Zoe insisted proved she had colic.

"I couldn't do this again, Zoe. I think Jaime is it for me." She looked at him sadly for a minute and nodded. It was early to bring it up, but the past two weeks had shaken them both.

"I've been thinking the same thing. I always assumed I could handle two or three children, but with everything there is to worry about, and that could happen to her, I think one is it for me too."

It seemed too soon to make the decision, but they were both sure.

"Nothing is going to happen to Jaime," Austin reassured her, and leaned over and kissed her. They had hardly spoken to each other in the last two weeks, except about the baby, or to argue about her. She had completely taken over their lives, and changed their easygoing relationship, which worried Austin. He didn't want to lose Zoe to the baby. He needed her too. And with more children, there would be less time for him. He could see that now. He felt as though he had lost a big part of Zoe. She was already more of a mother than a wife. He hadn't expected that from her. Having a baby was so much harder than they'd anticipated.

Her eyes filled with tears as he said it. "You don't know that nothing will happen to her. My parents thought that about Rose too. Nothing is sure in life. I learned that a long time ago. I **hope** nothing ever happens to her. That's the best we can do, and make sure that we protect her from danger." They already loved her, and Zoe would have given her life for her, even though the past two weeks had been difficult.

"You're a wonderful mother," Austin said gently, and kissed her, and she smiled at him.

"I want to be."

"You already are. The little vampire has turned your boobs into hamburger meat. Remind her that I want them back one day." Zoe smiled at that, and they managed to cuddle for a while, until Jaime woke up again. They were slowly getting the hang of parenting a brand new baby, and they were both pleased that she had gained weight.

The following week was Austin's last week at home from the office before he had to go back to work. Zoe had been grateful to have him there to encourage her, and watch the baby when she wanted to take a shower or wash her hair, or do a load of laundry. They had someone come in to clean twice a week, but the rest of the time, Zoe would be on her own when Austin went back to the office. She knew they'd have to hire a nanny when she went back to work herself, but she didn't want to think about that yet. She realized now how lucky her mother had been to have a husband who worked at home when their daughters were born. Zoe dreaded going back to work now and leaving the baby. Her life of running the shelter seemed like another person's. She missed the children, but being with her own child seemed much more real.

She was thinking about how scary it would be without Austin when he was at work, and managing it all on her own, as she looked down at the baby and let out a scream. She startled Austin, who was reading in bed next to her, and he saw panic on her face when he looked up, glanced at the baby, and saw that she was totally still, deathly pale and turning gray. He could tell that she wasn't breathing, and her eyes looked glazed. He grabbed her from Zoe and shook her gently as though to wake her up. There was no sound or reaction for almost a minute as Zoe's heart pounded while she watched, and then the baby took a breath and started crying heartily. She was breathing again, but still very pale, as Zoe leapt out of bed and ran to dress, and called over her shoulder to Austin, still holding the crying baby, and he looked as pale as Jaime. She had terrified them both.

"We have to get her to the hospital, or call 911," she said as she hastily pulled on jeans and a sweatshirt, put her feet into shoes, and went to take Jaime from him, so he could dress too. "Which do you think we should do?" He thought about it as he put on his own jeans, a sweater, and tied his running shoes.

"She's breathing now," he said in a shaking voice. "Let's take her to the hospital. It's only a few minutes from here."

Zoe quickly wrapped the baby in a blanket, put a little pink knit cap on her, and grabbed the diaper bag. A minute later, they were out of the apartment, dashed from the elevator on the ground floor, rushed out of the building, and hailed a cab. He handed the driver a twenty-dollar bill and told him to get them to NYU hospital as fast as he could. Jaime wasn't crying and seemed surprisingly quiet, but she was alert. They were at the emergency entrance to the hospital in minutes and rushed inside to speak to the nurse at the desk and explain what had happened. They were told to wait for a few minutes. Zoe held Jaime, while Austin filled out the forms, and Zoe called her mother in San Francisco. It was an unfamiliar reflex, but her mother was a pediatric ICU nurse, and would tell her what she thought might be going on. Zoe was terrified this could be serious, and Jaime might die. Luckily, Beth picked up when she saw Zoe's name appear on her caller ID. She was still at work. She was surprised to hear from her.

"Hi, Zoe, what's up?" Zoe told her mother, and Beth made a wild guess, based on her recent years of experience.

"Sounds like some form of apnea to me. It could be a seizure, but I doubt it. I'm not a doctor. And if they want to do anything dramatic, get a second opinion immediately. Don't wait," was the best advice she could give her. But she sounded calm, which reassured Zoe.

"What else could it be?" Zoe was panicked. She had only known and loved this baby for less than three weeks, and already Jaime was lodged deep in their hearts, and Zoe didn't want to lose her. The thought of that made her feel sick, and think of Rose.

"It's probably nothing. Call me after you see the doctor," Beth said and then had to go back to work.

An ER doctor examined Jaime carefully, and they were going to do tests. But he said his gut told him that it was some form of digestive apnea, where reflux from her digestive system backed up after she ate and may have caused her to stop breathing for a few minutes. "With any luck, it won't happen again, but you'll need to keep an eye on her now after she eats. There are some monitors available on the market that will warn you if she stops breathing. But they have constant malfunctions and false alarms. They'll drive you crazy all night, and in the daytime too."

"I'm with her every minute, I can sit up with her all night if I need to," Zoe said immediately, already a devoted mom, ready to sacrifice herself.

"She's more at risk now, at her age, than she would be as an adult or as an older child, after an episode like that. Eventually her digestive system will mature, and this won't happen anymore. It happens to some babies, and they grow out of it."

"I hope it never does again," Zoe said with feeling and Austin nodded. He had never expected something like that to happen. She had nearly died right under their noses, and what if they hadn't been watching her? Thank God Zoe had seen it quickly and reacted.

They called Cathy Clark and she came to see Jaime too and insisted she wasn't overly worried. She said bouts of apnea happened to some babies, and often never happened again. They were going to keep an eye on it and see if it recurred before subjecting her to intense testing. Austin liked her conservative approach, although Zoe questioned if they should do the intensive testing now and not wait.

They spent the night in the hospital with the baby so the staff could observe her. And in the morning, the attending pediatrician told them to keep her upright for half an hour after she ate before they laid her down, which made sense, so her digestive system didn't back up, causing her to stop breathing.

Zoe ordered a monitor for her from Amazon right from the hospital on her phone, even though the doctor said it was unreliable. It was better than nothing, and Zoe would rather be annoyed by a malfunctioning machine than lose her only child. And it would alert them in the event of sudden infant death syndrome, SIDS, too. The episode made Zoe think that maybe they should have another child, as protection if something happened to Jaime. But it affected Austin differently. It made him even more certain that he could only deal with the worry over one child, and not more. Jaime was definitely it for him. He was adamant about it now. The apnea incident had terrified him.

The baby slept on the way home, and when they got back to the apartment, Zoe and Austin talked about it before the baby woke up, and came to an agreement. One child was enough. Maybe even too much for them. They had had a rough start. But they had her now and were both determined to be the best parents on the planet. They owed her that. Austin was only just beginning to understand what that meant, a lifetime of vigilance and dedication to keep her safe. His heart was fully in it, and he was badly shaken by knowing they could have lost her the night before when she'd stopped breathing.

Zoe called her mother, mother-in-law, and sisters-in-law to tell them how close they came. If she hadn't been holding her and seen it when she stopped breathing, Jaime would have been dead by then, like the thousands of babies who died of SIDS every year. Austin readily admitted that Zoe was the hero in the story, since she had seen it when Jaime stopped breathing, otherwise they would never have known until too late, which was a horrifying thought. The fact that he had shaken the baby back to consciousness went unmentioned as a minor detail. Zoe had seen the baby stop breathing and turn gray and had screamed. She had won her first gold star as a mother and saved her baby's life. How many mothers had a chance to do that?

Her own mother had tried and been unable to turn the tides for Rose. Amelia, Austin's oldest brother's wife, had done it when one of their twins choked on a piece of hot dog at a birthday party, and she'd done the Heimlich maneuver on him, and saved him. And now Zoe had joined the elite. She hadn't worked the nursing out yet, but she had saved Jaime when she stopped breathing. It was a great feeling as she lay in Austin's arms that night and drifted off to sleep. The best feeling ever. From this moment on, Jaime was alive because of her, she had saved them from tragedy, and the whole family knew it, and so did Austin. Her instincts had finally kicked in. She was a mother after all. It was the best feeling in the world. Better than any she had ever known. Suddenly all the pain and confusion she had experienced for the past few weeks were worth it.

Chapter 3

Nursing remained complicated for Zoe, more so after Austin went back to work and she had no one to help with the baby. And the apnea episode made it all much scarier. Zoe never took her eyes off Jaime for an instant, and diligently held her upright after she ate, night or day. The breathing monitor she'd bought added a constant note of panic when the alarm went off. As the ER doctor had warned her, it sounded false alarms constantly, and drove them insane, waking them up during the brief times they were asleep, as they leapt to the Moses basket to grab her and would find her gurgling happily, or pink and peacefully sleeping. Austin objected to the monitor and thought it was worthless, but Zoe used it religiously. Their pediatrician, Cathy Clark, had suggested a night nurse again, to no avail, and finally gave up. Zoe was determined to be a full-time hands-on mom until she went back to work. She hadn't started looking for a childcare person yet, and Austin knew it wouldn't be an easy process to find someone to satisfy Zoe's diligence about their baby, but it was too soon to worry about it. Zoe still insisted that Jaime was colicky. Zoe had become an anxious person and worried ever since Jaime was born. It had changed the nature and tone of their relationship from peaceful, happy, and easygoing to frantic, tense, and argumentative. He blamed it on lack of sleep and hoped that he was right.

Despite the pediatrician's reassurance that it wasn't necessary, two weeks after the apnea episode, after doing research on the Internet, Zoe took Jaime to a pediatric gastroenterologist to have him check the baby out for a possible gastric obstruction. She reported to him that the baby didn't nurse well, usually fell asleep before she got to the second breast, and vomited most of what she ate. But after a conversation with Cathy Clark, and from his own examination of the baby, he deemed further testing unnecessary, unless she had a second episode of apnea after she nursed, or developed chronic projectile vomiting, which was not the case. Zoe had even gone so far as to ask him if he thought a gastric feeding tube might be necessary to nourish her if she continued vomiting, and he looked stunned by the suggestion. He explained that was only for extreme cases where infants were getting inadequate or no nourishment and losing weight steadily. Her baby was thriving and gaining weight, and normal babies vomited. He told her too that he considered the monitor she was using inefficient and unnecessary, but Zoe planned to continue using it anyway, as a safeguard. Although the constant false alarms were unnerving, she had a belt and suspenders approach to motherhood, and wanted to do everything possible to keep Jaime safe. She had the feeling that the gastroenterologist found her anxious and neurotic, but she really didn't care, if it was for Jaime's benefit.

She told Austin about the visit after the fact, and he looked shocked.

"Why didn't you tell me before you went?" He looked mildly hurt that she hadn't, and most of all surprised.

"I didn't want to worry you. I just wanted to get her thoroughly checked out. I thought Cathy Clark was a little casual about it. It seemed better to see a specialist and be sure that Jaime is okay." He was sure that her over-diligence, as he considered it, was due to her sister's early death and didn't want to bring it up. Losing a sister to leukemia at seven, while Zoe was only ten herself, had to have marked her, and given her a fear of illness in young children. He knew how her sister's illness and death had decimated her family, so he didn't fault her for being overzealous, but he would have liked to have known about a medical visit for their child, and to share Zoe's concerns, whether well-founded or not. But his happiness to hear that the baby was fine overrode any objections he might have had, and he didn't make an issue of it.

He had lunch with both his brothers once he went back to work, and marveled at how calm they were about their children. He shared how anxious Zoe was, how difficult the nursing had been so far, and how everything in their lives had changed. To some degree, he felt he had lost his wife, and they were only partners in a challenging venture now, like climbing Everest. And Zoe's hypervigilance was stressful. Their previously sexy, loving, playful relationship had disappeared. Zoe had become a one-person police force to protect their child, on duty 24/7.

His brothers were impressed by the apnea incident a few weeks before, and said that nothing that dramatic had ever happened to any of their kids at that age. They also commented that their wives were less perfectionistic than Zoe, and more relaxed, which was part of it. Austin admitted that a month into fatherhood, he could no longer imagine having more than one child, which they thought was too bad. They each enjoyed having several, even his brother with twins. They both suggested that if Jaime were to be an only child, Zoe might become too obsessive about her. She might be calmer with two.

"Or twice as anxious," Austin said with a rueful grin. He barely recognized his wife now. "She's read every book on the planet about child rearing, and has very definite ideas. Her younger sister died of leukemia when Zoe was ten, so she's very nervous about health issues. She has a million theories about everything." It sounded to both his brothers like he had a long rocky road ahead of him, but they didn't want to be critical of his wife, whom they all liked. Zoe was a terrific woman, just a little intense for them, but Austin didn't seem to mind it, and she was an expert in the field of child abuse, which was compatible with his interests and career too. They were happy for him that he had a baby now. They all loved the idea of the cousins being close as they grew up, and it was going to be fun having a little girl in their midst, with all the boys.

The nights were long at their apartment, with Zoe sitting up with Jaime, keeping a close eye on her, vigilant about another episode of apnea, and only dozing off herself between frequent feedings. Jaime wasn't sleeping through the night yet at two months, and Zoe insisted she was going to continue using the monitor for the first year, just to be safe. It finally led Austin to sleep in the small guest room he used as a home office when he brought work home on a case. There was no way he could get a full night's sleep with Zoe sitting up all night, the baby crying, the alarm going off randomly, and a light on next to their bed. He would have been crippled the next day at the office. He had tried it, but it just didn't work. He missed sleeping next to her, but only did that now on weekends, and they hadn't been able to resume their sex life with Jaime either in Zoe's arms, or between them in bed.

They no longer sat down to dinner together either, she was too busy tending to the baby, so he either bought food from a deli or nearby restaurant on his way home from the office, or cooked for them himself, something his brothers hadn't had to do either. But none of their children had apnea, and they had au pairs who took care of the children and lived in. He had suggested it to Zoe for when Jaime got a little older, but Zoe pointed out that his brothers' au pairs had no formal training, were usually foreign and around twenty years old, and she would never trust Jaime with someone like them. He didn't argue the point, and wondered who Zoe would find that she would trust with Jaime. It was going to be hard to fit the bill, and it would have to be someone who respected all her theories and rules. She wouldn't even let Austin hold Jaime now after a feeding. She held the baby upright herself, and never took her eyes off her. And she was planning to nurse for at least a year, which seemed like a long time to him.

He couldn't help wondering at times if the peaceful, happy, stress-free life they had shared for six years before Jaime was born would ever be normal again. A new, constantly tense, hypervigilant side of Zoe had emerged. She was not the same woman she had once been, but he loved her just as much, and forgave her quirks. After all, they were both committed to giving their daughter the best life they could. Who could fault Zoe for that? And he was sure that she would relax as Jaime grew older. It was just a bumpy start. His brother had said that to him too. His brothers and their wives had been younger when they'd had children. At thirty-four, in her line of work with abused children, and with two years of medical school, Zoe approached it more intellectually. And she had enough knowledge of the risks and downsides and medical dangers to fuel her fears. But he was sure that in time she'd relax.

His mother had suggested to her that Zoe be careful about what she ate while she was still nursing, and try to avoid onions, garlic, spicy food, cabbage, some dairy products, and even chocolate. She didn't think that alcohol would do any harm, and might even make the baby sleep better. And although Zoe liked Constance, she found her suggestions offensive and intrusive, and said they were all old wives' tales and would have no positive impact on Jaime's gastric disturbances, which Cathy Clark still said were in the normal range. Jaime threw up a lot, but Cathy said some babies were just vomiters and spat up a lot of their milk.

Austin didn't comment when he saw Zoe eat the forbidden foods mentioned by his mother and thought it might have been worth a try to avoid them, which Zoe flatly refused. She loved chocolate and spicy food, garlic and onions, and continued to eat them liberally despite her mother-in-law's advice. She rejected all of it as myths. It annoyed Austin, but he thought it best not to engage in battle with Zoe over it. Things were tense enough about Jaime's feedings as it was. And he didn't think she vomited unduly, no more than his nephews had at the same age, but Zoe insisted that Jaime threw up all day long, and less at night, so he didn't see it, and he assumed she knew what she was talking about.

Jaime was all smiles when he came home from work, and he loved playing with her. She was progressing at normal ages for infant development, and learned to smile and roll over when she should, and she laughed uproariously when Austin played with her. She had a deep, wonderful giggle that brought a smile to her parents' faces. Her happiness was contagious, and she loved it when her father blew raspberries on her stomach and she squealed with delight.

Everything was going smoothly and starting to get easier, even Zoe's breasts had finally adjusted to Jaime's needs and rhythm, when disaster struck. Zoe was changing her, and took her hands off the baby for a split second to reach for a fresh package of diapers high on a shelf. She took one short step away from her, and before she could step back, Jaime demonstrated her newest skill and rolled off the changing table onto the hardwood floor and gave her head a resounding crack when she landed with an ear-piercing scream. Zoe scooped her up with a look of panic, the baby was alert but it took long minutes to calm her.

There was no rug under the changing table or in the room where they kept Jaime's things, since Zoe was afraid of allergens and asthma, which she had had as a child, so the room was all hard surfaces, which could be wiped down, and Jaime's quick trip to the floor had been unforgiving. Within a short time, Jaime had a huge bump on her head. Zoe didn't stop to call Cathy Clark, she put Zoe in her quilted sack, grabbed a blanket and her purse, and rushed out the door to take her to the emergency room. She was sure Jaime had a concussion, given how hard she had hit, the awful sound it made, and the size of the bump on her head.

She called Austin from the cab, confessed to her own stupidity in stepping away from her. Jaime had never moved on the table before. Zoe told him where she was going, the emergency room at NYU, and he promised to get there as fast as he could. His office was in midtown, and Zoe would get there first.

They only made Zoe wait a few minutes before a pediatrician at the emergency room saw Jaime. He had a nurse get them an ice pack. Jaime seemed content by then, but there was no denying she had a big bump on her head, and Zoe cried guiltily as she explained what had happened, and how stupid and irresponsible she had been.

"Babies do things like that." The doctor tried to calm her and saw how terrible she felt about the accident. "Her pupils look fine. She doesn't have a concussion. Keep an eye on her, and if she throws up, call me. It's just a bump on the head," he said reassuringly, and was startled when Zoe asked them to call in a pediatric neurologist, just to be on the safe side. He told her he didn't think it was necessary, but Zoe insisted, so he did. Zoe asked the neurologist if he thought Jaime should have a CT scan, and he concurred entirely with the pediatrician. There was no sign of a concussion, Jaime had a nasty egg on her head, but she was fine. Both doctors were in the examining room when Austin walked in half an hour later, in time to hear that Jaime was fine, and he looked enormously relieved. From Zoe's description of the event, he was imagining her in a coma by the time he got there, and possibly brain damaged. He was thrilled to find that wasn't the case, and held her in the cab on the way home, as Jaime grinned at him and giggled when he kissed her. She seemed none the worse for the experience, although Zoe looked shaken up, and felt acutely guilty for Jaime's fall. She kept repeating how stupid she had been.

"She's going to get bumps and bruises over the years. You can't prevent them all." He kissed his wife, as they rode home, and made a comment that had occurred to him recently. "I think your medical school training makes you worry about her more. You have enough knowledge to terrify yourself, Zoe. Maybe you need to disconnect from that, and read fewer books. You're smart and sensible, and careful with her, to an extreme degree. You can't assume the worst every time. She's fine, and every bump on the head doesn't mean a concussion. Sometimes, most of the time, it's just a bump on the head. My brothers' boys would be brain dead by now if they got a concussion every time they knocked each other down or ran into something."

"But those things happen. You can't ignore them. That's how tragedies happen, when people assume that something is nothing, when in fact they're not seeing the danger signs."

"Not every situation is dangerous," he argued his case. "You're a great mom, Zoe. You don't need to worry so much."

"Even great moms lose their kids," she said softly, and he kissed her. He knew that was the root of Zoe's constant anxiety about Jaime, her fear that she would die. It caused her to be overzealous about everything, and had become her only role in life, to guard their child. And in spite of that, accidents happened anyway. It was inevitable, and making Zoe seem neurotic.

She nursed Jaime when they got upstairs, and Austin went back to the office. For once, Jaime didn't throw up after Zoe nursed her. The bump was ugly and a constant reminder to Zoe of her terrible mistake, but it absorbed in a few days, and was a dim memory after that. Zoe took it as a warning to be even more careful with Jaime, and she never stepped away again while she changed her. It alerted Zoe again too to how careful she would have to be in hiring a nanny for her, so she could go back to work. If a nanny had done what she had, and Jaime had fallen off the changing table, Zoe would have fired her on the spot. She had a month to find a nanny before her maternity leave ended, and she cried every time she thought of it. She loved her job, but she loved her baby more, and couldn't bear the thought of leaving her every day. It was going to be wrenching, and she was going to continue nursing even after she went back to work. Austin thought she should end it then, and Jaime would have gotten all the immunities she needed from her mother's milk at four months, but Zoe disagreed. She had read that a year would be better, and Cathy Clark thought six months would be a good compromise, but Zoe was set on a year. Austin didn't argue with her about it. Zoe was the best, most dedicated mother he had ever seen.

Even if he got less attention from her than he used to, less time with her, and none alone, and their sex life had dwindled to almost none at all, Jaime was the lucky beneficiary of her mother's passion and vigilance. Zoe's mothering was superb.

Chapter 4

After interviewing more than twenty candidates for in-home daycare for Jaime, Zoe concluded that Jaime was still too young for her to leave her, and she extended her maternity leave by two months, which was an enormous relief to her. She missed her job now, and the challenges it provided her on a daily basis, and the children she saw there, but being with Jaime was so much more important to her that she wasn't ready to go back. And the thought of separating from Jaime made her feel anxious. The person replacing her was delighted to stay for an extended period. The shelter was running smoothly, and Zoe called in frequently and was available for consultation on important decisions. And once she explained that due to Jaime's apnea, she needed another two months at home with her, no one begrudged her the extra time. She'd never had another episode since the first one, but it was the perfect excuse to get two more months of caring for her daughter on a full-time basis herself, one to one, and more time to find the right nanny, which was beginning to seem like an impossible task.

In the next two months she interviewed more than thirty applicants from four agencies, and finally found a woman whom she liked, who had no objections to Zoe's many rules and theories and said she was willing to adhere to them. She was a warm, loving woman in her fifties from Jamaica, with years of experience as a baby nurse and six grown children of her own. Her name was Jamala. She had a musical, lilting accent, talked to the baby and made her giggle, and Jaime took to her immediately, and didn't object when Jamala picked her up and held her, which surprised Zoe. She often resisted when her grandmother tried to pick her up, and had cried when Brad and Pam came to visit. She wasn't used to strangers. Austin's father seldom came to visit and said he enjoyed his grandchildren better when they were old enough to talk. Beth hadn't come from California yet. She said she had been working double shifts in the ICU and couldn't come until the summer, but she had seen the baby on Skype and thought she was beautiful.

Sadly, she and Zoe had never grown close again after her years of being disconnected and drowning in her own grief, but they had a friendly relationship. Zoe had been closer to her father for most of her life, while her mother was so involved with Rose, and then nearly catatonic in her sorrow after. The chasm between them had never narrowed after that, and all that Zoe remembered were the years of her mother paying no attention to her, both before and after Rose's death. There was no animosity or bitterness between them, just distance, in a cordial way. Her not coming to see Jaime by the time she was six months old hadn't helped to bring them closer again. It was a missed opportunity Beth hadn't seized, yet again. She had been an extraordinary mother to Rose, but not to Zoe, once Rose got sick. It was too late to rewind history.

Austin and Zoe had found Jamala through friends, and not an agency. She had worked for them for six years and they raved about her, how careful she was, how loving and devoted. All of their children were in school now and they no longer needed her. The wife of the couple she had worked for didn't have a job, and was home when the children got home from school, or their housekeeper babysat for them. So Jamala was thrilled to find a job with a six-month-old baby, starting all over again where she was needed. All of her children and grandchildren lived in Jamaica and she missed her family. And Zoe was relieved to have someone who came so highly recommended.

Zoe had Jamala start two weeks before she was due back at work, so she could observe her, and she liked what she saw. And to be sure that she really did follow the rules, they had six nanny cams installed in hidden locations throughout the apartment, so they could check on what she was doing. It was Zoe's idea, and Austin thought it unnecessary and excessive, but if it reassured Zoe, he was willing to do it. He knew how hard it was going to be for her to leave the baby every day. She hadn't left Jaime for an instant since she was born. She hadn't been to lunch with a friend, or even gone shopping without her. She and Austin hadn't been to a movie, and the only restaurants they went to were the ones where they could take Jaime in her stroller. Zoe wanted to be with their baby 24/7, and felt it was crucial for her early development.

It had curtailed private adult time for her and Austin, but he was hoping that Jamala would be willing to work some nights and weekends, so that he and Zoe could get out for some "date nights." He was longing for that, and Jamala said she would. Austin was really looking forward to it, and couldn't wait to spend time with his wife again. He had missed it terribly, and it was irksome at times to have to share her so constantly, although he loved their baby too. But their life had gotten very different very quickly, literally overnight, and he wanted to recapture some of the romance in their relationship. Zoe said that sounded good to her too, but so far had done nothing about it. Her first priority was Jaime now, not Austin, who often felt like the forgotten man.

Jamala followed all of Zoe's rules during the two weeks that Zoe observed her closely. And she was confident that Jamala knew what she was doing, but she still looked bereft the first day she had to go back to work. She had left a freezer full of breast milk and had been pumping for weeks before. There was enough in the freezer for her to leave the baby for a month, which she would never do. She had the smaller pump boxed to take to work with her, so her nursing wouldn't get disrupted and her milk wouldn't diminish. She had left dozens of additional instructions she wrote up the night before, and every possible emergency number.

Austin thought he'd never get her out the door on her first day back at work at the non-profit that had been so important to her, but not as important as their baby, who was her all-consuming passion now. Zoe cried as she got dressed, couldn't eat breakfast she was so upset, and gazed at Jaime as she nursed her as though she might never see her again.

"She's gonna be happy to see you tonight, Miz Roberts," Jamala said as Zoe handed the baby over to her with tears streaming down her cheeks, and Austin shepherded her out of the apartment. He had offered to drop her off, and Zoe looked beautiful. She had her figure back six months after she'd given birth, and she looked better than ever and had lost a few extra pounds from the exercise classes she went to in the Village where she could take Jaime in her stroller. She was wearing black jeans and a red sweater, her eyes looked vibrant and alive, her dark hair shone, and she'd had it trimmed to shoulder length. As he looked at her, Austin felt he had his wife back. She was no longer hanging around the apartment in worn-out exercise clothes or a nightgown with breast-milk stains on it. She looked as vital and crisp as she always did when she went to work. She was the consummate professional, with a new facet added. She was a devoted mother too, and they both suspected it was going to give her new depth when dealing with the children who required her attention.

Austin was currently handling two pro bono child abuse and custody cases for them, with appropriate grandparents who were anxious to have custody of their grandchildren and deserved to, in opposition to convicted felon fathers and negligent mothers who were in jail. Zoe had fresh passion to bring to the situations they dealt with. He rode all the way uptown with her to keep her company in the cab, so she wouldn't be crying alone, and then went to midtown to his office. And he kissed her lovingly when she got out.

"Have fun . . . see you tonight." He smiled at her, prouder of her than ever, and he loved having her back in her old life. It gave him hope that their married life would return to a semblance of their old life too, which hadn't happened yet, since they'd had no help when they were home alone together. Every time he tried to make love to her, the dreaded apnea monitor went off with another false alarm, or Jaime woke up on her own timing and cried, and Zoe went to pick her up, and that was the end of their lovemaking until the next attempt, which would be interrupted again.

They had only made love a few times in the last six months, and he missed it dreadfully. Zoe kept promising that things would calm down again, but they hadn't yet, and at times he wondered if they ever would. He'd asked his brothers about it, and they said the au pairs they hired had saved their marriages, and gave them time alone with their wives. His oldest brother had sheepishly admitted that he'd had an affair after the twins were born, when he felt that there was no longer time or room for him. But they had gotten past it, and he said that their marriage was back on track again, the affair had been a big mistake, and he regretted it. Austin had no intention of making the same mistake, but he appreciated his brother's honesty. They had a warm relationship and Austin had confessed that things were up and down with Zoe, she was obsessed with the baby, and had turned into an uber mother overnight. He missed the woman he could make love to whenever he wanted, but he was confident they'd get back to their old rhythms soon.

"Yeah, like maybe when Jaime goes to college," his brother teased him, and Austin hoped that wouldn't be true for them, or even close to it. Austin had high hopes of getting their marriage back to where it had been before Jaime, until lunchtime, when Zoe called him in a fury.

She had gone home for lunch unannounced, to nurse the baby instead of pumping. And she had found Jaime, just fed and looking milk drunk, sound asleep in Jamala's arms, and the Jamaican woman crooning to her.

"What's wrong with that?" Austin interrupted her. It sounded just right to him, and exactly the kind of person they wanted. She wasn't some teenybopper wearing headphones and dancing to music, or on the phone with her boyfriend. "Did she give her your milk from the freezer?" Maybe she had given the baby formula, which would have been a felony to Zoe.

"She had her lying flat in her arms, not propped up as I showed her because of the apnea, and she wasn't wearing the monitor." Zoe was almost in tears as she said it, but it sounded reasonable to him. If Jamala was holding her, she would see if she stopped breathing, which had never happened again anyway, and he was sick of the malfunctioning monitor too, which constantly woke the baby, and all of them, out of a sound sleep. "She **didn't** follow my rules. It could have killed Jaime."

"She was holding her, Zoe. She could see what was going on with her. She didn't leave her alone in the room in her crib." Jaime had outgrown the Moses basket by then, and slept in a crib. They had an additional crib in their now cramped bedroom, so she could sleep in the same room with them, which Zoe wanted most of the time, so she could watch her. She didn't trust their video monitors, which they had in every room, in addition to the six hidden nanny cams, which Austin felt was overkill, to say the least.

"I don't care. She didn't do what I told her. I can't trust her. I want to fire her. I canceled my afternoon and sent her home. I told the office I had a child-care emergency at home and my nanny got sick."

"Don't fire her, Zoe. The Johnsons raved about her, and they're careful with their kids." He had recently learned that many people they knew weren't, especially by Zoe's standards. "You know how hard it was to find her. How many people did you interview? Thirty? Forty? Fifty? Give her another chance. You'll never get back to work if you keep firing nannies." He was discouraged at the thought and how rigid Zoe had become.

"I'm questioning if I even should go back. I'm not sure there are decent nannies out there." She was appalled by the level of incompetence of the au pairs her sisters-in-law hired and had told Austin she wouldn't leave a dog with them, if they had one, which they didn't. She thought it would be unsanitary for Jaime, and cats were known to carry diseases that could be lethal to kids, so pets were out for the moment. Austin wanted Jaime to grow up with a dog, as he had. His brothers had a chocolate Lab and a golden retriever for their kids, but they were older than Jaime. Austin thought it was a great way to teach kids responsibility. But Zoe hadn't had a dog as a child or as an adult, so she wasn't sympathetic to the idea. He was planning to work on that in the future.

"Why don't you give her another chance?" he said gently about Jamala. He could only imagine the commotion if Zoe had to take more time off to find another nanny, and he liked Jamala, and thought she was perfect with Jaime, loving, kind, and competent.

"I'll think about it," she growled at him, her voice shaking with anger. She was still livid when he got home that night, and was holding Jaime after a feeding, so she couldn't put her down for another hour, and then put her in her crib. She sat in the kitchen with Austin to have the dinner he had brought home. He had worked late and was too tired to cook. She was too upset to eat, but she listened to his arguments in favor of Jamala, skeptically, and finally agreed to keep her and give her another chance. She called the woman at home, who cried when she answered and apologized again. Zoe told her to come to work in the morning and they'd start over, but she had to respect the rules Zoe set for her, and Jamala assured her she would.

Jaime squealed with delight when she saw her the next morning, and Jamala looked happy and relieved as she took her from Zoe, and apologized again. The atmosphere between the two women was chilly, on Zoe's side, and as they left for work together, Austin could see that the handwriting was on the wall. Zoe had made her mind up, and at the first slip Jamala would be out the door, for good next time. It seemed inevitable.

She lasted a month, until Zoe came home and found evidence that she had given Jaime applesauce from a baby food jar instead of making it herself. She gave Jamala a lecture on the chemicals in commercial baby food and the kind of damage it could do, both physically and mentally, to Jaime in the future. In Zoe's mind, prepared foods, for an infant Jaime's age, were akin to poison. At the end of the speech, she gave Jamala three weeks' notice until she could find someone to replace her. Jamala left that night looking dejected, but she could see that it was a battle she couldn't win. She loved Jaime, but Zoe was impossible to please and sooner or later there would be some new unforgivable offense that would cost her the job. She didn't argue to keep it this time. She thought Zoe was too hard to work for, and she and Austin exchanged a despairing look when she left that night. He didn't say anything to Zoe except that he thought she was making a mistake. Jamala was a loving, reliable, experienced, honest, trustworthy woman and Jaime adored her. He thought Zoe would be hard-pressed to find someone as good. She had reviewed their nanny cam videos and all she'd seen were hours of Jamala being loving and responsible with her daughter, but Zoe thought her offenses were serious enough to warrant terminating her, whether Austin agreed or not. He wasn't going to add stress to their marriage by fighting for the help.

Miraculously, two weeks later, they found a thirty-six-year-old Irish hospital nurse, recently arrived from Dublin with a legal green card. She hadn't found hospital work yet, and she wanted the more stress-free life of a nanny. She listened to all of Zoe's theories about feeding, the apnea monitor, baby food, no schedule, and agreed to follow all of it. She wasn't as warm and kind as Jamala, who'd cried when she kissed Jaime goodbye, but she was reliable and efficient, showed up for work on time, and followed Zoe's rules to the letter. She didn't talk to Jaime much, which Austin thought was disappointing, but Zoe thought the rules and Jaime's safety and health were more important, so she hired Fiona.

Jaime was leery of her at first, and seemed to sense her lack of warmth, but other than that, there was nothing wrong with her, and she did as Zoe told her. So there was peace in the house, which was at least something. Austin had noticed that instead of softening her, or maintaining the gentleness Austin had loved about his wife when he'd met her, motherhood had somehow made her rigid, less flexible, and tougher with him and everyone else. She was unforgiving and merciless about any mistake. Her theories meant everything to her, in order to protect Jaime. She was obsessive about them, and everything that concerned their baby, to the point of being harsh at times, and he noticed how possessive she was of Jaime. Zoe was always tense when her mother-in-law came to visit now, didn't like any of Constance's more relaxed ideas and didn't welcome her suggestions. It was Zoe's way or no way, and Constance felt the chill between them, and tried not to interfere. Zoe invited her over less and less often, and Constance didn't complain to Austin. She didn't want a hostile relationship with her daughter-in-law, for fear of losing her son. She could see that Zoe didn't want anyone too close to the baby or too loving with her. She wanted Jaime to herself, and the only person she was willing to share her with was Austin, and even with him, under close supervision.

After the visit, Constance mentioned it to George, her husband, who always told her to relax. He reminded her that Zoe was a very bright young woman. She had come to motherhood later than their other daughters-in-law, and had a different personality, and ran a complicated non-profit perfectly. He felt sure she'd relax and get the hang of motherhood eventually. He thought Constance was being oversensitive about it. He always gave Zoe the benefit of the doubt, he liked her. Constance liked her too, but there was something so rigid and intense about her, ever since she'd had the baby.

Austin had seen it too, but he and his mother never discussed it. It would have seemed disloyal to him to do that. He loved Zoe, she was a wonderful mother, and if she was a little too zealous about their baby, how could he fault her for that? She was super-mom to the letter.

Chapter 5

Fiona worked out well for them as a nanny. She wasn't an exciting person, didn't have interesting ideas, and wasn't creative with Jaime. She was used to being a hospital nurse, not entertaining a baby or toddler. The baby was always clean and well cared for, combed and brushed in clean pajamas when they got home. She took her out for walks in the fresh air, and followed Zoe's orders to a T. She never asked questions unless she had to, and wasn't chatty. When Jaime was eleven months old, Fiona asked Zoe how long she was planning to nurse her or if they were going to start to wean her.

"It's working well," Zoe answered her. "I originally planned to nurse her for a year, but I think it might go longer. She's happy with it, and so am I. Maybe a few more months." Fiona nodded. She didn't care one way or another. She had no opinions about babies. She'd been a post-surgical recovery nurse for adults in Ireland, so she wasn't invested in any theories, unlike Zoe, who had many. And at this point, the nursing was a comfort for Jaime, but no longer a necessity. And they were still following the precautions for apnea, although it had never happened again, and Zoe had her still wearing the annoying monitor. They had told her she could give it up at a year, and she planned to.

When Jaime took her first steps, Fiona sent a cellphone video to both parents at work, and Zoe cried when she saw it, and was crushed she hadn't been there to witness the moment herself. But she was loving her job, the complex meetings she attended daily, both internally and with foundations for grants, the judicial system, and city government for funds. And she loved going home to Jaime at night. Her life felt complete with a baby and husband she loved, and work she knew was meaningful. And her contact with the children at the shelter was a bonus. The long-term ones were dear to her heart.

Austin's reaction to Jaime walking was different, although he was sorry he had missed the first steps too. He knew it was time to think of safety, which was usually Zoe's province, but he got involved this time.

"I want to get gates this weekend," he said that night over dinner, after Jaime had gone to sleep. She had drunkenly demonstrated her new skill to her parents, and they applauded when she walked across the room to them at Fiona's urging. But when Austin saw Jaime staggering toward them on unsteady legs it reminded him that the short staircase to their bedroom would be dangerous for her now, and they needed to close it off with a gate at the bottom of the stairs, so she wouldn't climb them, fall, and get hurt. Gates were easy to get in any hardware store, or store with furnishings for children. Most people used them to confine their toddlers in a safe space.

"She'll crawl up the steps for a while, she won't try to walk them," Zoe said confidently. While she'd only been crawling, she'd been easier to distract from the stairs, but Austin could see an accident waiting to happen. "I think we can wait awhile, and I don't like them anyway. Gates are for dogs, not children, like leashes. I hate them, when you see a kid on a leash at an airport or the zoo. Besides, if they're the stretchy accordion kind, she'll pinch her fingers in a gate."

"Better that than landing on her head. Let's not do that again." He was referring to her fall off the changing table, eight months before.

"She's not going to fall down the stairs, she'll stay away from them, she won't know how to negotiate them. Toddlers are smarter than that," Zoe said confidently. Austin looked annoyed but didn't comment. They still had a solid marriage, but their sometimes different opinions about Jaime gave them things to argue about, which they'd never done before. Now there were little squabbles and differences of opinion about their child, which weren't serious, but annoying and frequent.

As promised, he came home with three gates, of the scissor-accordion kind, which stretched out to fit the doorway. There was one for the flight of stairs to their bedroom, and two extras in case they needed them, now that Jaime was walking.

"Those are exactly the ones I told you I didn't want. She's a lot more likely to hurt her finger in them, or cut it really badly, than she is to fall down the stairs. And why three of them? Are you planning to lock her in her room?" Zoe looked disapprovingly and instantly critical of him.

"No, but now that you mention it, if she wakes up before we do, and ever gets out of her crib, she could wander all over the apartment and hurt herself. A gate on her room would be a good idea." In the larger apartment they'd moved to when Zoe was pregnant, there was lots of room for her to move around, and get into trouble if unsupervised.

"I won't allow a gate. We have to respect her as a person, we can't treat her like a prisoner," Zoe said angrily.

"We need to treat her like a one-year-old with more mobility than sense," he said firmly, irritated by Zoe's take on everything, that schedules were abusive and gates were for dogs. For someone so obsessed with safety and Jaime's well-being, she was ridiculous sometimes, but he didn't say that to her. Instead he installed the gate on the stairs that night, after telling Zoe that he couldn't get the flat kind, which wouldn't have been the right size for their doorways anyway, as they were unusually wide. He put the two extras in a storage closet in case they needed them later.

Zoe was furious when she saw the already installed gate on the stairs, got out a screwdriver, and took it down, which made Austin even angrier, and led to a fight. The first bad one they'd had in a while, maybe the worst one yet.

"If she falls down the stairs and gets hurt, you'll be calling me crying from the emergency room. We don't even have carpeting on those stairs, she could really get hurt. And God knows what she'll do if she gets out of her room before we get up. She could cut herself, or bang her head, or anything."

"I've childproofed the house," she said confidently.

"Not entirely. You can't, she could knock a lamp down on herself by pulling on the cord. We can't live in an empty bomb shelter, Zoe, the gate makes sense."

"They're offensive, they disrespect our daughter," she said fiercely. "I'll get carpeting, if you want."

"Until you do, I want that gate up," he said angrily. "She's my daughter too."

"Then treat her like one, and not your dog. I won't have those things in my home."

They went to bed angry at each other that night, after she called him abusive, insensitive, and disrespectful, and he called her unreasonable and nuts. But he didn't put the gate up again, he knew she'd just take it down. And they were chilly with each other when they left for work on Monday. The battle of the gate had been a bad one, and neither of them had recovered yet.

Fiona called Zoe at eleven-thirty, while she was in a finance meeting with a city official. Fiona sounded flustered at first, which Zoe had never heard before. Zoe was surprised and Fiona cut to the chase, knowing she was busy. "Jaime's all right, nothing serious, but she got hurt. I was putting the breakfast dishes in the dishwasher, and she ran away from me. I went to find her immediately. I think she was looking for you. She got up your bedroom stairs, and before I could get there, she fell. She's cut her lip, and I think she hurt her arm. The lip might need a stitch, though. I'm going to take her to the hospital now. I called Dr. Clark first, she's meeting me there in five minutes. I just wanted to let you know." By the end of her recital of events, Fiona sounded cool and efficient again, although apologetic. Knowing how extreme Zoe's reactions were, she hated having to report an accident to her, even a minor one.

"I'll get there as soon as I can," Zoe promised, feeling terrible. Austin was right, the stairs were dangerous for her, more so than Zoe had realized, or had wanted to admit to him. Being right had seemed more important at the time. But she'd been wrong and now Jaime was injured.

Zoe excused herself from the meeting, explaining that her daughter had had a minor accident. They'd almost concluded their business and agreed to finish without her. She rushed outside to hail a cab.

Fiona had called Austin too. He got to the hospital before Zoe and Cathy Clark was already there, with Jaime and Fiona. Jaime had been crying, Fiona was holding an ice pack to her lip, and Jaime held her arms out to her father and started crying again.

"We have a busy young lady here." Cathy smiled sympathetically at him. "I've called in a plastic surgeon for her lip, and we need an X-ray for her arm."

"A plastic surgeon? Why? Is it that bad?" He hadn't seen the cut yet, and Cathy reassured him.

"Just a few stitches, but a good rule to follow: Always get a plastic surgeon for injuries to lips and ears, especially lips. You don't want a scar there later, lips and ears are funny that way. Once you interrupt the lip line, it always leaves a scar. And we don't want her beautiful smile affected later on. He said he'd be here in a few minutes. And I have a feeling her arm is broken." Austin looked crushed, it brought to mind his argument with Zoe all weekend, and he was angry at her again. He looked like a storm cloud when Zoe walked in ten minutes later, and he explained the situation to his wife. They both knew it could have been avoided with the gate he had put up and she had taken down. Zoe looked sick at the thought.

Cathy took Jaime to get the X-ray then, and she was right, Jaime's arm was broken, it was a clean break, but needed a cast for the next six weeks.

"She's so young to have broken a bone. I didn't do that till I played football in college," he said sadly.

"You were lucky," Cathy said kindly. "She's a busy bee, some kids are adventuresome. She'll keep you busy now that she's walking." He didn't tell her that he had put up a gate that would have avoided the whole thing. He kept silent out of loyalty to his wife, but he was furious with Zoe. The X-ray confirmed that the arm was broken just as the plastic surgeon arrived. Austin held her while they numbed her lip and sewed it up. It only took two stitches, but was traumatic nonetheless.

After that, the attending orthopedist put on a fluorescent orange waterproof cast. Cathy stayed with them the entire time, and appeared not to notice that Jaime's parents hadn't spoken to each other since they arrived. They thanked Cathy when they left, and went back to the apartment. Fiona made Jaime lunch, and Austin and Zoe went to their bedroom to talk.

"I'm sure you know what I'm thinking," he said coldly. "If you'd left the goddamn gate up, this wouldn't have happened. You have to run everything and decide everything, with all your goddamn theories about respecting a one-year-old, so now she has two stitches in her lip and a broken arm. I hope you're satisfied."

Zoe just sat on the bed and cried. "I'm sorry," she said softly. "I just don't like gates for kids," she said meekly. He felt terrible for shouting at her, and sat down next to her on the bed and put his arm around her.

"I'm sorry too. Sometimes I'm right, though. We're in this together, Zoe. You can't always call the shots. She's my daughter too."

"I know. I'm sorry. I feel terrible. I can't believe she broke her arm and cut her lip."

"At least it wasn't worse," he said generously, calming down. He could see how awful Zoe felt.

They both had to get back to work and left together after kissing Jaime, and thanking Fiona for handling it so well. At least the war between them was over, as they shared a cab uptown. He kissed her when she dropped him off.

He told his mother about the incident the next day when she called him to say hello and she was shocked.

"Why didn't you put gates up now that she's walking?"

"I didn't have the time," Austin said, covering for his wife. He'd rather look like an idiot to his mother than have her know that Zoe opposed him and took it down, particularly since Jaime had gotten hurt.

"I thought Zoe was careful about those things." She sounded surprised. She sensed that something was off, but she couldn't tell what. She knew him well.

"We both misjudged it. We'll be more careful from now on."

"I hope so," she said and they hung up a few minutes later.

That night, he and Zoe made love for the first time in months. He felt closer to her than he had in a long time, and she seemed so vulnerable and so sad. He wanted to make it better, for both of them, but he wasn't sure how.

Once Jaime was walking, the next few months were hard on her. She constantly had a scrape or a bruise, or a "boo-boo" somewhere. She'd had a hard time teething, with pain and fevers that Zoe had reported to Cathy Clark. And with all the minor injuries from walking and falling on unsteady one-year-old legs, Austin said she looked like a child abuse victim when he gave her a bath one day. But her broken arm had healed well, and there was no scar from the cut on her lip.

Zoe took her to the playground one Saturday afternoon and had fun with her. Austin was playing tennis with a friend, and Zoe swung Jaime in a circle around her, holding firmly to her hands as Jaime squealed with pleasure, and then let out a blood-curdling scream, let go of her mother's hands, and clutched her elbow. Jaime was crying as Zoe dropped to her knees in the sand beside her, trying to figure out what had happened. She was alone with Jaime, Fiona was off on the weekends, and not knowing what else to do, Zoe left the playground with Jaime and headed to the emergency room. It was the opposite arm of the one she'd broken, so she hadn't reinjured that. She was sobbing and hiccupping in the cab on the way to the hospital, as Zoe held her. She paid the fare and carried Jaime into the hospital, running with her. And as they walked in, one of the nurses smiled and waved at them.

"Hi, Jaime," she said with a warm look. "How've you been?"

"She just hurt her arm at the playground," Zoe explained, looking stressed.

"Same one she broke?" the nurse inquired, and Zoe shook her head. "I'll get the pediatric attending," she said, heading for the desk, as Zoe went to sign in. They were in the computer so it didn't take long, and the nurse put them in an exam room five minutes later. Jaime was still crying when the doctor walked in. He remembered Jaime from last time too, as soon as he looked at the chart.

"What happened? Did she fall?" he asked Zoe and she shook her head.

"I was swinging her around by her arms, and all of a sudden, she screamed and grabbed her elbow." The minute she said it, he nodded.

"Easy one this time." He looked at Jaime then. "This is going to be an owee for a minute, Jaime, but then it won't hurt anymore." As Zoe watched, wondering what he was going to do, he held Jaime's small upper arm firmly with one hand, pulled on her lower arm with his other hand, turned it sharply, and moved the lower part of her arm upward, and suddenly Jaime stopped crying instantly, like magic. "Dislocated elbow," he said to Zoe. "It happens to toddlers all the time. You'll have to keep an eye on it, if she has a tendency toward that, it could happen again. Their joints are loose at this age. It can happen reaching for a spoon or putting on her pajamas. It doesn't take much to pull an elbow out of a socket. No more swinging her by the arms after this."

"I promise," Zoe said, looking subdued. What the doctor had done had hurt her, but he did it so quickly, Jaime didn't have time to react, and the relief was total after he did, with her elbow back in place. Zoe's stomach felt upside down, as the nurse walked into the room and he explained it to her.

"You can give her some baby aspirin tonight if she needs it, but I don't think she will. It's back in place now. There should be no residual pain. Bye, Jaime, thanks for the visit, take care." He waved at her as he left the room, and Jaime waved back with the arm that had been excruciating a minute before.

"Well, that was quick," the nurse said as she lifted Jaime off the table, and smiled at Zoe. "She keeps you on your toes, huh?" She could see that Zoe was a great mom, she always came to the hospital with her. They left a few minutes later and went home.

Zoe gave Jaime some juice and cookies. She had just stopped nursing six weeks before at fourteen months. She had given it up on her own, and Zoe was sad about it, but it was time. Austin had been relieved, his mother kept telling him that Jaime was too old to be nursing, a message he did not pass on to his wife.

"How was the park?" Austin asked when he got home, still wearing tennis shorts and a white Lacoste shirt. He looked tall and handsome, and his face was still flushed from the game he had won.

"Not so good, I guess," Zoe said as she kissed him. "We were playing and Jaime dislocated her elbow. We just got back from NYU, the doctor said it can happen easily at this age. He put it back in place and it was fine. She scared the hell out of me, she just started screaming. I was swinging her around when it happened."

"Jesus, I do that all the time. I'd better not anymore. I can't believe how often she gets hurt," he said, looking worried. "I wonder if all kids are like that. I don't think my nephews were, and they play rough."

"Cathy says it's all normal, she's a lively little girl."

"I guess so," he said and went to shower, still thinking about it. He got to see how easily it happened a month later, when Zoe was putting Jaime in her pajamas after a bath, and the same arm dislocated again, just as the doctor had warned Zoe it could. Austin watched in horror at Jaime's extreme pain as she screamed. They made a quick trip to the ER, with Jaime in her pajamas, and the pediatrician on duty put it back in place again. Zoe didn't look as upset this time, since she knew instantly what had happened and that it wasn't serious. But Austin looked distraught seeing Jaime in such acute pain.

The same nurse was on duty that night, and greeted Zoe and Jaime by name, which Austin commented on after they left. "I'm not sure it's a good thing that half the staff in the ER know us by name. I think it means we're there too often. Does that ever worry you, Zoe?"

"I can't put her arm back in place myself at home," she said simply.

"Of course not, but she gets hurt all the time."

"No, she doesn't. We've had a few incidents, but that happens to all kids." He didn't think so, but he didn't argue with her.

He brought it up with Cathy Clark the next time he saw her, when Jaime was due for a vaccination, and Zoe didn't have time to take her, so he said he would. He'd been wanting to talk to her for a while, without Zoe. The opportunity was perfect.

Austin brought it up after the shot, Jaime only cried for a minute, and he lingered to talk to Cathy when she asked how Jaime was doing.

"It's a little like **The Perils of Pauline.** I feel like she gets hurt every five minutes. She's dislocated her elbow twice recently, the broken arm a few months ago, stitches in her lip, apnea, colic, teething. Zoe says it's normal, but is it?" He looked harried and concerned and Cathy was sympathetic. She was a quiet, low-key, serious woman, with a wonderful way with children. She had mentioned at one of their meetings that she came from a medical family in Columbus, Ohio. Both of her parents were doctors, and her two brothers. Her grandfather had been a doctor married to a nurse. Austin liked her style. She had a down-to-earth, unpretentious manner. She was patient with Zoe's many theories, and equally so with Austin's concerns. She had said she didn't have a husband, and was married to her job. She was attractive without artifice in a very natural Midwestern way.

"They're not serious injuries, fortunately," she reminded him, "more like the perils of childhood. Some kids are more accident prone than others, just like some adults. She's active and lively, and curious about the world around her. Usually, boys get into more mischief, but some girls do too. She's delicate, but she's also energetic and fearless. It's a tough combination. She'll stop falling and getting injured when she's steadier on her feet." She didn't sound worried and Austin was relieved.

"I'm glad to hear you say it. I have five nephews a little older than she is, and they've never had a stitch or a broken bone. And we can't even blame our nanny, most of Jaime's injuries have happened while we were with her, except for the fall down the stairs, and that was our fault, since we didn't put up a gate fast enough." He shared the blame with Zoe to be kind, and not out her to the pediatrician they both liked. Cathy liked them too. She could tell they were devoted parents, and she had no questions in her mind about abuse.

"She'll grow out of this stage," Cathy assured him and he nodded. He felt more peaceful about it in the cab on the way home. He played with Jaime until Zoe arrived from work and asked how the shot went, and Austin said it was fine. He didn't mention his conversation with Cathy but it rang in his ears a week later, when Zoe gave Jaime a bath, turned her back for an instant to reach for the shampoo, and Jaime slipped, hit her cheek on the side of the bath, and hurt her wrist, when she landed on it and it twisted. They made yet another trip to the ER where almost everyone recognized her this time. The wrist was only a sprain, and the doctor said she'd have a bruise on her cheek the next day, but none of her injuries were serious, and the pediatrician in the ER called her a slippery little fish. Austin looked embarrassed, and told Zoe they had to be more careful with her. She just got hurt too much.

"Hell, Zoe, the whole ER knows her and us. What does that tell you?"

"That I'm a rotten mother?" she asked him with tears in her eyes, and he felt terrible for mentioning it, but he had to.

"Of course not. But it means we don't watch her closely enough. She gets injured a lot."

"I can't put her on a leash or lock her in her room. She's still a baby, she falls down a lot. She's a toddler. Do you think it's my fault?" She looked crushed as she asked him, and Austin winced. He didn't want to hurt Zoe's feelings, but he was worried about Jaime. She was always getting hurt.

Zoe was still crying when they got back to the apartment, and after they put Jaime to bed, he apologized to Zoe and told her he thought she was a wonderful mother. He didn't know what else to say. The truth was that Jaime was getting injured too often, whatever the reason. His loyalties were divided between his daughter's safety and his wife's bruised feelings.

The next day, Jaime had a noticeable black eye from the bathtub incident. It was a harsh reminder to Austin of what was at stake, Jaime's well-being, or Zoe's tender heart. And if it came to a choice between them, Jaime won, hands down.

Chapter 6

Austin was in Washington, D.C., speaking at a convention for child advocacy attorneys and chairing a panel, when Jaime came down with her first serious case of the flu at eighteen months. She had a high fever, an earache, a cold, and was miserable. Zoe was alone with her, and called Cathy Clark at midnight to tell her that Jaime had had a febrile seizure, with a fever of 104.2. The pediatrician wasn't panicked about it and said it wasn't unusual, but she told Zoe to bring her into the ER and she would meet her there. She wanted to see her after the seizure.

Zoe bundled Jaime up in a blanket and took her to the hospital in a cab. The fever was already down to 102.1 by the time they got there, Zoe said she'd given her baby aspirin. It wasn't an excessive fever for a sick child her age. She didn't have another seizure in the ER, but Cathy decided to admit her for the night so they could observe her in case she had another one, and Zoe could stay at the hospital with her. She texted Fiona and told her she'd let her know when they were coming home. She didn't text Austin, so as not to worry him. Cathy said Jaime wasn't in danger, and there was nothing he could do.

Cathy left after they settled Jaime into bed. She was asleep within minutes, as Zoe sat in a chair and watched her, and the nurses made up a bed for her. They were impressed by how attentive she was. She didn't leave Jaime for an instant. The fever came down during the night without incident, and no further seizures. Zoe reported the whole episode to Austin by text when they got home. Fiona was waiting for them. And Zoe went to take a shower and dress for work.

Austin called her when she was in the cab, and asked about the seizure. She said that Cathy had said that febrile seizures weren't dangerous even if they looked frightening, which Zoe said it had.

"I wish I'd been there," he said, sounding unhappy and guilty for being away. "I'll be home late tonight. I'm sorry I wasn't with you."

"She's fine. Her fever was normal when we left the hospital this morning. She's on antibiotics for the earache. It's just a nasty flu." Zoe had been sick with a cold the week before, but without earache or fever, and they agreed Jaime must have caught the cold from her, which left her vulnerable to the flu.

He was happy to come home to his girls late that night, and Jaime looked bright eyed and lively the next morning when he saw her, and her earache seemed to be better. He watched her on Saturday while Zoe did errands, and his mother came by for a visit. Austin told her that Jaime had been in the hospital for a night with flu and a high fever, and had had a seizure at home, and his mother looked worried. They put Jaime down for a nap after Constance had played with her for a while, and it gave them a chance to talk before Zoe got back. Constance had been wanting to say something to him for a while.

"I'm worried about Jaime," she said gently, and looked at her son with troubled eyes, not sure how to approach the subject. She had a doctorate in psychology, but hadn't used it professionally, and it was challenging to broach sensitive topics with one's own adult children. "She gets sick a lot, and injured," she said cautiously.

"According to our pediatrician, whom I trust, she's delicate because of her size as a toddler and her age, but she's also very active and curious and fearless. That's a tough combination. And some of it is just bad luck."

"It seems to be. I had three boys, and you were all very active, but we never had the number of injuries with the three of you that Jaime has had in eighteen months." She tried not to sound judgmental but was concerned.

"I've thought of that myself, Mom. And in part, I think Jaime is just a busy kid. And we end up in the ER a lot because Zoe is hyper-vigilant and very nervous. I think losing a sister who was so young marked her deeply. She's terrified that something could happen to Jaime." It was easy to explain that way, and made sense to him.

"Maybe she's not vigilant enough, just nervous. There are only a handful of reasons why children get hurt that often, and Jaime has had some real injuries, stitches, a broken arm, sprains, a lot given her age, more than her fair share. Children get hurt from child abuse, which I know isn't an issue in this case, with the two of you, and Jaime has gotten hurt more often with you than the nanny, so it's not that. Negligence or poor supervision is another reason, parents or caretakers who don't watch children closely enough, or underestimate the risks of what they're doing. I don't know how closely you and Zoe watch her, but she sounds like a child who needs close supervision if she's that active, and Zoe watches her like a hawk whenever I see her with Jaime. But there are other more complicated, less obvious, psychological reasons that could be an issue here. Maybe related to her sister's death when they were both children, or some trauma with Zoe's parents. I don't think she had an easy time of it when her sister was sick, and afterward when they got divorced. Her mother told me at the wedding, in confidence, that she was a basket case herself for years after Zoe's sister's death, and after she and Zoe's father split up. He remarried very quickly, and had two more children. Zoe must have felt completely abandoned growing up, and it's hard to say how that scars someone." She was being very careful about what she said, so as not to offend Austin, who was a deeply loyal person and loved his wife.

"What are you saying, Mom? That Zoe has a screw loose, or neglects our daughter?" He looked hurt as he said it, and Constance's internal yellow flags went up, to advance with great delicacy.

"I don't know what I'm saying, or seeing, except what I said, that Jaime gets hurt a lot and it worries me."

"It worries me too. And maybe I'm the guilty party here," he said valiantly. "Maybe I'm not as careful as I should be." But she hadn't gotten hurt with him. She had only gotten injured with Zoe, in the bath, in the park, the gate she wouldn't let him put up because of her crazy theories about "respecting Jaime," the febrile seizure when he was away on business. But he didn't like what his mother was intimating. "Zoe loves Jaime more than anything in the world, even more than she loves me sometimes. She wouldn't do anything to hurt her." He sounded defensive and Constance knew she'd lost the battle, but at least she had planted a seed in his mind. She hoped he'd think about it. Someone had to.

"Of course not," Constance said innocently. "I can see how much she loves her. Maybe the rules just have to be a little tighter, or the boundaries," she suggested, and Austin relaxed when she said it.

"That's a whole other story. She believes in freedom and respect, even for babies. She thinks rules are abusive, and gates are for dogs. She thinks Jaime should have the freedom to go where she wants and do what she wants. I don't agree with her, but Zoe is adamant about it," and then he admitted something to his mother. "We fight a lot on the subject. I don't want Jaime to get hurt either, even if Zoe thinks rules are disrespectful to her at eighteen months. It's a philosophical issue, and I strongly disagree with her." Constance was relieved to hear it.

"I hope she gives it some thought, before Jaime gets injured more seriously." They both knew it was not an easy subject to bring up with Zoe. She was very touchy about her theories on child rearing, and rigid about them.

"I hope so too, Mom," he said sincerely. "Thank you for worrying about it. Everyone in the ER knows us by our first names. That tells me something too. Maybe things will get regulated better when Jaime starts preschool," but that was a year and a half away, a long time to wait, and expect someone else to lay down rules for Jaime, because her mother refused to. And yet she had been so heartbroken and remorseful when Jaime broke her arm, because Zoe wouldn't let him put up a gate on the stairs. She knew she had been wrong, but only **after** Jaime got hurt. "Anyway, just know that it's a work in progress but it's not an easy negotiation, with someone with ideas as strong as Zoe's."

"Her ideas are too modern for me," Constance said simply.

"For me too sometimes," he admitted. Zoe came home a short time later, and after a few minutes of polite chitchat, Constance left. It hadn't been a bad conversation with her son, but she didn't know if it would be fruitful, or if he had any influence over Zoe. It didn't sound like it.

Constance brought it up to her husband that night but as always, he was skeptical about Constance's psychological theories. He saw things more pragmatically, without looking deeper.

"I don't think lack of supervision is the issue," he said simply. "Every time I see her with Jaime, she's on top of her, she hardly lets the poor kid breathe."

"She's very attached to her," Constance conceded, "and appears to be a doting mother. But that doesn't mean she's careful enough. There's some reason why that child keeps getting hurt, and sick. Think about it, not one of our other grandchildren has had everything happen that she has, and she's only eighteen months old, and a girl, and girls are usually less active. Think of your own sons, they never had constant injuries, broken bones and stitches, or had to go to the hospital. None of them has ever had a seizure."

"Maybe she's just fragile," he said, which wasn't impossible either. But in that case, she was very fragile to an alarming degree. "What are you thinking, really?" he asked his wife and she hesitated. She knew he would pooh-pooh it, and Austin would too, for different reasons.

"If I told you what I'm thinking, you'd say I'm crazy," she said hesitantly, and he nodded.

"You're probably right," he admitted, "if it's one of your complicated, academic psychological theories that never make sense to me. You know what they say, 'If you hear hoofbeats, don't look for zebras.' The right answers are usually pretty simple. Don't go looking for convoluted reasons, Connie. Our son and his wife probably don't supervise their kid properly, and need to watch her more effectively, even if he is our son. It could be as simple as that. Don't make yourself crazy trying to figure it out. And whatever the reason for Jaime's injuries, there isn't a damn thing we can do about it." Listening to her husband, Constance knew it was true. He had a way of breaking things down to the basics. She was their child, and they got to make the rules. It didn't matter who was responsible for her injuries. It had been heartening to hear from Austin that he was trying to talk Zoe out of some of her absurd theories too. Maybe that was all

Constance could do. As a grandmother, she got to sit on the sidelines, sometimes in a front row seat, and say as little as possible, or even nothing at all. She knew from experience that Zoe didn't welcome comments and advice from her mother-in-law.

Constance had understood that as soon as Jaime was born and Zoe couldn't work out the nursing, but she wanted no advice from her or anyone, even her sisters-in-law, just from "specialists," whose theories sounded as off base as Zoe's. All Connie could do was pray and hope that they would get more sensible about parenting and the simple rules of safety regarding Jaime. Beyond that, she could do absolutely nothing, except what she had done today. Plant a seed with Austin, and hope it would grow.

For several weeks, Zoe was busy with some reorganization at the children's shelter that involved changes of staff, new systems and techniques they were adopting, a new computer setup, and a board meeting. Zoe had to work late several nights, Austin was home alone with Jaime, and he really enjoyed it. She was a bright, affectionate little girl, and he loved spending time with her, and taking care of her.

Thanks to Zoe, all his wishes had come true. He had a wife he loved deeply, and a beautiful little daughter. He could tell how bright she was, even though she couldn't speak clearly yet. She said a lot of words. He could hardly wait until she could communicate with them in sentences. Then she'd really be fun. She was more daunting as a baby, when he didn't know what to do with her. But the older she got, the more he enjoyed her. Fatherhood was everything he had hoped it would be and more, even if it had been confusing in the beginning.

When Zoe got home that night, she told him about the changes they were implementing at the shelter. Since he was on the board, he would hear about them at the upcoming board meeting, but he liked the insider information he got from Zoe. They were getting more hardcore cases from the courts now, children who had been severely physically abused, some of whom came to them directly from hospitals after they'd been injured, and many of whom were too damaged to put into foster care, and couldn't adapt to normal family life. A number of them had been serially raped by older family members, even their fathers, brothers, and uncles. Some had been viciously attacked by their mothers and had crippling defects as a result. One had been blinded by bleach sprayed in her eyes. In dealing with all of them, Zoe showed remarkable wisdom, dignity, and compassion, and great medical judgment. She also had a strong alliance with several judges who trusted her implicitly and admired the way she ran the shelter.

As Austin listened to her, he remembered everything that he loved and admired about her, and how remarkably capable she was. There were few women he respected as much as he did Zoe, except maybe his mother, who was the smartest woman he knew. He could sense that his mother didn't understand Zoe. She was so discreet and so modest, she rarely talked about her work and all that she accomplished. He often wished that his family knew more about her, but much of what she shared with him was confidential. She was the soul of discretion, and incredibly humble. He often thought that her own suffering as a child helped her understand the children she worked with. She knew about human suffering more than anyone he'd ever met, including some of his clients.

She asked him to take on three new court cases for them, during her reorganization. She wanted to see some of the offending parents brought to justice, and wanted him to be the advocate for the injured children, guiding them through the process. He was brilliant at what he did, and incredibly compassionate with the children.

The board meeting that came after Zoe's months and final weeks of revision was electric, it was so exciting. Even he hadn't realized how much she was doing, how lofty her goals were, and her ultimate vision for the children. She was organizing an alliance with a school, to ensure that their clients had a real education, which would prepare them for a better life in the future. Several people cried at the board meeting, they were so moved by what she was doing, and how powerfully she was implementing her plans for the shelter and how eloquently she expressed them. Austin was proud to be a part of it, and to be her husband. At the end of the board meeting, he looked at her, and remembered his mother's concerns about the reason for Jaime's frequent injuries, and if there was some hidden psychological reason in Zoe for them. He realized now that wasn't even remotely possible. She was the most extraordinary woman he had ever known. She was the kindest, best, most honorable woman he knew and the champion of abused children. His mother had no idea how remarkable she was. Whatever his mother's concerns were, he realized fully now that they were absurd. Zoe was as close as it got on earth to being a saint. And he was the luckiest man on earth to be married to her, and Jaime the luckiest little girl on earth to have her as her mother. Austin had total faith in Zoe as a woman, a wife, and a mother.

Chapter 7

For Jaime's first birthday party, they had had a small family celebration. It was really more for the parents anyway, Austin and Zoe had decided. So they had a cake for her with two candles in it, one "to grow on," and Connie and George had come by for a slice of cake and to wish them well.

But for Jaime's second birthday, Zoe decided to go all out. She invited Austin's parents, his brothers, and their wives and children. Her father and Pam were going to be in town to see his agent, and they had promised to come by. Their children weren't going to be with them. Christopher had graduated from UCLA the previous year, and had an internship with a graphic designer in London. He was an artist like his father. And Ashley was a senior at Northwestern. Beth had come to meet Jaime once, but admitted to Zoe that it was painful for her. It brought back too many memories to be close to a child that age. She saw children every day in the ICU where she worked, but that was different. This was too close to home, and the memories it brought back were too much for her. And Zoe didn't go to San Francisco for the same reasons. They were each part of a painful past that both of them had put to rest. It was easier just talking on the phone, and on Skype occasionally. Zoe and her father had overcome the painful past and never talked about it. Pam had helped him deal with it. Zoe was able to have a superficial relationship with her father, and saw him when he came to New York on business. And he had promised to be there on Jaime's birthday, which coincided with his meetings with his agent and publisher.

Cathy Clark had become Zoe's closest female friend and was coming too. She enjoyed both Austin and Zoe, and wished there were more parents like them in her practice. They were so caring and concerned, and doted on their daughter. It was always a pleasure for Cathy to spend time with them, and Jaime was an adorable little girl and the image of her mother.

She had stopped getting hurt every five minutes in the last six months and was steady on her feet now, although constantly in motion. Fiona was still with them and kept a firm eye on her. She liked working for the Robertses, they were kind, considerate employers, even though she admitted that

Jaime was a handful, and some of Zoe's theories about child rearing made no sense to her at all. But she followed most of them, and enjoyed her job.

When the guests arrived at Jaime's birthday party, there was champagne for the adults, and ginger ale or Coke for Austin's nephews. The boys had agreed to come to humor their parents, on the condition that they didn't have to stay long. Austin put them in front of the TV to watch sports. He had been passionate about all sports as a boy too, growing up. He had played football, baseball, and ice hockey, and played tennis and squash now as an adult, and still loved watching football and basketball on TV, and shared his love of sports with his brothers and nephews. Zoe didn't share his love of sports with him. The apartment was too small for five exuberant boys, so watching TV would keep them busy.

Constance and George enjoyed seeing all of their grandchildren in one room, and George joined his grandsons at the TV and teased them about their haircuts and baggy pants, and asked even six-year-old Seth about his girlfriend, which made him laugh.

Brad talked to George for a few minutes when he could tear himself away from the TV after a touchdown. He enjoyed talking to Constance, who was an intelligent, elegant woman, down-to-earth and pleasant. She and Pam had a great deal in common, with Pam's therapy practice as a marriage, family, and child counselor. She was still in practice with the same partners in Santa Barbara twenty-three years after they'd moved there.

Zoe's sisters-in-law, and she and Cathy, hovered around Jaime, and brought out the birthday cake that looked like the face of a doll. They took pictures while Jaime blew out her candles, and Constance watched, and almost stepped forward as Jaime's long dark hair hung near the flames. Connie was afraid her hair would catch fire, which Zoe didn't seem to notice. But Fiona was standing closer and pulled her hair back for her as she blew the candles out and then laughed happily. She had a big vocabulary for a two-year-old and enjoyed her party. She got pink icing all over her face. There were no children there other than her cousins, because she had no real friends yet, except the children she played with at the park. She had another year before she would start preschool. Zoe was applying to all the best ones, and talking to her sisters-in-law at the party about how hard it was to get in, and how extensive the applications were.

"It was easier to get in to Yale, and medical school at Duke, than applying to preschool," she said, they all laughed and agreed that it was true.

"I had to prostitute myself for reference letters for us. No one cared about Tommy. They wanted our tax returns and a bank statement. They hit us up for a donation the minute he got into the school, and they haven't stopped asking us for money ever since," Amelia said.

After the cake had been served, Zoe's father came up and put an arm around her. He loved seeing her happy, and Austin had been telling him about the work she was doing at the shelter and how much she had accomplished. And then she and Pam chatted for a while. She was relieved to see Zoe happy too. She had been so dark and depressed as a teenager that Pam had worried about her for years. But she had blossomed into a beautiful, content woman, and it was obvious how happy she was with Austin and their little girl. She was a woman fulfilled after her lonely youth.

After she disappeared for a few minutes, Zoe came back and scolded the men in the group. "Who left the toilet lid open?" She asked as though she expected a full confession, but didn't get one. "That's the most dangerous thing you can do with a toddler in the house," she informed them, and they looked startled. "A two-year-old can fall in the toilet headfirst, since they're top-heavy, and suffer a 'near drowning,' and when they get stuck head down in the water, they drown. I learned that in the Red Cross first-aid class I took last year. So the message is, 'Next time, gentlemen, put down the lid, so Jaime can't fall in.' " It was an unnerving announcement that stunned everyone into silence, and Austin lightened the moment by teasing her that the apartment was so thoroughly childproofed that he couldn't get into a cupboard or a drawer.

"I call her the safety warden," he said, and everyone laughed as he gave them humorous examples. A few minutes later, Seth, the youngest grandson, spilled his ginger ale, and Constance went out to the kitchen to get something to mop it up. She looked under the sink when she saw the cabinet open, with no child lock, and found all the household poisons and chemicals there, within easy reach for Jaime. There was no lock on the door at all, and she was stunned by how dangerous the products were, in sharp contrast to how careful Austin had just said Zoe was. There was always a strange contradiction between her theories about safety and the reality of Jaime getting hurt so frequently.

Connie grabbed a handful of kitchen towels and a sponge and went back to the living room to clean up the ginger ale her grandson had spilled. But what she had seen in the kitchen made her wonder just how childproof their home actually was, and how careful Zoe really was. It all sounded good, but what was the truth? If Jaime ever got in to the cabinet under their kitchen sink and ingested any of it, she'd be dead. And there was no gate on the kitchen door either to keep her out.

When Constance came back from leaving the wet towels in the kitchen, she saw Jaime winding the long strings from the balloons around her neck.

Fiona was in the kitchen putting away the cake. And Zoe was deep in conversation with Cathy Clark about whether or not vaccines really caused autism, and how dangerous was it not to get children vaccinated at all, but then you couldn't get them into a school. And could they really force you to vaccinate your child? Meanwhile, Jaime was continuing to wind the sturdy ribbons from the balloons round and round her neck, and Connie walked across the room and stopped her, and unwound them before she could strangle herself. No one had been watching her at all, until Austin saw his mother intervene, and walked over to thank her.

"She can get in to mischief faster than anyone I know," he said, looking sheepish. "She put peas in her ears last week, and we had to take her to Cathy to get them out." Cathy overheard him say it, and turned to Constance with a grin.

"Ah yes, the great pea caper. I had another patient who put them up his nose. Children can be very creative with food." They laughed about it, but Constance didn't think that peas could kill Jaime, ribbons wrapped around her neck and household bleach could. There was a strange dichotomy between what they said and what they did. It made Constance uneasy, and in a quiet moment when no one else was paying attention, Constance said something to Zoe about the toxic household products under the sink.

"I wasn't snooping, I was looking for some cloths

and a sponge to clean up the mess Seth made," Constance said in a soft voice no one else could hear. "And I found all your really dangerous cleaning products there. You need to childproof the cabinet or put a lock on it, before Jaime gets in to it." That would be a tragedy, not just another trip to the ER, they both knew.

"She has to learn what's dangerous, and where she can't go. It's about respecting boundaries," Zoe said, as Constance stared at her in disbelief. "I respect her intelligence. She has to know I trust her. We can't lock everything up. She could fall into the toilet by accident, but she would have to **choose** to open those bottles. She knows she's not supposed to do that, and she respects my rules on that."

"I wouldn't trust a two-year-old to make that choice," Constance said firmly, feeling panic rise in her throat. What were they thinking, to trust a two-year-old to respect their rules and learn boundaries, with poisons within easy reach? She wondered if Austin was just as foolish as Zoe about it. She hoped not. They needed to empty that cabinet in the kitchen immediately. She wanted to do it herself, but she didn't dare interfere in their home. She felt as though her granddaughter was living with a time bomb waiting to go off. What if she played with any of those toxic substances? Constance wanted to cry as she thought of it. "But thank you for your advice, Connie," Zoe said and walked away as Austin approached.

"What was that about?" he asked his mother in an under voice. He could see that Zoe was annoyed. She covered it well, but she looked furious at her mother-in-law.

"I just discovered that you keep all your toxic household products under the sink without a lock. I told her she needs to put a child lock on the cabinet or move them somewhere out of reach."

"I know, she thinks Jaime has to learn to respect what's dangerous and stay away from it. It makes me nervous too," he admitted, feeling awkward and as though he was betraying his wife. "Maybe she's right. Jaime doesn't go near it. Zoe told her that she can't."

"She hasn't gone near it **yet.** You can't trust a two-year-old with rules like that. Hell, you can't trust a fifteen-year-old with them. You and your brothers got into our liquor cabinet every chance you got. But bourbon wasn't going to kill you. Rat poison and bleach would. Austin, be sensible for heaven's sake. She's an adventurous kid, and she's only two. Move that stuff." Connie looked at her son with fear in her eyes.

"I will. I promise. I've been meaning to." He had intended to move all of it, but Zoe had made such an issue of it, so he didn't. But he knew his mother was right. Zoe had blind spots about some things, and respect, even of a two-year-old, was all important to her. It was a theory he didn't espouse, like not having gates on the stairs, which had led to a broken arm.

"Thank you," Constance said quietly, and went back to talking to Pam.

He walked out to the kitchen then, looked under the sink, and realized that his mother was right. He hadn't checked it in a while and there were products in easy reach and plain sight that could kill a grown man, let alone a two-year-old. He didn't hear Zoe come up behind him, and she was glowering at him when he stood up and turned around.

"Did your mother complain about me to you? She told me to move the products under the sink. Jaime never goes near them. She knows she's not supposed to."

"Come on, sweetheart. She's only two. This is like the gate on the stairs. I understand how much you love and respect her, but some of those theories are downright dangerous and just don't make sense, like this one. Let's not take the chance."

"Fine. Do whatever you want," Zoe said, and walked out of the kitchen in a huff. But the way she did it and her icy look spoiled the party for him then and there. They went through the motions after that until all the guests left. And then he went out to the kitchen and put it all on a high shelf. He had noticed that Zoe was chilly with his mother when his parents left.

Zoe saw what he was doing and didn't comment as she got Jaime's dinner ready.

"You don't need to be mad at me," he said gently. "My mom was right on this one."

"She doesn't like me, that's what this is about. She never has."

"That's not true," he defended his mother, hating the position he was in between the two. "She loves you, but she's the original safety warden, and she's old school, and so am I. The new theories are fine when they deal with how you handle bedtime, or discipline your children, not when dangerous substances are involved. I always stick up for you and your theories, Zoe. But this isn't about nursing or preschool, these are poisons."

"And Jaime's never gone near them, has she? She understands."

"And what if she doesn't, or forgets? This is a crazy conversation and it makes no sense. Don't make me the bad guy here, or my mom, it's common sense. You're worried about the goddamn toilet lid, this is just as dangerous. Why can't you see that?"

"I respect my daughter's intelligence. You don't."

"Then leave the toilet lid open and tell her not to put her head in it," Austin said, raising his voice. He hated their fights, but it was crazy talking to her about issues like this, especially with their daughter's safety on the line. He didn't usually disagree with her, but this time he did.

"If she winds up headfirst in the toilet, it will be

because she fell in, not because she decided to put her head in the toilet."

"Do you realize how crazy this sounds?" he said, frustrated beyond belief. "You gave a beautiful birthday party for her," he said, changing the subject and she looked at him, still angry at his mother for causing the problem by bringing it to his attention.

"Thank you," she said icily. "I thought so too, and I enjoyed it, until all this came up."

"Why don't we just let it go? The stuff is put away. That's good enough." He tried to be pleasant about it to calm her down.

"Good enough for who? Your mother? Is she coming back to check?" Zoe was being nasty about it, which she often did when she was wrong.

"No, good enough for me, Zoe. If that matters to you." He sounded so sad as he said it that she felt bad, and walked out of the room. She looked unhappy too. They had left Jaime alone the whole time they were arguing, and they went to look for her and found her in her room, playing with her toys. She looked like a dark-haired cherub as she gazed innocently up at them.

"Did you like your birthday party?" Austin asked her as she nodded with a smile.

"Cake . . . blow . . . I'm two." She held up two fingers then, to show how old she was. She was irresistible, she was so cute, and even her five male cousins had thought so. They didn't see her often, but they liked her.

One of his brothers lived in New Jersey, and the other in Connecticut, in the suburbs. He and Zoe had agreed that they wanted to live in town, even with a child. It was more stimulating for them, and would be for Jaime one day. They lived in an apartment on Charles Street instead of a house out of the city, but they didn't need more than that with only one child. Having only one was a decision they had stuck with and were glad they'd made. They both knew they couldn't have handled more, and didn't want to try. Jaime was enough for them. He had started later than his brothers. Austin had just turned forty-four, and Zoe was thirty-six, and didn't want to be pregnant again or go through the early months with a newborn and all that it entailed. Jaime was easy now.

Zoe gave Jaime a bath after the party, and Austin read her a story and put her to bed. They ate leftover sandwiches from the birthday party, and Zoe was still chilly when they went to bed. His mother's criticism and interference had rankled her, and she didn't like Austin's reaction to it. But neither of them brought it up again.

They watched TV in bed for a while without speaking, and he finally put an arm around her and tried to pull her closer, but she resisted him. It always took her longer to get over their arguments.

She viewed them as betrayals, particularly this time with his mother involved and Zoe's policies in question.

"I hate fighting with you," he said gently, and she didn't answer for a minute.

"Then don't." It sounded simple but it wasn't, and it always amazed him that he could love someone so much, respect her profoundly, and disagree with her so vehemently at times, particularly about their child. She had very different ideas than he did about freedom and respect and what to teach them, even though their fundamental values were the same about morality and honesty, and good and bad.

"I like your dad a lot," he said to change the subject.

"He means well, although he made some tough decisions a long time ago, but they were right for him. It almost killed my mom when he left her, though. I think he was drowning with her. I can see now that Pam is better for him, although I didn't see it then. They just up and left when they moved to Santa Barbara. They always invited me to come and visit, but my mom made it clear that if I went, I was betraying her, so I stopped going. My parents had a lot of baggage after Rose. She doesn't talk about it, but I think my mom still does. I don't think you ever get over losing a child. She didn't, although I think she's better now." Austin nodded, not sure what to say. It was delicate ground for all of them, and a minefield of sorts, with some very old mines buried deep in the ground. "I like your father a lot too," but not Austin's mom. She smiled at him then, there was tension between them that was hard to explain. Austin knew his mother sensed something about Zoe that worried her, although she'd never fully put it into words. But it came through and Zoe felt it too, no matter how diplomatic Connie was. And she'd only worried about Zoe since Jaime was born.

They watched TV together for a while, and Zoe fell asleep. He lay in bed and looked at her, loving her as he always had, more each year, but he knew that part of her would always be a mystery to him. No matter how much he loved her and tried to understand her, there was a part of her he could never reach.

Chapter 8

Two weeks after Jaime's birthday, Austin had to go to the office on a Saturday to work on one of the custody cases he was handling for Zoe. She took Jaime to the playground near their apartment, and allowed her to run around to let off steam and get some exercise. Jaime loved hanging around the big kids and watching them, and she ran as fast as she could to impress a group of older girls, who paid no attention to her. They had bigger things on their mind than a two-year-old in a pink down jacket. Jaime was fascinated by them, and Zoe didn't tell her to slow down. She was having fun, as Zoe chatted with some of the mothers she saw there regularly. One of them had a brand new baby. It was his first time out and all the mothers were admiring him. He was a strapping ten-pound boy, her fourth. Zoe had no pangs of envy as she looked at him. All she could think of was that he would be a nightmare to nurse. Jaime had been hard enough with her reflux and apnea, falling asleep at the breast, and vomiting. She enjoyed Jaime at two a lot more than she had in the early days. Eventually, Jaime came over to look at the baby too. Jaime looked at her with wide eyes and pointed at him.

"Baby, Mama? For Jaime?" Zoe laughed and shook her head. "No, you're all I need. You're my baby." She walked her toward the swings then, but all the ones for babies and toddlers were taken. The only empty one was one of the big kid swings that someone had just vacated, and Jaime looked at it longingly.

"Big girl swing?" she asked hopefully, and usually Zoe said no, but it looked like it was going to be a long wait, there were a lot of toddlers and mothers in line for the baby swings, so she relented.

"You can go on the big girl swing, but you have to hold tight." There was no way to attach her to it, and no safety belt, but Jaime had a good grip, and she knew how to pump, and there were interlocking rubber pads under it that fit together like a puzzle, so she wouldn't get hurt if she fell.

Zoe sat her on it and gave her a push, and Jaime squealed with delight, and pumped with her short toddler legs.

"Higher!" she called out to Zoe who gave her

another push, but not too hard. "More!" Jaime demanded, with a glance over her shoulder, just as Zoe gave her a bigger push, and as she looked back at Zoe, Jaime flew off the swing, and landed in a heap on the rubber mat. Zoe dashed toward her and picked her up, narrowly missing getting hit in the head by the swing as she pulled Jaime away from it. Jaime was crying, and holding one arm limply as Zoe pulled her into her arms. "My hand hurts, Mommy," she said between sobs, and Zoe could see it was at an odd angle, and was already starting to swell.

She carried Jaime clear of the swings, and sat her down on a bench to have a better look. It didn't look good to her. She carried Jaime out of the playground as the other mothers watched and waved goodbye to them. She hailed a cab as soon as they reached the street, got in with Jaime still crying, and asked to be taken to NYU hospital, the now all too familiar emergency entrance. They got there ten minutes later, and after paying the cab fare, she rushed straight to the nursing desk.

"What are you doing here again?" a familiar-looking nurse asked them.

"I fell off the big girl swing," Jaime said between sobs and gulps of air. Zoe was relieved that it wasn't the arm she had previously broken, and this time it seemed to be her hand that had gotten hurt. A nurse they didn't know walked Zoe into an exam room, where she gently set Jaime down on the table, and carefully took Jaime's down jacket off, which made her cry harder.

They waited fifteen minutes for the doctor, while several nurses they knew came to say hi to Jaime. Zoe hadn't called Austin yet, and decided to wait until she knew what the doctor would say about Jaime's hand. The doctor took one look at it when he walked into the room, and said he was fairly sure her wrist was broken, and ordered an X-ray to confirm it. A nurse's aide put Jaime in a child-size wheelchair and rolled her down the hall to the X-ray lab. Zoe and Jaime knew where everything was now.

The X-ray showed that her wrist was broken. It was a clean break like the last one, and the doctor met them back in the exam room. He was looking at a computer screen and glanced up at Zoe, taking in her sleek looks and well-kept appearance even in jeans, a sweater, and a black down jacket.

"Your daughter's had quite a list of injuries in the past year. Broken arm, dislocated elbow twice, now her wrist. And I see she was admitted for a severe case of the flu. She must be a pretty rambunctious kid. Have you had her checked for ADHD? That's quite a list for a two-year-old." Zoe stared at him with relief. For a minute, she thought they were going to accuse her of child abuse, instead he thought Jaime might be hyperactive, which Zoe knew she wasn't. Cathy Clark would have picked it up if she were but had never suggested it.

"I'll mention it to our pediatrician," she said soberly, and he asked Jaime what color cast she wanted. They had just added fluorescent pink to the options.

"Pink," she said, still holding her hand, but she had stopped crying. He put it on without calling the orthopedist on duty, he said it was a simple break, and the cast could come off in four weeks. They knew the drill now. They left the ER an hour later, with the nurses waving at them, and Zoe called Austin from the street and told him what had happened.

"She what?" he said in a tone of disbelief.

"She fell off the swing and broke her wrist." The first thought that ran through Austin's mind was how he was going to explain it to his mother.

"How could she break her wrist? They have sand under the swings, and they can't fall out of the basket once they're in it. Did she climb out when the swing was moving?"

"She wasn't in the baby swings," Zoe explained with a sigh, her stomach was churning having to admit it to him but she knew Jaime would tell him. "They were all full, and there was a line of kids waiting for them. She was on the big girl swings and she slipped off. They have rubber mats under them, but she must have fallen wrong on her wrist."

"Is it the same arm she broke before?" He sounded discouraged.

"No, the other one. She has to wear the cast for four weeks."

"Did they question you about it? By now, they must think we're child abusers. We'll have to start going to another hospital if she gets hurt again." He was only half joking.

"No, I thought of that too. But the doctor asked me if she had ADHD. Maybe she does."

"She's not hyperactive, Zoe. We're not supervising her properly, or this wouldn't be happening. She should never have been on the big kid swings." The reproach in his voice was clear.

"I know," Zoe said in a small voice. "I didn't think this would happen."

"We never do, and then it does. Where are you now?"

"Outside the hospital. We just finished. We've been here for an hour."

"I'll pick you up in ten or fifteen minutes and take you to lunch. I'm almost finished what I came in to do. I'll take care of the rest on Monday."

He looked serious when he drove up to the emergency entrance, and Zoe and Jaime got into the backseat. He didn't have her car seat in his car, since Jaime usually rode in Zoe's car, so Zoe put the seatbelt on her. Jaime showed him her bright pink cast, and he exchanged a look with Zoe. He wasn't angry at her, she could see, he was worried.

"Did you call Cathy?" Zoe shook her head. She was as upset as he was, and furious with herself for giving Jaime a harder push, so she fell off when she turned to see her mother.

"I didn't want to bother her on a Saturday. I didn't think it was broken."

"They'll probably report us to Child Protective Services next time, if there is one," he said seriously.

"Cathy would vouch for us."

"They might not give her a chance to, particularly if they find out we're friends." Zoe nodded, as he drove toward a deli they liked in SoHo. There were mobs of tourists and people from the suburbs milling around. He found a parking space two blocks away, and carried Jaime to the deli. They sat down at a free table in the middle of the restaurant, and Austin looked unhappily at Zoe. "I can't believe she broke something again. Maybe her bones are unusually brittle."

"I don't think so. It's just bad luck."

"Bad luck doesn't happen this often," he said as a waiter handed them the menus and dashed off to pick up someone's order. It was a busy place, but they liked the food there. They had great chicken soup, and Jaime loved the hot dogs. They were looking at the menus, when Austin glanced up and realized that Jaime had left the table. She was wandering down the aisles, smiling at people and showing them her pink cast, as waiters whizzed by her, carrying pots of hot coffee. Zoe smiled when she realized what she was doing, and Austin flew out of his seat, crossed the restaurant, grabbed her, picked her up, and brought her back. He set her down on her chair and spoke to her sternly.

"You don't get out of your seat again until we leave, do you hear me, Jaime?" Her lip started to tremble and tears filled her eyes, as Zoe looked at him in outrage.

"Why did you do that? You embarrassed her, it's humiliating to be carried away like that."

"Why did I do that? Are you kidding me? There were four waiters about to trip over her and pour hot coffee on her. Do you want to check out the burn unit at NYU next? We've worn out the charm of the ER, and met everyone who works there." His tone was harsh, but he had seen another disaster about to happen, and they had just barely finished the last one. "Don't you see that, when an accident is about to happen? You can't let her run around a busy restaurant."

"What do you want me to do? Tie her to her chair? She has a right to get up just like you and I do."

"She most definitely does not. I'm not three feet tall and going to trip a waiter. They wouldn't even see her until they fell over her and poured coffee on her." They filled coffee cups at the table, and the coffee they poured was boiling hot. He'd had it before. "You have to pay closer attention, and see the accidents before they happen, not after." He made her feel about two inches tall, and this time Zoe's eyes filled with tears as Jaime watched her. "This isn't about respecting a two-year-old, Zoe, it's about being a responsible parent."

"You think I'm irresponsible?" She looked crushed.

"We both are, if this keeps happening again and again. It's not her fault, it's ours. We have to teach her that some things are dangerous, like riding a swing for big kids, or running through a restaurant. We can't let her do whatever she wants."

"She just wanted to show those people her cast."

With that, Jaime piped up and agreed with her mother. "I told them I bwoke my wist, they liked the pink cast. I do too," she said, and her wrist didn't hurt once the doctor set it.

"She should be picking out sneakers or teddy bears or hair ribbons, not casts," Austin said miserably, as the waiter came to take their order. Zoe ordered chicken soup, Jaime said she wanted a hot dog and a donut, and Austin asked for a pastrami sandwich. They had the best in the city. When Jaime's hot dog came, Austin cut it in little pieces, which Jaime objected to strenuously.

"Why did you do that?" Zoe asked him, shocked. He hadn't listened to what Jaime wanted, and cut it up anyway.

"Because if she chokes on a bite of hot dog, and I have to do the Heimlich on her, I'm going to have a heart attack. We've had enough excitement for one day." Zoe nodded, and told Jaime it would be yummy anyway, and it came with French fries, which she loved. Zoe doused them in ketchup, just the way Jaime liked them, and she ate the little pieces of hot dog and dipped them in the ketchup too.

Austin looked relaxed by the end of lunch, and ordered a piece of cheesecake for dessert, while Jaime ate her donut with sprinkles on it. Zoe had hardly touched her soup. She was too upset by Austin's attitude. He was blaming her for all of Jaime's injuries, or that was what it felt like to her. She had texted Cathy by then, who called them at the end of lunch.

"What happened?" she asked, stunned by yet another broken bone after an accident, when Zoe explained it in detail.

"It's my fault. I shouldn't have put her on the big swing. I didn't think she'd fall off, but when she turned around to look at me, she lost her balance, and the swing was at the high point."

"It can happen." Cathy sounded discouraged too.

"The doctor asked me if she has ADHD. Do you think she does?"

"Of course not. She's just a busy two-year-old."

"With an irresponsible mother." Austin felt guilty when he saw the look on Zoe's face. She had taken every word he'd said to heart.

"I'll come by to see her later," Cathy promised. "I can't right now. I'm at a flea market in Brooklyn."

"We're out to lunch. Jaime just had a hot dog

and fries and a donut. Her appetite doesn't seem to have suffered." Austin almost said that she was used to breaking bones by now, but managed to restrain himself. "She'll come by to see her later," Zoe said after the call.

"She doesn't have to. She seems fine. I think you and I are more upset than she is." It was an accurate statement of how the adults were feeling. Jaime looked relaxed and happy by the end of the lunch.

They drove back to the apartment, and Austin put the car in the garage where he kept it, and walked into the apartment twenty minutes later. Zoe had put Jaime on her bed for a nap, and was going to lie down herself. It had been an upsetting morning, and Jaime had recovered faster than she had. Zoe still felt slightly sick. "What took you so long?"

"I got a call from my mother. I told her what happened, and had to explain it to her. She thought I was joking at first, she couldn't believe Jaime broke her wrist. Neither could I when you called me."

"I felt the same way when I saw her do it," Zoe said, looking exhausted. The hospital, and Austin's anger over the whole thing, had worn her out.

Austin went to watch TV in the living room then. He didn't even want to think, just focus on something else. He didn't tell Zoe that his mother had burst into tears when he told her, and she finally realized he wasn't joking.

"Something is really wrong here," she said to her

son when she regained her composure. "I don't know what it is, but I can feel it. No child has this many accidents." She had already said it to him several times, and it didn't feel good to hear it again, and he didn't entirely disagree with her. He just didn't know how to stop it. Every time he turned around, Jaime was in the ER again and had just been there. Now that they had made it through apnea safely after a year, it seemed like she was breaking something every five minutes.

He wanted to be angry at Zoe about it, but he couldn't be. She looked so devastated and remorseful that he felt like a monster continuing to make an issue of it. He peeked into Jaime's room and saw her sound asleep in her bed, looking like an angel. It had been a big morning for her too, and traumatic. Then he went to lie down on their bed, next to Zoe.

"You hate me, don't you," Zoe said in a hoarse whisper with the TV on in the background. She wasn't really watching, she just wanted the noise and the voices.

"Of course I don't hate you. I love you. I just wonder what we're doing wrong. Other kids don't get hurt this much, and their parents don't know every nurse in the ER." Zoe was always so nice to them that they remembered her, and Jaime. Austin reached over and took her hand in his, and saw that she was crying. It turned into sobs almost immediately, and he pulled her into his arms and held her.

"I'm so sorry, it was an accident. I promise it won't happen again." But suddenly he was afraid it would. He was frightened that something was happening he didn't understand.

"I believe you. And I'm sorry too. You're the best mother in the world," but for the first time it had a hollow ring to it. If she was, why did Jaime keep getting hurt? He told Zoe again and again what a good mother she was, and as he held her, there were tears rolling down his cheeks too, and the woman in his arms was starting to feel like a stranger to him. Maybe his mother was right.

Chapter 9

When Jaime was two and a half, having her normal checkup, Zoe asked to talk to Cathy Clark in her office and asked her a question which stunned her.

"I know this probably sounds crazy to you," she said to her friend almost shyly, "but would you do some bloodwork on her to check for leukemia?" Cathy frowned and looked worried. It was an odd request.

"Do you suspect something? Have you seen any signs that would indicate that?" She knew that Zoe had attended two years of medical school, was still interested in the profession, still occasionally read medical journals, and had a surprising amount of scientific knowledge. But in answer to Cathy's question, Zoe shook her head.

"No, I haven't," she said. "It's just that . . . afterward, my mother said that there had been some symptoms six months before they discovered my sister had leukemia. It probably wouldn't have made a difference, but who knows if with six more months jump on it, she might have survived it. She had the most aggressive form of the disease, so maybe it wouldn't have changed anything. Rose was three when they diagnosed her. I just don't want to miss something, and have a bad surprise later. It would reassure me if her tests come back clear."

"It's a very unusual request," Cathy said quietly. She felt sorry for her. Zoe was obviously still haunted by the loss of her sister, and terrified it could happen to Jaime, the same shocking news, the agonizing years, the tragic ending. "I don't normally like to put kids through unnecessary bloodwork. And I see absolutely not the slightest hint that there is anything wrong with Jaime. If I did, I'd tell you, Zoe. I'd want to get all the tests and consultations we could on her. But I understand why you're worried."

"I watched my sister fade away and die for four years. If we're going to face that, I'd rather know it so I can steel myself. My mother was amazing with her when my sister was sick. She gave her own bone marrow for a transplant. It got her three more years, but my mom thought it would save her. She would have done anything for her, and she never left her for a minute for the whole four years."

"That must have been tough on you," Cathy said sympathetically. Zoe didn't usually talk about it, although she had mentioned it once or twice after they became friends.

"It was. It changed my relationship with my mother forever. Before that, she was wonderful and totally attentive to both of us, and I was the favored big sister with all the privileges. Once Rose got sick, my mother had to be at the hospital with her, at labs or doctors' appointments, or getting chemo. I hardly ever saw her for four years. And afterward, it took her five years to get over it. She was in a daze for all that time. And when she woke up and could function again, she went back to work, which she hadn't done since I was born. So basically, I lost her from the moment Rose got sick. We couldn't ever put it back together again, and I think we remind each other too much of the bad times. Just seeing her or hearing her voice brings it all back, and I probably do the same for her. We talk on the phone occasionally, but I don't visit her, and she doesn't come to New York. It's better this way. After thirty years of loss and pain, it's too late to fix it. But I have to say, she taught me how to be a mother. I have never seen anyone give and do so much, or try so hard, as she did with my sister. I hope nothing like it ever happens to us, but if it does, I hope I can be like her. Everyone talked about what a great mother she was." There were tears in her eyes as she said it and Cathy's heart went out to her.

"You're a wonderful mother, Zoe," Cathy said

sincerely, "the best one I've ever seen in my practice. You're always right there for Jaime. And let's face it, she is a handful. She is curious and active, into everything. I know she's had some mishaps, but I think she would have had many more if it weren't for you. I know you do everything you can to keep her safe," including asking for testing for leukemia, although there was no sign of a problem. But Cathy could understand why now. "Normally, I'd discourage you from the testing you want for Jaime. As a physician, I can't justify it. But as your friend, I want to help you put your fears to rest. I'll give the lab an order for the tests, and then promise me you'll try not to think about it again. She's not your little sister. She's a healthy little girl with her whole life ahead of her. Try to believe that." Zoe smiled at her through tears, and was immeasurably grateful.

"I lie awake at night, terrified that lightning is going to strike us, like it did my family all those years ago. We all died in a way when Rose did, and it killed my parents' marriage. My father hung around for two years waiting for my mother to get better, she never did, and I guess he couldn't take it anymore. He left and married Pam a year later, that was the final blow for my mother. She sank even lower after that."

"I assume you all had therapy to get through it." She was shocked when Zoe shook her head.

"No, only my father did. He married his first

therapist. Pam. She's a nice woman. I never let myself get close to her once they were married, it upset my mom too much, so I hardly ever saw them. And they had two more kids. My mother refused to go to therapy with my father, which was why he left. He wanted them to try to recover, and my mother said she just couldn't. And they never suggested any therapy for me. I was ten when Rose died, and by the time my mom was halfway sane again, I was in my rebellious teenage years. I'm not even sure they thought of therapy for me. They were both so wrecked after it happened, they never talked to each other or to me. The ship had gone down, and it was every man for himself. My father got out, my mother was underwater for a long time, and I just paddled along on my own, trying not to drown."

"Did you seek therapy later on, as an adult?" Cathy had never dared to ask her these questions, but somehow in her office she felt she could, even though they were there to talk about Jaime, not about her. But they were also friends, which made it permissible in her dual role.

"I never saw the need," Zoe answered quietly. "Eventually, I went to college. I got my life on track. Then I was busy in medical school, and came to New York after that. I was working, I met Austin, we got married and had Jaime, and now here we are. We're happy, we get along, and Rose is a distant memory now. There's not much left to say."

"You had a tough childhood, Zoe, and a lonely

one it sounds like. A brutal shock when Rose died. That was a lot for a kid that age to sort out, and even later, the divorce. You must have felt abandoned by everyone." Zoe nodded but didn't comment at first.

"It's all water over the dam now. I'm not that sad, lost kid anymore. I'm a wife and a mom, with a child of my own. My only fear is that she'll get leukemia like my sister, and our whole world will come crashing down." Cathy didn't see it the way Zoe did. The years of emotional pain Zoe had lived with had to have left deep emotional scars, and she thought therapy would have helped her at any point in time, even now, to resolve the past. She was amazed that she had never sought counseling, and had dealt with it on her own. In her opinion, performing open heart surgery on oneself would have been easier than surviving that kind of trauma without help.

"I'll order the bloodwork on Jaime, and then you can put that fear out of your mind." They both commented that Jaime seemed to be navigating being two better, and had had no injuries in several months.

Zoe felt so relieved after talking to Cathy that she mentioned the blood tests they were going to do on Jaime to Austin that night. The moment she said it, he looked panicked.

"Oh my God, is something wrong?"

"No, not at all. She's fine, or she appears to be.

My sister was a few months older when she got sick, with no warning. It's always worried me, if I had a child. I just want to know concretely that she's fine. This is about my history, not about anything Cathy or I have observed. I just want to stop worrying about it." He looked calmer after she said it, but unhappy nonetheless.

"It's too bad she has to get a blood test just to reassure you." He didn't really approve of it, but he understood. "Did Cathy think that it's okay?" He trusted her completely with their daughter's health.

"She said it won't do her any harm, and it's important to me."

"I wish there was some other way to put your mind at ease."

"There isn't," she said softly. "I want her to get the tests." She was definite about it, and he saw that he couldn't change her mind.

"You're not hiding anything from me?"

"I promise I'm not." He nodded and they finished dinner, but it preyed on Austin's mind afterward. Getting a blood test for symptoms Jaime didn't have, just for her mother's comfort level, seemed unreasonable to him. But he didn't object.

Since there was no rush, Jaime went to the lab and had the blood test two days later, and she cried when they did it, but Zoe bought her a toy afterward. She picked a baby doll with a bottle and a diaper, and its own bathtub, and she slept with it that night, after giving it a bath. She told her father all about the blood test when he came home. And when the tests came back, predictably, they were fine. Jaime was perfect, a totally healthy little girl, and Zoe slept peacefully that night, as she hadn't in years, and dreamt of Rose.

Zoe was increasingly busy at the shelter in the following months. They had been able to obtain three new grants, and one large bequest from a private donor, which made life both easier and more difficult. The influx of money expanded their budget and allowed them to hire more staff, which always brought problems in its wake. Some of them were wonderful additions, others were challenging to work with. But Zoe always balanced her responsibilities at work to perfection, and had flawless judgment about people and plans. She knew how to organize, encourage, and control her staff and kept a tight grip on the reins. She spent time with each of the children who came through their doors, and worked closely with Austin on the abuse and custody cases he was handling for them, as well as the other attorneys whose services they required.

She managed to keep all the balls of her complex job in the air, and never dropped a single one. And her relationship with the children at the shelter was compassionate and strong. She knew their histories and their names, and they all loved her. Oddly, she was always less sure of herself with her own child, which she shared with Cathy privately one day over lunch. After two and a half years of motherhood, she still questioned all of her decisions, and constantly second-guessed herself, which she never did at work.

"I think it's harder with people's own children. I see it all the time with my patients. Parents who run major corporations can't decide what time their kids should go to bed, or what they should be eating. Or what school to send them to, and then they argue with each other about it."

"At least Austin and I agree about what school we want her to go to." Zoe had just been accepted at an excellent school, three blocks from their home, for September. It was kindergarten through twelfth grade, but had a small preschool where they accepted students who had an interest in staying on from kindergarten through the upper grades. Zoe had mixed feelings about it. Jaime still seemed too young to go to school, and Zoe hated to see her baby days end so soon. Austin felt the same way, but they both had demanding jobs, and she was at home with the nanny without them anyway. Fiona was going to become part-time in the fall, and work for another family as well.

"Get ready to see Jaime with a runny nose for the next two years," Cathy said, laughing. "They get sick constantly when they start school."

"Do you think we should wait another year? We don't have to send her yet. We just thought it would be more interesting for her than going to the playground every day, and playing with Fiona at home. I think the structure will be good for her, and the challenge. She's so bright."

"I think school at three is fine. It's the right age. You don't want her to be too old or too young when she starts, and she'll have consistent friends and a social life. And yes, they catch flus and colds, but it'll strengthen her immune system. I think she'll love it," Cathy said easily, and then went on to tell Zoe about her recent breakup from a disappointing boyfriend she had just dated for six months. They had met on a dating site for people in the medical profession. He was a heart surgeon and a narcissist, according to Cathy, and he was dating a slew of women he met online and had lied to her about it. She found out from another doctor friend he was dating too. She was turning forty in a few months, and was startled at how fast time had flown.

"It feels like I was a resident just a few years ago, and now suddenly I'm old."

"Don't be ridiculous, you're not old." Zoe was about to turn thirty-seven, but it was different being single, when you hadn't found the right man yet, and still wanted children, although Cathy always said privately to Zoe that she wasn't sure she did.

"I give at the office. I'm not sure I need children of my own. I'm not even convinced I'd be good at it."

"How can you say that? You're great with kids," Zoe said.

"They're not mine. It's easy to be great with other people's kids. From where I sit, it's not as easy to be consistent and make the right decisions with your own children. The parents do the hard part, I just take care of their kids' health. Maybe that's all I know how to do." Medicine and her practice were her life. She was still close to her family in Ohio, and had three nieces and two nephews she loved. But she didn't get home as often as she liked, and had drifted away from her old friends in Columbus. Zoe had become her closest friend in New York.

"Why don't you figure out about having kids when you meet the right guy?" Zoe said gently, and then they talked about other things. They had a number of interests in common, art, books, movies, fashion. They really enjoyed each other when they had time to get together, which wasn't often, but they texted and called when they could. And their daily messages to each other were fun and light, often about something silly or humorous they had seen.

In addition to its geographic location, the school Austin and Zoe had selected for Jaime turned out to be the perfect one for her, or so it appeared. She loved it right from the first day. She was crazy about her teacher, Mrs. Ellis, and the young teaching assistant they called Mr. Bob. The school had traditional principles and structure, but also incorporated some modern views and new techniques, which satisfied both of Jaime's parents, and she announced with delight after the first day that they had great toys and good juice. Austin or Zoe was going to drop her off every day, and Fiona would pick her up at two.

Cathy's prediction proved to be true. Jaime caught a cold three weeks after school started which turned into a nasty ear infection with a high fever a week later, and Jaime missed two weeks of school. Her absence didn't matter in preschool, but Zoe hated to see her so sick, and worried that she'd have another febrile seizure when her fever went over a hundred and two. Cathy prescribed amoxicillin for the ear infection, which Jaime had never had before and turned out to be allergic to. She'd had another antibiotic, but not that one. She threw up violently for twenty-four hours, until they switched her to a different antibiotic, and five days later, she was healthy and back in school. The ear infection had been acute, and Jaime had howled in pain for two long nights before Cathy put her on the antibiotic.

Remembering what Cathy had said about Jaime being sick constantly for the first two years of school, and having taken it to heart, Zoe called an ear, nose, and throat specialist as soon as she was well. She didn't want Jaime going through something like that again, and there were colds and coughs and earaches going around, only a month after school had started. And this was the second ear infection in her life.

They went to Dr. Parker uptown in the East Seventies, whom one of Zoe's co-workers had recommended. She said that her son had had chronic ear infections for two years until they saw him, and she said he was a miracle worker. Zoe wanted his advice.

She picked Jaime up at school herself and took a cab uptown the day they went to see him. He had a toy box and an aquarium in his waiting room, so he obviously had a number of children as patients in his practice. Earaches were so common in little kids. He explained why, using a plastic model, once they got to see him. He said that children's ear passages weren't always fully developed at Jaime's age, and ear infections happened more easily. Zoe asked if they would damage her hearing. He was young and attractive and great with Zoe, as he answered her questions.

"Chronic infections could eventually damage her hearing, but more than likely, she'll outgrow them. I usually put in ear tubes if it happens too often. It's a minor surgical procedure that takes a very short time, there's very little recovery, and it works brilliantly to avoid further infections." It was the procedure Zoe's co-worker said her son had had, and he'd had no problems since. "Has Jaime had frequent ear infections? Sometimes it begins as babies, or when they start school."

"She just had a very bad one, it kept her out of school for two weeks, and she was in agony for the first two days."

"Earaches can be very painful, in children or adults," he said sympathetically, but she hadn't answered his question, intentionally. Zoe didn't want him to know that Jaime had only had two in her life. She wanted to get ear tubes for Jaime, **before** she had chronic infections. It seemed like a great prophylactic measure. Why wait for her to get another one, if he could prevent that from happening again? It was why she had come to see him, the procedure was a minor one and would do Jaime no harm. He had said so himself. "How many infections has she had, say in the past year?" He repeated the question, and smiled at Zoe. She was enjoying talking to him. He had already examined Jaime, who was back in the waiting room, playing in the toy box, while Zoe and Dr. Parker chatted in his office.

"I can't remember how many," Zoe said vaguely, "but she's had a number of them. I'm afraid she'll miss a lot of school if it keeps happening."

"She sounds like a perfect candidate for tubes," he said, making a notation on Jaime's chart, and then he glanced up at Zoe. "Are you worried about a surgical procedure for her?"

"Not really. My co-worker says you're a magician." He smiled at the compliment.

"It's really very minor. She'll be under general anesthesia for fifteen minutes, long enough to position the tubes correctly. And then she'll have about half an hour recovery time. We can remove them at any time, but I think you'll find that they'll keep her from getting the frequent ear infections she's had till now. The tubes are the magic, not the doctor in this case. When would you like to do it? I do it at the hospital, and I can do it on a Saturday morning, if you like. That way, she won't have to miss any school." He picked up the phone on his desk, and asked his nurse a question about his schedule. "I can do it on Saturday, two weeks from tomorrow, if that works for you." He was easy and accommodating, and Zoe looked pleased. She had made a decision that was going to spare Jaime years of pain from ear infections, like the misery she'd just been through. No matter that she'd only had two before, she would surely have more now that she was in school. It was good preventive medicine. The only problem was that she hadn't mentioned it to Austin, but when she explained it to him, she was sure he would agree.

"That's perfect," Zoe agreed to the date he suggested. They shook hands, and he told her that the nurse at the desk would give her all the pre-surgical information she needed. And then she went to find

Jaime at the toy box, she had building blocks and Legos all over the floor and a doll with tattered hair.

They went back downtown, and Zoe was satisfied with the appointment. Now all she had to do was tell Austin about the surgery, and sell him on the idea. She was certain they were doing the right thing. She hadn't mentioned it to Cathy either but she told herself she would approve too. It was preventive medicine, after all.

Chapter 10

Zoe mentioned the ear tubes to Austin on Saturday night while they had a late dinner, after they put Jaime to bed. They'd had a busy day with her, doing errands, and Zoe took her to a birthday party for one of her new friends in school. Her social life was about to expand exponentially with twenty children in her class, which Zoe thought was a good thing. All the more reason not to be out sick all the time, with coughs and colds and ear infections.

"I took Jaime to see an ear, nose, and throat doctor this week, by the way," Zoe said casually.

"What for? Are her ears bothering her again?" He looked surprised.

"No, she's fine. Just some preventive medicine before it happens again. He suggested ear tubes as a prophylactic measure. Apparently, they work brilliantly."

"That sounds simple enough. But won't she pull them out?"

"That's the whole point. The doctor inserts them, and we leave them in as long as we want, until she outgrows the need for them or they fall out on their own. Cathy warned me that she'd be sick constantly for the first two years of school, from exposure to other kids. At least that would rule out ear infections. I don't want her to go through that again, she was miserable. And I'm sure you don't want that either."

"The doctor puts them in? Is it a big deal?"

"He says it only takes a few minutes. They give her a general anesthetic to insert them, and a few minutes later, it's all done." She made it sound incredibly easy, as Austin looked at her hesitantly.

"They give her an anesthetic to do it? That sounds like a big deal to me. I don't like the idea of them putting her out."

"You'd rather have her screaming in pain from an ear infection every few weeks?" She made it sound like those were the only two options, but Austin wasn't convinced.

"What does Cathy think? Did she suggest it?"

"She said she's going to be sick almost constantly for the first two years of school."

"You told me that. What does she think of surgically implanting ear tubes?"

"Lots of kids have them," Zoe said blithely. "She thinks it's a good idea." It was a bold-faced lie and Zoe knew it, she thought the end justified the means. And the end in this case was a good one. She hadn't mentioned it to Cathy, because she didn't want to argue with her, in case she thought it unnecessary or premature. But Zoe didn't want to wait for another ear infection to do it. Why let Jaime go through all that pain again if it could be prevented? With Cathy's alleged endorsement, Austin agreed. He trusted her medically a hundred percent, even more than he trusted Zoe or himself. She had far more experience than they did, and he liked how cautious and conservative she was. She didn't rush into anything, overprescribe medication, or do anything they didn't have to do. So if she thought the ear tubes made sense, he wasn't enthusiastic about it because of the anesthesia, but he reluctantly agreed.

"I don't think any of my nephews had them," Austin said pensively as they cleared away the dishes.

"Maybe they don't get ear infections," she said lightly.

"That's true. I never asked."

"And with the high fevers she'd run with an ear infection, we have the risk of another febrile seizure in her case," Zoe reminded him.

"She's never had one again," he said staunchly.

"I think we're doing the right thing," she said seriously.

"When do they want to do it?" He still looked unhappy about it. He believed in natural solutions whenever possible, particularly for such a young child, not surgery.

"Two weeks from today. We'll be in and out in an hour." He nodded and left the room, still digesting what they were planning to do.

He asked his brother about it the following week. He said that one of his boys had had them too. "The poor kid had constant ear infections, and he wanted to be on the swim team, which made them worse. The only way he could swim on the team was if he got the tubes inserted, with plugs in his case. They work well for him, he still has them. It's not a big deal." After that, Austin was reassured. He had been unnerved by the way Zoe had sprung the plan on him as a fait accompli, and making him feel like a bad father if he wouldn't agree. But if his nephew had them, they must be okay. He had gotten them at six and was now twelve. But Jaime was only three, still a baby to him, and had had only two ear infections in three years, which didn't seem like a lot to him.

The night before the surgery, Zoe reminded Austin that Jaime couldn't have anything to eat or drink after nine o'clock that night. They didn't want her to vomit and aspirate it while she was under general anesthesia. The surgery was at nine A.M. the next day. It was going to be done at Lenox Hill Hospital uptown. Austin was feeling panicked about it, and didn't want to admit it to Zoe. She was totally calm, and elated every time she talked about the painful ear infections Jaime was going to avoid.

They told Jaime about it in the morning when she woke up, and Zoe couldn't give her cereal, fruit, and juice as she always did.

"We have to get ready," she told her. "We're going back to see the nice doctor with the toys who looked in your ears. But we're meeting him somewhere else. He's going to give us little tubes for your ears."

"No, Mommy," Jaime said seriously. "I'm not opposed to put things in my ears." Cathy had told her that after the peas.

"That's true. But the doctor can do it. It won't even hurt." Jaime put her hands over her ears then and shook her head, and looked at her mother with a question. "Will I get a cast?" She brightened at that. "I want pink."

"Not this time. No cast. They can't put a cast on your ears, or you won't hear me tell you how much I love you," she said and kissed Jaime's neck.

"I want a cast." Jaime pouted. That was something she knew, and it made Austin's heart ache as she said it. At three, she had broken bones twice.

"Don't be silly, you don't need a cast." Zoe continued the banter as she got Jaime dressed in a pink tracksuit with pink sneakers and a pink coat with toggles on it. She looked adorable and so small as Austin carried her outside, and they hailed a cab to take them to the hospital. It was eight o'clock on a Saturday morning.

When they got there, they went to same-day surgery. Zoe got Jaime undressed, a house pediatrician examined her, and the anesthesiologist came to talk to all three of them. He said that Dr. Parker was already in surgery. He'd had a case before them, but would speak to them after the tubes were in. The anesthesiologist asked if Zoe and Austin understood the procedure, and they said they did. He said it would be brief, and then he talked to Jaime, and told her she was going to get sleepy for a few minutes, the doctor was going to put little tubes in her ears, and then she would wake up and she'd come back to her mom and dad, and they could go home.

"You're not coming with me?" Jaime looked suddenly panicked and leapt into her mother's arms, as Austin watched, looking grim.

"May I?" Zoe asked the anesthesiologist and he shook his head.

Two attendants came to take her to surgery then, and Jaime tried to cling to her mother and looked imploringly at Austin. He felt like a monster as he let them take her away on a gurney, and then he and Zoe sat down in the small room to wait for her. Her clothes were neatly folded on the bed.

"I don't know why we had to do this now," he said with the sound of Jaime screaming for them still ringing in his head. "Why couldn't we wait to see if she had more ear infections? This seems so extreme, and premature to me." The only reason he had agreed to it was because Zoe said Cathy thought it was a good idea.

"It's not extreme, it doesn't hurt, and ear infections do. It's the smart, responsible thing to do," Zoe said convincingly, as they waited.

"She's only three, for heaven's sake. My nephew didn't have it done till he was six." Austin stood and stared out the window, and Zoe sat quietly in a chair, and forty-five minutes later, Jaime was back. She looked wide awake and had already come out of the anesthetic. Dr. Parker was with them, as the attendants rolled her into the room, and she sat on the bed and smiled. Austin looked enormously relieved, as he picked her up and held her with tears in his eyes.

"It went perfectly," the doctor assured them as he took off his surgical cap. He was still wearing scrubs as he smiled at them both, and then at Jaime. "She was very brave, but when I was talking to her, she fell asleep. She can do whatever she wants today, normal activity, and a big breakfast, I'll bet. And no more nasty ear infections like all the ones she's had till now. Too many for mom to even remember how many there were." He smiled at Zoe, as Austin glanced at her with obvious surprise. "Give me a call if you have any questions or problems. I don't think you will." He shook hands with both of them and rushed out, as Austin stared at his wife, and gently set Jaime down on the bed.

"Did you tell him she's had a lot of ear infections, 'too many to even remember how many,' in order to convince him to do it?" Austin asked her in a low voice.

"I can't recall what I said. I told him how bad the last one was, that was enough," she said as she started to get Jaime dressed.

"But she's only had two in her whole life," Austin said, trying to hide his anger from their child. "You lied to him, Zoe, didn't you, so he'd do it?"

She turned to him and looked him in the eye. "I don't want her to get any more ear infections. Is that so terrible?" Austin didn't answer her, and as soon as Jaime was dressed, they went home in a cab. He didn't say a word on the way downtown, as Jaime chattered, and Zoe avoided his eyes.

Zoe was giving Jaime breakfast when Austin went for a walk, and as soon as he left the building, he called Cathy on her cell.

"How are you?" she asked, surprised to hear from him.

"Pissed, I think."

"Is Jaime okay?" She put her doctor's voice on immediately, ready to focus on the child.

"She seems to be, she came out of the surgery in less than an hour. Was this your idea or Zoe's, and did you really think it was a good idea?"

"What surgery? What happened? Did she get hurt?" She sounded surprised.

"We just had ear tubes surgically implanted, with Jaime under general anesthesia. I have the distinct impression that Zoe told the specialist Jaime had recurring ear infections. And she told me you thought it was a good idea."

"I don't know anything about it, in this case. I have patients who've had the procedure, but only after chronic ear infections. It's not dangerous, and the tubes won't harm her. They'll take them out eventually or they'll fall out on their own. But in Jaime's case, after two episodes, it seems very premature, and unnecessary, to be honest. I'm surprised the ENT was willing to do it."

"Zoe told him Jaime had had more infections than she could remember. And she told me you suggested it as a preventive measure against future infections."

"Shit," she said, reverting to his friend and not just their doctor. "She never told me she was considering it. Probably because she knew I would have discouraged her. Jaime doesn't need that yet, and maybe never will. It won't do anything bad to her, but she didn't need to go through it. And I never encourage general anesthesia unless it's absolutely necessary."

"That's what I thought." Austin was livid and Cathy could hear it.

"I think she overstepped on this one. Can I talk

to her about it? I don't like her using me to convince you of something I knew nothing about."

"Neither do I. Bluntly put, she lied to me, she used you to convince me to do it. Once she told me you liked the idea, I endorsed it blindly. She lied to all of us, you, me, and the doctor."

"She didn't lie to me," Cathy corrected him, "she just didn't tell me."

"Okay, a sin of omission in your case, and of commission in mine," he conceded.

"You must be very upset," she said sympathetically. She loved Zoe as a friend, but this wasn't right, just to get what she wanted. It was cheating.

"Furious is more like it. My wife lied to me, and my three-year-old just had a general anesthetic unnecessarily and under false pretenses. How would you feel?"

"Probably as mad as you are. Although knowing Zoe, she had good intentions. She just went a little too far. I'm sorry I didn't know, I would have told you, and we could have talked her out of it. If anything like it ever happens again, you can count on me to let you know." He believed she would. At this point, he trusted Cathy more than his wife. "I'm really sorry, Austin."

"Thank you."

Cathy suspected that the sparks were going to fly between them that night, and she was right. As soon as Jaime fell asleep, Austin quietly closed the door to their bedroom, and turned to his wife with his eyes blazing. Until then, he had avoided her all day, but he was face-to-face with her now.

"What the hell were you thinking? You lied to me to get me to agree to a surgical procedure for our daughter. You told me Cathy thought it was a good idea, and she knew nothing about it. And you lied to the doctor and told him she'd had recurring ear infections, when she's had only two. Are you crazy? You conned me into agreeing to general anesthesia by lying to me. Zoe, what are you doing? It's so goddamn unfair. I would never do that to you."

"I don't want her to be sick all the time, like she was with the last one. Why wait until she's had a bunch of ear infections? I wanted to prevent them in the future."

"By lying to me and the doctor, and not telling our pediatrician? How am I ever supposed to trust you again? How would you feel if I did that to you?"

"I'd realize that you did it for Jaime's good. I was doing the right thing for her, whether you think so or not," she defended herself hotly, and justified everything she'd done.

"The end does not justify the means in this case, when you lied to everyone involved. I would **never** have agreed to a general anesthetic, even for five minutes, if I'd known the truth. You took away my right to make an informed decision as her father.

You're not her only parent, Zoe. I'm here too, and the decisions about Jaime have to be ours, jointly, and if we don't agree, we'll have to work out some kind of compromise. But don't you **ever** do something like this again."

"I promise, I won't," she said in the voice of a chastised child. "I love you, and I'm sorry. But I knew it was the right thing for her."

"That's not for you to decide on your own. You're only half that voice, and I'm the other half. Don't forget it again." He stormed out of their bedroom then and slept on the couch in his small home office. Zoe didn't try to convince him to sleep in their bedroom. She knew he needed time to cool off.

On Sunday, he told her he was taking Jaime to visit his parents at their house in Sag Harbor, and said in a stiff voice that she was welcome to come. But she knew that the time in the car with him would be tense, which wouldn't be good for any of them, least of all Jaime, and she didn't want to see his parents, particularly his mother.

"I've got some work to do," she said quietly. "Why don't you and Jaime enjoy your parents. Give them my love." He didn't argue with her or insist that she come, and he hadn't asked her before he'd called his parents and suggested the visit. One of his brothers was going to visit them that day too, and it would be nice for Jaime to see her cousins, since Zoe never took Jaime to New Jersey or Connecticut to see them, and he always had to organize it. He and Jaime left half an hour later. He didn't mention the ear tube incident again. There was nothing left to say about it, it was done, but he hadn't swallowed it yet, which Zoe could see. She had no regrets about it, she still believed she had done the right thing, even if her methods had been somewhat dubious. She knew her motives were pure. It was all for Jaime's good, which justified everything, even if Austin couldn't see that. At least not yet.

Cathy called a little while later, as Zoe was working on some papers for the shelter.

"I'm calling as your friend, not your doctor," she said clearly at the outset. "How's Austin?"

"Not happy. He'll get over it," Zoe said coolly. "I gather he talked to you yesterday."

"He did. Zoe, please don't use me to justify medical procedures for Jaime unless you talk to me first. I would have tried to talk you out of it, which is probably why you didn't ask me. It may prove to be the right thing for her, but not now, after only two ear infections in three years. It was way too soon."

"I just didn't want her to go through all that pain again," she said with a sigh, "she screamed in agony for two days."

"And it stopped when we got her on the right antibiotic. I just don't want to get in the middle of things between you and Austin. I love you both, you're my favorite friends, and the best parents I know. And the three of us trust each other. I want to keep it that way."

"He'll calm down," Zoe said confidently, with no apparent remorse.

"I'm sure he will, but he sounded very pissed."

"He is, or was yesterday. All I want is what's best for Jaime."

"I know you do. But you may have to go about it a little more openly, to give everyone a chance to vote." Zoe didn't answer. They talked for a few moments, and then hung up, and Zoe went back to the papers she was working on. They were applying for a federal grant, which would benefit the children they protected.

Austin and Jaime had gotten to his parents' house by then. His brother and his family hadn't arrived yet, and his parents were happy to see them.

"Where's Zoe?" Constance asked as she poured apple juice into a glass for Jaime.

"She had homework," Jaime answered her grandmother. "She said to send you and Grampa George her love."

"Send her ours." Constance smiled at her. Jaime went out to the garden with her grandfather then to play with their dog, a little Maltese named Molly. Constance looked at her son after they went outside. "Everything okay?"

"Yeah. Sure."

"You look stressed," she said cautiously, wondering what was going on, and why Zoe hadn't come.

"I had a long week. I'm doing a bunch of pro bono cases for the shelter, with some nasty characters. They always are. By the way, Jaime had ear tubes put in yesterday." He decided that he'd better tell her before Jaime did.

"Patrick has them too, and they were thinking of doing them for Seth. I didn't know Jaime had ear problems, other than the infection she had a few weeks ago."

"Zoe thought we should do it." He looked tense as he said it, and his mother nodded and didn't comment. At least Jaime hadn't gotten injured recently, which was an improvement, and made her think that she had been too extreme with her worries. Maybe Jaime had just been a rambunctious toddler, as they said.

His brother arrived shortly after that, and they talked about their respective plans for Thanksgiving. Both his brothers were going to their in-laws' and his parents had decided to go on a cruise for the first time. Usually, they all got together in Sag Harbor for Thanksgiving, but not this year. Zoe's father and Pam always invited them to Santa Barbara, but they never went. Zoe didn't want to be forced to make a choice of which parent to visit, so she visited neither. And her mother was working that day. She hated holidays and had ever since Rose's death.

Austin and Zoe would be spending the holiday at home, which was different but didn't displease him.

After a big lunch, and time for the children to play, Austin and Jaime drove back to the city. Zoe had set the table and bought Mexican food for dinner, which they all loved. While they ate, Jaime reported on her day with her cousins, uncle, aunt, and grandparents, and her account of the day made both her parents laugh. Little by little they relaxed. After dinner, Austin stayed to talk to Zoe for a few minutes. They didn't speak of the ear tubes again, but Austin knew that from now on, something would be different. The person he trusted most in the world had lied to him, and he knew that no matter how hard he tried, he wouldn't forget it, and he would never fully trust her again. He was no longer rabid about it, or even angry. He was just sad.

Chapter 11

Despite Zoe's good intentions with the ear tubes, from September until Christmas, Jaime was constantly sick, with illnesses she picked up at school from the other kids. Nothing serious, colds, flu, bronchitis, croup where she barked like a seal each time she coughed, and a stomach bug. She was absent as often as she was present. She was even sick over Thanksgiving. She didn't get another ear infection, but she had everything else. She was sick for all of Christmas vacation and had roseola, to add insult to injury, which wasn't serious, but unpleasant. All their Christmas photos showed Jaime in pajamas with a red rash on her face. She spent most of the time in the bath, with Zoe putting calamine lotion on her afterward. As an only child, she had had no exposure to other children and their maladies until then, except at the playground. Austin called it the Disease du Jour, and

Cathy tried to encourage them. She said it was totally normal for her first year at preschool. The school expected it too.

They had a nice Christmas anyway, although they couldn't go to Austin's parents as usual, which was disappointing. Jaime wasn't well enough to go, and his parents didn't want to catch any of her maladies. Santa Claus showed up right on schedule and left everything that Jaime had asked for in a letter she had mailed to him on December 1. She even got a pink bike with training wheels which Austin assembled for her at midnight. They took it to the park for her to try out, with a matching pink helmet, on the first day after her roseola had disappeared. She got to go ice skating with her parents at Rockefeller Center on the last day of Christmas vacation too. Santa had brought her new skates, and had been extremely generous with her. She said it was the best Christmas of her life, and in fact, the only one she remembered. Santa had left her a letter too, which Zoe wrote in red pen, telling Jaime how proud he was of her, and Mrs. Claus and the reindeer sent their love.

The atmosphere between Austin and Zoe had relaxed again. He had forgiven her for the ear tubes incident, and realized it was well meant, and she had solemnly sworn not to lie to him again. He believed her. He thought she had learned a lesson. It had taken them a month to get close again. But the holidays had been very special, and even Jaime's roseola and cold hadn't ruined them.

Jaime reported on all of it to her friends at school, and told them about the cold and rash she'd had, which several of her classmates had had before her, which was how she'd gotten it just in time for Christmas. She got ten solid days of school in, when she woke up one morning with a raspy voice and said she had a sore throat. When Zoe checked, she had a blazing fever, all of which had come on quickly with no warning.

Zoe went to work late so she could take her to see Cathy, who did a quick test, and said she had strep throat. They did a culture too, which would take longer, and she prescribed a broad spectrum antibiotic in the meantime. Her throat was so sore Jaime could hardly swallow. Zoe sent Fiona out to buy popsicles for her, and Zoe took the rest of the day off from work so she could care for her herself. Cathy warned her to be careful she and Austin didn't catch it, since it was highly contagious. Austin had had a recurring cold since October. Every time Jaime got sick, he did too. Preschool was proving to be tough on both of them. Zoe was hardier, and seemed to have better immunity, since she saw kids at work every day, and she had only caught one cold since the epidemic of illnesses that had felled Austin and Jaime. She warned Austin when he came home that night not to kiss Jaime or he'd be sick again, and he groaned at the prospect.

"Why didn't someone warn us that children are dangerous? They're germ farms. How could she get sick again? She just went back to school."

"Cathy says everybody has it," she reassured him. He blew Jaime a kiss from the doorway but didn't go into her room, and Cathy had told Zoe to warn him to wash his hands frequently and take his vitamins. She was beginning to feel like Florence Nightingale, Zoe teased him.

"More like Nurse Ratched," he said, teasing her back, and kissed her as he went to wash his hands.

The broad spectrum antibiotic Cathy had prescribed was very effective, and in two days, Jaime was bouncing all over the house, wanted to bake cupcakes, was fever-free, and said her throat felt all better. She'd eaten all the popsicles. Zoe kept her home for two more days, and then sent her back to school, fully recovered. And miraculously, Austin had managed not to catch it.

That night, Jaime reported in detail about her first day back at school. They were going on a field trip to the Museum of Natural History the following week, and she was going to be Person of the Week, with a poster where everyone in the class had to say nice things about her and the teacher would write them down. And the big news of the day was that Mr. Bob, the teaching assistant, had strep throat too. Austin felt sorry for him.

"Poor guy," he commented. "You couldn't pay me enough to be a preschool teacher, I'd need a resident doctor to get me through it. How long do you suppose this will go on?"

"Cathy says two years," Zoe said, laughing at him.

"Oh God, don't tell me that. Can't we fast-track her into high school? I may not survive till first grade."

Jaime was in particularly good spirits the following week when she was Person of the Week, and came home with a poster, with a self-portrait she had done in crayon in a pink dress, and the comments the teacher had diligently written on it, of all the nice things Jaime's classmates said about her. "They weren't allowed to say bad stuff," Jaime explained, "like when I had an accident at school and wet my pants." Austin and Zoe loved listening to her. She was a whole person with her own ideas and opinions now, and expressed them well. And she had lots of friends at school.

She had been healthy for an entire week after the brief bout of strep throat. Austin asked Zoe if she was still on the antibiotic, and Zoe said she had stopped it after four days. She said Jaime didn't need it anymore since the sore throat was gone and she felt fine, and Zoe didn't like abusing antibiotics, in case she got immune to them and they wouldn't be effective in the future when she needed them. It sounded reasonable to Austin, and Jaime seemed fine.

Jaime ate a big bowl of pasta and meatballs that night, which Zoe had picked up at a nearby restaurant on her way home from work. She was dealing with assorted crises at the shelter and didn't have time to cook, and Austin had four new cases, and was swamped, so takeout from local restaurants worked well for them. Sashimi, sushi, Thai, Italian, Chinese, roast chickens from their favorite deli, and pizza in a pinch. The spaghetti and meatballs had been delicious and Jaime ate a lot of it, and so did they.

Everything seemed fine, until Jaime woke up in the middle of the night crying that her stomach hurt. She threw up shortly after, all over the room, and then screamed that her stomach hurt even worse. It was four in the morning, Jaime was crying, and Zoe was trying to clean up her room when Austin came in to see what was happening. Jaime said she had a terrible stomachache, and Austin looked at Zoe, exhausted.

"Should I call Cathy?" he asked her.

"I hate to call her at this hour," Zoe said, as she took the towels to the laundry room to soak them, and when she came back, Jaime was crying even more. At first Zoe thought it was stomach flu, but this seemed worse, Jaime was writhing in pain, which she had never done before.

"Maybe we should go to the ER," Zoe said, trying to assess the situation.

"At least we haven't been in a while," he said

sleepily, but he was starting to get worried too. Jaime's face was very pale.

Zoe gently tried to touch her abdomen, and with a question in her mind, she touched her on the right side, and Jaime screamed in agony. Zoe glanced up at Austin and they both had the same thought at the same time. Appendicitis, with her abdomen tender on the right side.

"I'll get dressed," he said without further comment, and was back in two minutes in jeans and loafers and a heavy sweater, and Zoe dressed just as fast. They wrapped Jaime in a blanket and Austin carried her. She continued to cry all the way to the hospital, and she was doubled over in pain when they walked into the ER, which was bustling with activity at five A.M.

Austin sat down holding Jaime, while Zoe spoke to the nurse at the desk and told her that her daughter had severe stomach pains, and then suggested appendicitis. The nurse nodded and said that the pediatrician on call would be with them in a few minutes. He was admitting a six-week-old with pneumonia, and Zoe went to fill out the familiar forms. A nurse's aide took them to an examining room they had seen before as soon as she got back.

"This is where I got my pink cast," Jaime said, remembering. It had been a landmark in her life, and whenever she got hurt, she asked for another one.

The doctor walked in five minutes later, and was a resident on call that night. Zoe reported Jaime's symptoms and said that she was experiencing acute pain, particularly on the right side, and this was much worse than the stomach flu she'd had two months before. And as though to illustrate it, Jaime let out a scream, followed by a long whine, and was crying.

He talked to Jaime for a minute and then to Zoe again. "Has she complained of pain lately?"

"No, she hasn't."

"Nausea?"

"Yes," Zoe confirmed, and Austin frowned.

"When was she nauseous?" He was surprised. "She ate a huge dinner of spaghetti and meatballs last night."

"Which she threw up eight hours later. She's complained of nausea a couple of times in the last few days, but nothing came of it, so I didn't think much of it, until now."

"I think we have a hot appendix here," the resident said seriously, and Austin felt his own stomach turn over, worried about his daughter. "We may not have time to lose, we don't want it to perforate. I'd like to get it out fast, these things can move quickly." He was very definite about it, and Zoe nodded in agreement.

"I agree," Zoe said quickly, she didn't want to waste time either, and suddenly Austin intervened.

"I want a second opinion before we move on this. Is there an experienced surgeon in the house?" He was cold and calm and serious. He didn't want to be railroaded into surgery by a panicked resident with limited experience.

"Of course," the resident said, visibly offended, and left the room to page a surgeon on call.

"If it's her appendix, we need to act fast," Zoe whispered to him.

"Not that fast. That guy looks twelve years old. I'm not agreeing to surgery till someone else tells us it's the only option." It was five-thirty A.M., and he wanted to call Cathy, but he agreed with Zoe that they should wait another hour.

The resident returned ten minutes later with a doctor roughly Austin's age, and he scowled as he looked at the chart, after greeting Austin and Zoe with a cursory glance. "Wait a minute here, folks. Let's go about this sensibly," he said, looking at the resident. "I want an ultrasound so I can see if her appendix is hot or not. It could be anything, intestinal flu, colitis, something she ate." He looked at Austin then. "I had a six-year-old boy come in last year, and we saw a tiny turtle swimming around when we X-rayed him, he had swallowed it. Kids do weird things. I had a four-year-old who had ingested a Lego. Let's get an ultrasound now." There was a sonography lab on the same floor as the ER, and the four of them rolled down the hall to it with a nurse, with Jaime on the gurney, crying. She was frightened and in pain.

They set up the ultrasound for her, and the surgeon studied the sonogram with the technician, as

Zoe and Austin stood to one side. She was convinced they should operate immediately, before Jaime's appendix burst, and she risked septicemia which could kill her, she told Austin. But the surgeon turned to them and shook his head.

"No turtle," the surgeon said to Jaime, and he turned to her parents. "Nothing shows on the sonogram. Her appendix isn't inflamed. Has she eaten anything strange in the last twelve hours?"

"Spaghetti and meatballs," Austin answered for her.

"A bad oyster? Seafood that might not have been fresh? She has no known food allergies," he mused, and thanked the sonography technician. "I'm not taking a kid into surgery for an appendectomy with nothing on a sonogram. We may have to observe her for a while. I want to keep her in the ER." They rolled her back to the exam room, and Zoe looked panicked and whispered to Austin after the surgeon left the room.

"What if he doesn't know how to read the sonogram, and her appendix bursts?"

"I don't know," Austin said, running a hand through his hair. "I'm calling Cathy." He walked away to call her on his cellphone and Zoe stayed with Jaime, who was still in excruciating pain.

Austin called Cathy on her cell, apologized for waking her at an ungodly hour, and told her what was going on. "They thought it was appendicitis at first, and so did we. She's screaming in pain. The hothead resident wanted to operate immediately, and Zoe agreed with him, Jaime is tender on the right side. Zoe still thinks it's appendicitis. They called in a surgeon and he ordered an ultrasound. He says her appendix looks fine and isn't inflamed, so he's not going to operate. No one knows what this is, Jaime looks like she's in agony."

"It could just be a bad case of stomach flu. There's a lot of it going around. I'll be there in twenty minutes," she promised and showed up in fifteen. She conferred with the surgeon, and the resident to spare his ego, and then the surgeon turned to Zoe again.

"Has she been sick recently, or on any medication?"

"She had strep throat, and was on an antibiotic," Zoe answered, and as she said it, Cathy looked like a light had gone on.

"Wait a minute! Did you finish the course of antibiotics?" she asked Zoe. "All seven days?"

Zoe looked mildly sheepish. "I gave it to her for four days. I didn't want to overdo it."

"You can't do that with an antibiotic," Cathy chided her. "What may have happened is that you got the strep subdued but didn't knock it out, and when that happens, the strep can travel, and go to your stomach lining. It's not dangerous but it's excruciatingly painful, and the timing is about right. I think that may be what happened."

"Bingo." The surgeon smiled at her. "Good detective work, Doctor. I'll bet that's it. It's just as painful as appendicitis," he explained to Zoe and Austin.

"What do we do for that?" Austin asked them, looking hopeful and somewhat relieved.

"Put her back on the antibiotic," Cathy answered him. "She'll be better in twenty-four hours, out of pain in a few days, and fine in a week. And all seven days this time," she said, looking at Zoe, who wasn't convinced of the theory.

"Don't you think it would be safer to take her appendix out now anyway, in case you're wrong? If it bursts, it would be dangerous. I'd rather play it safe here," she said firmly and Austin looked shocked.

"With surgery?"

"Her appendix shows no sign of inflammation," the surgeon said sternly, "there is no valid reason to take it out. And what would **you** rather have? Surgery or an antibiotic? I don't know about you, but I'd go for the pill every time."

"Jaime's mom just wants to be cautious," Cathy translated for her. Zoe was coming across as hysterical and unreasonable, but Cathy knew her well. She was an ultra-caring mother who would go to any lengths to protect her child. "We'll keep her here for a few hours, and start her on the antibiotic. I think she'll respond to it very quickly. She did well on it before," Cathy said calmly.

"Sounds like a plan to me," the surgeon said. "You don't need me, then," he said and left the room, and Cathy stayed with them for an hour, and then left them, and Austin walked her out.

"Thank you for coming. Christ, Zoe would have had her in surgery if you hadn't come in."

"The surgeon wouldn't have gone along with it. People with a little medical training react like Zoe. They think they know all the obvious answers. But the real diagnosis is usually something more subtle than that, like in this case. I'm sure the strep has gotten into Jaime's stomach lining, which hurts like hell."

"Well, all's well that ends well. I'm glad she didn't have her appendix out for nothing," Austin said, relieved.

"Me too." Cathy smiled at him. "You can always call me, at any hour. Glad I could help." As always, he appreciated her calm demeanor and cool head. She was great in a crisis. And they had a lot of them.

"You came up with the right answer." The conservative one, as usual, which was why he liked her as a doctor. Zoe was willing to go along with more extreme measures, but he wasn't, not where his daughter was concerned, or even for himself.

He went back to Zoe and Jaime then. She had just been given the antibiotic. They let her leave the hospital at noon. She was feeling a little better.

"I hope Cathy is right," Zoe said in the cab on the way home.

"I do too, and I'm glad Jaime didn't have surgery for nothing. The surgeon was smart too."

They put Jaime to bed, and she fell asleep immediately, and Zoe went to lie down until Fiona came in. Austin had to leave, he had a court appearance that afternoon on a case for the shelter. He kissed Zoe before he left and smiled at her.

"We came out winners on this one," he said with relief.

"I hope you're right. It would be terrible if they made a mistake and should have operated." He nodded, but didn't argue with her. Jaime was home safe and sound in bed. That was all that mattered. He was sure that Cathy was right, and Jaime would get better quickly. Zoe always favored more extreme measures, but he knew what was behind it. She didn't want to lose another little girl she loved, whatever it took to save her.

And as it turned out, Cathy was right. A week later, Jaime was fine, for real this time, and back in school. She told everyone about the boy who had swallowed a turtle.

Chapter 12

They limped through the rest of the winter with fewer illnesses than they had had before Christmas. Another cold for each of them and not much else. And once again, Zoe was unscathed. But Austin was tired and had lost weight, and Jaime had had more than her fair share of winter miseries in her first months of school. Austin suggested that they go to Florida for Jaime's spring break, and it sounded like a great idea to all of them.

Austin found a resort just outside Miami that had a beautiful pool, a spectacular beach, and lots of activities for children, and he reserved a two-bedroom suite for them for Jaime's vacation. They could hardly wait and were in high spirits when they flew to Miami, and were picked up by the van from the hotel.

Jaime got all excited when she saw the pool and the people having fun around it, and she wanted to play on the beach too. There was a high-end shopping mall near the hotel, which Zoe wanted to explore, and Austin just wanted to relax and enjoy his wife and daughter. He was exhausted by months of hard work, and had won two of the custody cases he was handling for the shelter.

They changed into their bathing suits as soon as they arrived. Zoe slathered sunscreen on Jaime and Austin, and they went out to the pool, where Jaime insisted her father take her swimming immediately. She was wearing floaties, inflatable armbands, since she couldn't really swim yet, and Austin held her and showed her how to kick while holding on to the side of the pool. She'd had a few lessons, but all she could do was dog paddle while her armbands kept her afloat. She started to run when she got out of the pool, and Austin stopped her instantly and told her she'd have a time-out if she ran at the pool.

"Let her have some fun," Zoe said, lying in the sun in a bikini that showed off her figure.

"It won't be fun for any of us if she falls and hurts herself," he answered Zoe. "You can't be lenient with her here. One of us has to have our eyes on her at all times," he reminded her.

"Obviously," Zoe said and closed her eyes as she lay in the sun, since she knew that Austin was watching her. And later that afternoon, they went for a walk on the beach, with Jaime running ahead and then coming back to them as Austin and Zoe walked hand in hand, and Jaime stopped to pick up shells.

Austin promised to buy pails and molds and shovels at the gift shop the next day and build a sandcastle with Jaime. She was already having fun on the first day.

The next day, Austin and Jaime got up early and went down to the beach. After a stop at the gift shop, he built a sandcastle worthy of a princess, and then waded into the ocean with her, holding tightly to her hand. There were lifeguards both at the pool and the beach, and dozens of children everywhere. It was the perfect place for a family vacation, and by the end of the second day, Jaime had made several friends her own age. They played in the pool together, with their mothers standing next to them, and while Zoe took her turn with her, Austin lay in the sun and went to sleep. It was the perfect vacation for tired, busy people from New York.

At night, they explored nearby restaurants, and Jaime joined them for dinner. Austin arranged an outing on a glass-bottomed boat, so they could see the fish.

They put Jaime in an arts and crafts class for three-to-five-year-olds, making shell necklaces, and Austin and Zoe went snorkeling in the ocean while she was busy. They hadn't had as much fun together in years. It reminded them both of their early days together where they'd been carefree and madly in love. And now they had Jaime to make it even better.

"We should have invited Grandma Connie and Grampa George to come with us," Jaime said generously, and Austin and Zoe smiled at each other. They loved being just the three of them, and they bought postcards for Jaime to show her class when they went home.

They spent an afternoon at Seaquarium, and then went back to the pool at the hotel so Jaime could meet up with her friends again. Two of them were from New York and Jaime was already clamoring to see them again. They had to remind her every day not to run at the pool, where the wet surface was slippery, and several children had already fallen and gotten hurt, but with Austin's stern warnings and close supervision, Jaime had been pretty good. And he was proud of the fact that Jaime had been well behaved at the hotel and the restaurants they went to, she had gotten much more manageable since she'd started school, and used to following directions. She was more grown up and reasonable than she had been at two. She was a pleasure to be with, and all three of them had enjoyed the trip. There were even several couples they'd met around the pool with children the same age that Zoe and Austin hoped to see again. Zoe rarely had time to meet up with other women, except at work. And it was nice meeting people away from their jobs, and enjoying them socially. Zoe loved having time to just be a mom and a wife, without all the pressure and demands of her job. She hated to see the vacation end.

She was talking to three of the women, while Jaime and the three other children were playing nearby, on the last day. Zoe was smiling and relaxed, she had a deep tan and looked beautiful, as the four women were chatting. And Austin had gone to play tennis with one of the men they'd met.

They were comparing the schools their children went to, one of them in the suburbs and two in New York, when Austin came back from his tennis game, and spotted Jaime racing around the pool with her friends on the wet cement. Zoe had her back to them and didn't see them, and was wearing sunglasses and a big hat. She looked like a movie star, and Austin could see that Jaime and her pals were going wild, and none of the mothers were watching them.

He called out to Jaime and she didn't hear him, as he rushed across the pool area to stop her from running, and before he could get to her, he saw her stub her toe and trip, slip across the wet cement, hit her face on the side of the pool, fall into the water, and go down like a rock to the bottom of the pool at the deep end. She didn't have her armbands on, and no one had noticed her yet. She was so small and had fallen in so fast. Zoe still had her back to her, and the lifeguard was helping an elderly woman with a deck chair and hadn't spotted Jaime when she fell in. Austin was at the pool within seconds, kicked off his shoes, jumped in, wearing his tennis clothes, swam down to the bottom, grabbed Jaime, and rose to the surface with her, as she spluttered and coughed. The lifeguard had seen Austin dive in and rushed to the side of the pool to pull Jaime out when Austin handed her to him. The lifeguard laid her on the ground, as Austin hauled himself out of the pool and picked Jaime up in his arms, as she coughed up the water she'd swallowed, and as he held her, he realized that he was covered in blood. She had split her chin wide open on the side of the pool as she went down. By then people were looking and asking if they could help. Austin was shaking, as he realized that if he hadn't seen her, she might have drowned.

A man came over to them and said he was a doctor, took a quick look at her chin, and told Austin she would have to be stitched up. The wound was bleeding profusely, as Austin pointed to Zoe and asked the lifeguard to go and get his wife.

She looked shocked when he came to get her, still talking to the other women, and rushed to where he pointed to Austin and Jaime, and she almost slipped herself on the wet surface, knelt down next to them, and tried to reach out for Jaime, but Austin had a firm grip on her, and spoke to Zoe in a harsh voice.

"Get a car and driver from the hotel," he said to her coldly, "she needs to be stitched up. She's got a gash on her chin. And while you were talking to those women, she damn near drowned."

"I was watching her," Zoe insisted.

"No, you weren't. I saw you. You were talking to them with your back to the pool. You didn't see any of it, she was running around the pool, and she didn't have her floaties on." All week they had made her wear them anytime they were near the pool, and on the very last day, everything had gone wrong. It was Murphy's Law, but it wasn't new to them. "Just get a car, we can discuss it later," he said, as Jaime sobbed and clung to him. It was a sad end to their wonderful vacation, and he couldn't believe how irresponsible Zoe had been with a three-year-old in her care at a swimming pool.

The women Zoe had been chatting with were all crowded around them by then, holding tightly to their children. Jaime had served as a lesson in what could happen in an instant if you ran around a swimming pool.

"What can we do to help?" one of them asked him.

"We need a car to get to the hospital. My wife is taking care of it," he said, as Jaime continued to bleed all over him and the lifeguard handed him a towel, which was instantly drenched with blood.

Zoe had run to the front desk on bare feet. She came back five minutes later with the assistant manager of the hotel, who insisted on escorting them to the car they were providing them. There were signs everywhere that said "Do Not Run at the Pool," which all of the children and half the parents didn't observe, including his wife, Austin thought, as he thanked the assistant manager. Austin was barefoot, dripping wet in his tennis clothes, and covered in Jaime's blood. But she was alive and hadn't drowned, which was a lot to be grateful for.

As soon as they got in, the car took off and headed to the nearest hospital, as Zoe tried to place the towels so Jaime didn't bleed on the seat. They were at the hospital ten minutes later, and Austin carried Jaime inside in his bare feet. He hadn't bothered to retrieve the tennis shoes he'd kicked off near the pool before he jumped in. He didn't care. They went to the emergency room and stood at the front desk, while Jaime's chin bled all over the floor.

"We'll get you in right away," the nurse on duty told him, "we can get your information later." She immediately led the way down the hall to a room, while Zoe followed, looking pale beneath her tan, and a lot less glamorous than she had looked half an hour before.

"What in hell were you thinking?" Austin asked her in an icy voice as they waited for the doctor. "She's three years old and she can't swim, and you weren't even watching her. What if she was dead by now, or brain dead because she drowned?"

"I'm sorry, the last time I looked she was sitting on a lounge chair with her friends."

"And you assumed she wouldn't move? When I

got there, she was racing around the pool at full speed, and she fell in at the deep end." Zoe shuddered as he said it. Jaime was whimpering by then and had stopped crying. Zoe was holding a towel to her face, and the bleeding had slowed down. Austin was in his wet tennis clothes and Zoe in a bikini.

The doctor came into the room then, and looked at the wound carefully after introducing himself. "It's a clean slice," he said looking into it with a light, "but it's deep. No jagged edges. There will be a scar under her chin, but it won't show for about fifty years, till her chin starts to sag." He smiled at them. You could cut the tension between Austin and Zoe with a knife. "We're going to have to stitch her up, but we'll numb it, unless you want us to put her to sleep for a few minutes."

"I'd rather not," Austin said without consulting Zoe, and she didn't say a word.

"That's fine, you'll have to hold her firmly," he said to Austin, got his equipment ready and then turned to talk to Jaime, with a shot of novocaine held out of her line of sight. "Young lady, we're going to make some little tiny pinpricks, they won't hurt in a minute, and then we're going to sew you up, and send you home." She started to cry as soon as he said it and Zoe stroked her hair and spoke soothingly to her, and kissed the top of her head. Austin got a grip on her, and she screamed as they gave her the novocaine shot to numb her face, they let her sit for a while until the doctor was sure it had taken effect. Austin held her face, as Zoe held her hands down, and the doctor put twelve stitches in her chin, and covered everything below her mouth with a large bandage. Jaime was hiccupping with sobs by then, but it was over, and she reached out to Zoe, who picked her up and held her tight.

Austin looked like a train wreck, as they thanked the doctor. He gave them instructions for caring for the wound, and said the stitches should be removed in about ten days. Then Austin went to fill out the forms they had neglected when they came in. They were back in the car an hour after they had arrived. It was a familiar scene to them by now, their daughter injured, and either stitches or a cast, which made Austin feel a wave of panic wash over him as he thought of it. And when she wasn't injured, she was sick.

He and Zoe didn't speak to each other on the way back to the hotel. They laid Jaime on her bed when they walked into the suite. She looked drugged, she was so exhausted from the trauma, as her eyes fluttered closed within minutes and she drifted off to sleep. She had been through the wringer, nearly drowned, cut her chin wide open, and had twelve stitches. It would have been extremely trying even for an adult. Her parents looked nearly as bad. They walked into the living room of the suite, and Austin poured himself a stiff drink from the minibar. He looked devastatingly handsome with his wet dark hair and powerful athletic body. But what did it matter? Zoe wondered if he'd ever forgive her. It seemed like a long time before he sat down and looked at her. She was sitting across from him and didn't move. She looked like she was waiting to be whipped.

"What do you expect me to say to you?" he asked her in a low voice, so Jaime didn't hear them, but she was sound asleep. "I'm sure you're sorry, but that was the most irresponsible, neglectful thing I've ever seen. How am I supposed to trust you with our daughter's life when you do something like that? Do you know how many times she's been injured? I can't even count anymore. She's had more stitches and broken bones than any child I've ever heard of, other than the kids at the shelter. I don't understand it. I don't know if we're neglectful parents or she's a particularly active child, but I'm beginning to think we're unsuitable parents. Zoe, something has to change." He looked devastated and so did she.

"It will, I'm sorry. I don't know what happened, I was talking to those women, it was only for a few minutes, I was having fun with them, and the next thing I knew, the lifeguard came over and told me she almost drowned, and you were holding her and she was bleeding."

"I think we have to hire a full-time nanny," he said with a look of desperation, but the truth was that she had never gotten hurt with Fiona, except when she fell down the stairs because Zoe wouldn't let him put up a gate. And she had never gotten injured with him. It only happened with Zoe. And she always had a reason, a ready apology, or an excuse. For a terrifying moment, he wondered if she was subconsciously trying to kill her, if there was some deep psychological reason why she wanted to hurt their child, like jealousy, or fear, or something deeply psychotic. But whatever the reason, he no longer trusted his wife with their daughter. And after the scene at the swimming pool, he wasn't sure if he ever would again. It wasn't Jaime's fault. She had never gotten injured at school. It only happened at home, or when Zoe took her out. He didn't dare tell her what he was thinking. It sounded too sick.

"I swear to you, Austin," she said with a pleading look, "I will never take my eyes off her again."

"I don't believe you," he said sadly. "You're a wonderful mother in a lot of ways, and I know you love her, but we're not responsible parents. I'm scared, Zoe. You have to watch her better. That shouldn't have happened today."

"It won't again. I promise you." As he looked at her, he saw the woman he had loved for nine years, the champion of abused children, and the best mother in the world. But was she? What if nothing he believed about her was true? He wanted to believe it, to cling to who he thought she was, but all he could think of now was Jaime at the bottom of the pool, while Zoe laughed with the other women and didn't even know where Jaime was. What if she had already been dead when he got there? He started to cry as he thought of it, and Zoe came to sit next to him and put her arms around him, and she was crying too. "I love you and Jaime more than anything in life," she whispered, and he nodded, and prayed that it was true. But he was no longer sure.

Zoe and Austin were both very quiet as they flew back to New York the next day. Jaime sat between them and played on Zoe's iPad, as Austin watched them, trying not to think about the day before. If he had come on the scene seconds later, they could have been taking her body back to New York in a coffin. Jaime said her chin hurt. She had bumped it hard when she'd split it open and the doctor had warned them it would be bruised and hurt for a few days.

They got back to the apartment at three o'clock. Zoe unpacked and did laundry, and Jaime played in her room. She looked tired after the events of the day before, and some of the shine of their vacation had worn off. Jaime had returned as the walking wounded, and was going back to school the next day with her big bandage on her chin.

Zoe went to buy groceries after she unpacked, and Austin sat down on their bed and called his mother after she left. As she always did, his mother picked up immediately when she saw his number.

"Hi, Mom, how are you and Dad?" he said in a tired voice, trying to sound cheerful.

"Fine. How was Florida?"

"Wonderful. We had a great time." He could tell her the truth when he saw her. He didn't want to tell her on the phone. Not again. Listening to him, she thought he sounded sad and subdued, and as though he was lying to her. She had no idea about what, but she could tell something was wrong. "I was thinking on the way back. We haven't had lunch in ages. Do you have time for a date this week?" He tried to seem casual about it, but the invitation sounded stilted to him too.

"For you, my darling boy, my dance card is always free. When do you have in mind?"

"Does tomorrow work for you?" There was something desperate in his voice that he couldn't hide.

"Sure. Our usual?" There was a small Italian restaurant near his office that they both liked. Da'Giulio. They had lunch there from time to time.

"Perfect. Noon? I have to be in court in the afternoon."

"Noon it is. See you then."

"Thank you," he said in a soft voice.

"For what? Having lunch with my son?"

"For making time. For being you," he said gratefully.

They hung up, and she sat looking worried and pensive as George walked by.

"Something wrong?"

"I don't know. I have a feeling there might be. Austin wants to have lunch with me tomorrow. He hasn't done that since my birthday."

"Don't be so paranoid. He probably feels guilty for not calling more often."

"I don't think so," but she hoped he was right.

She was already at the restaurant, waiting for him, when he walked in the next day, looking tall and handsome in a dark suit, white shirt, and navy tie, since he had to go to court.

"You're a good-looking man," she said to him, and smiled as he sat down, and leaned over to kiss her. She could also see that his eyes looked strained, and she thought he didn't look well despite the tan.

They ordered quickly, and she smiled at him again. "So Florida was fun? Did Jaime love it?"

He didn't answer for a minute and looked his mother in the eye. "Until the last day. Zoe was watching her at the pool, except she wasn't. She was talking to some women, while Jaime ran around with some other kids her age, she slipped and fell into the pool at the deep end, without her floaties on, slit her chin open, went straight to the bottom, and nearly drowned. I just happened to come back from tennis then. I saw it, jumped in, and pulled her out. Even the lifeguard didn't see it. If I hadn't come back then, she'd be dead. And she has twelve stitches in her chin." There were tears in his eyes when he said it, and his mother ached for him, as she touched his hand. "I'm not going to clean it up for you, or cover for Zoe this time. Mom, I don't know what it is, but I'm scared. Something's wrong. Maybe with her. Jaime only gets injured with Zoe. I don't understand what's happening, or maybe even who she is." Tears slid down his cheeks as he said it, and he wiped them away. "I don't know what to do." It brought tears to her eyes just looking at him as they held hands across the table and he fought to regain his composure.

"I've been worried for a long time." She spoke softly. "I think there's a part of Zoe broken so deep down inside that you can't see it. On the surface she looks like the perfect mother, or wants to be. She runs the non-profit brilliantly. She's a loving wife, a bright girl, a charming woman, but I think part of her is badly damaged. I feel it, more than see it. I think Jaime's injuries are proof of it."

"Do you think she hurts Jaime intentionally?" He was willing to consider any possibility.

"It's more complicated than that, I think." She said it as their lunch arrived and neither of them touched their food. "I wanted to talk to you about it a year or so ago, but you weren't ready to hear it then. There's a form of mental illness or a personality disorder that's hotly debated in the psychiatric community. It's called Munchausen syndrome by proxy."

"I've heard of it, but I never knew what it was." Somehow he'd had a feeling that his mother would know what was going on, better than he did, and he hoped that was true.

"People who suffer from it often make their children sick in a very serious way. They poison them, and do some frightening things to cause illness—not feign it, cause it. That's the most severe form. Or they create or allow dangerous situations, where a child will get injured. They don't injure them themselves, but they set it up, and let it happen. Or when a child is legitimately sick, they exaggerate the symptoms and insist they're sicker than they are to make the illness seem more important. Some of them even set up surgeries that aren't necessary." He thought immediately of the ear tubes Zoe had engineered, and the appendectomy she wanted Jaime to have for her stomachache, and if he hadn't objected, she might have had it.

"I think Zoe fits in that spectrum somewhere," Connie said. "She puts Jaime in dangerous situations and the inevitable happens. And then there's the apnea, the febrile seizure no one ever saw, the appendicitis that wasn't. It's a plea for attention for the mother. A desperate need to be noticed, appreciated, and comforted. Once the child is genuinely sick or injured, or appears to be, they rush forward and are the perfect mother and astound everyone with how attentive they are, and become the child's savior and hero. They appear to be fabulous mothers, and it's mostly women who suffer from this disorder—and no one sees that they have caused the child's injury or illness in the first place. Some of them have had medical training in some form, so they know what they're doing," she continued. "The debate among psychiatrists is whether it's a mental illness, a personality disorder, or a form of child abuse. Maybe it's the degree of it that makes the difference. I've done a lot of reading about it for the last three years, since Jaime was born. I think Zoe fits the pattern. You'd know better than I. But it occurred to me three years ago—the difficult nursing, Jaime rolling off the changing table and bumping her head, falling down the stairs, the broken arm and wrist, the story you just told me. I've suspected it for a while.

"These women usually cover their tracks carefully and are very clever. There is always another explanation. They're practiced liars. And I hate to tell you, but some of them kill their children. Or the children die in an accident they allowed to happen. I don't think Zoe is at the extreme range of the disorder, but I'm not sure of that, and maybe you aren't either. I understand why you're scared, I am too." Constance was quiet and calm and sane about it, which made everything she said worse and more real. She wasn't hysterical or accusatory, she was, as always, intelligent, well informed, and made perfect sense. And what she described sounded all too familiar.

"Do they know they're doing it?" he asked in a strangled voice.

"That's debatable. Even the psychiatrists don't agree on that. It's a form of compulsive behavior."

"Her mother donated her own marrow for a transplant when her little sister was dying of leukemia, and everyone thought she was heroic during her entire illness. Maybe Zoe wanted a piece of that kind of admiration, and the only way she could get it was by making Jaime sick, or letting her get hurt. Mom, are you sure about this, I mean about Zoe?"

"No, I'm not," she said honestly, "which is why I haven't talked to you about it. From everything I've read, the puzzle pieces fit, and she's a match with the pathology, but you'd be a better judge of it than I. I have a book about Munchausen by proxy in layman's terms, if you want to read it. It's frightening, especially when you read the case studies. People with this disorder can be, or become, extremely dangerous. And after what you tell me happened in Florida, I think you need to watch Jaime closely. Does Zoe know how upset you are?"

"Maybe. I've only just started figuring it out myself. I'm not sure what I think." Constance nodded, and picked at her pasta, and he did the same.

"There's also a different form of the disorder, which is simply called Munchausen, where adults pretend to be ill, but they aren't, they just want attention. In Munchausen by proxy, the illnesses and injuries are not pretend, they're real, caused by a parent, usually a mother, and it is far more scary. They can also attack the elderly. Most victims are under the age of six, because they don't understand what they're seeing, and can rarely report it accurately. People with Munchausen by proxy are usually accomplished liars and get away with it. And what they do, and how they do it, is extremely difficult to prove. They're often above reproach and no one would suspect them," which was true of Zoe, champion of abused children and devoted mother. Nothing his mother was telling him was good news, but in some ways it was a relief, to finally hear the truth, if it was the truth about Zoe. It sounded to him like it was. He trusted his mother and valued her opinions immensely.

"How do you stop them?"

"You can't. You can't change them. The child or the victim has to be removed from them to be safe. That's the bad news for you here. If we're right, you may have some hard choices to make at some point, for Jaime's sake." He nodded, but didn't comment. After all, he wasn't sure yet. This was just a theory. "Some of them wind up behind bars, sometimes for murdering their own children. Most of them go undetected, and you just have to hope the child survives, physically and psychologically. Some cases are less extreme. I thought that about

Zoe at first, but I'm more concerned now. If Jaime had drowned, she could have played the grieving parent. It's always about playing a role, star mother mostly. What they want is praise and attention heaped on them. They appear to be perfect, but they're severely damaged. The old saying 'too good to be true' seems to apply here. I'll lend you the book I mentioned, if you want to read it."

"I want to," he said with a look of determination. "Christ, Mom, I hope you're wrong about this."

"So do I, Austin. But I don't think I am. I'll drop it off at your office. Don't let her see it," Constance said wisely.

"I won't. I promise." Austin looked frightened and his mother's heart ached for him.

"You know, the poisons under your kitchen sink were a perfect example. She left them there so Jaime could get in to them, and if she had, they would have killed her. And she did it after bragging about being the safety warden. Not exactly." He shuddered as he thought about it and remembered Zoe saying that they had to respect Jaime, and teach her boundaries, and leave the poisons in plain sight so she could learn not to touch them, as a two-year-old. It was crazy, and he'd had to move them himself. And there was the gate she had taken off the stairs after he'd set it up. There were so many examples he couldn't even begin to remember them all.

Austin looked even more sober when he hugged his mother and left her after lunch.

She went home afterward, put the book in a manila envelope, and dropped it off at his office an hour later. He read the description on the jacket flap when he got it, and it was even worse than his mother had described. Munchausen by proxy was terrifying, and if Zoe was suffering from it, he had to figure out what to do, now. He couldn't wait till a tragedy happened.

Chapter 13

Austin read the book his mother gave him during his lunch hour the next day and on his way to and from work every day. He hid it in his locked briefcase at home, and only read it when Zoe was out or asleep. Too much of it already sounded familiar and painfully apt, and so much like Zoe, even the reasons for it. She had been starved for attention and affection for years during her youth and childhood and now she wanted to shine as a mom, as a savior and protector. He hadn't come to any conclusions yet, but there was a huge question in his mind now. Was Zoe hurting Jaime intentionally, or just letting it happen in order to draw attention to herself once Jaime was injured? She claimed to be so diligent and careful, but he had evidence now that she wasn't, like the incident in Florida. She played innocent every time, and was so convincing about it. Maybe there was a part of her he didn't know. And if so, how dangerous was she to Jaime?

He was reading the book on Saturday, while Zoe and Jaime were at the playground, when a call came in from a doctor's office, with a message for Zoe, confirming an appointment for Jaime. It caught his attention and when he asked what kind of doctor it was, the woman on the phone said he was an orthopedic surgeon. The appointment was for Tuesday, and they had managed to squeeze her in, in response to an urgent request from Zoe.

He didn't beat around the bush and asked Zoe about it immediately when they came home for lunch.

"What's this about? Why is Jaime seeing an orthopedic surgeon? And why wasn't I told about it? That sounds pretty major."

"It's not major yet," Zoe said calmly. "And I didn't tell you because I didn't want to worry you. I want him to check out Jaime's spine," she said when they were out of earshot of Jaime, while she ate her lunch at the kitchen table. At least she had returned from the park unharmed. He was grateful for that now. A day without injuries.

"Why would you want him to check out her spine?" Austin asked her.

"For scoliosis," she said simply.

"What's that?"

"Curvature of the spine. I've noticed hers is a

little off. And I want to get on it early if she has a problem."

"Did you talk to Cathy about it? Does she think she has it?"

"It's not her area of expertise. I want to see the orthopedic guy first." Austin didn't comment, but checked it out online and saw that scoliosis was sometimes repaired surgically, by inserting metal rods along the spine to prevent it from curving further. He felt sick as he read it. He had never noticed anything unusual about her spine, and he saw Jaime in the bath all the time. He felt panicked that Zoe was even taking her to the doctor, and called Cathy about it on Monday and told her about Zoe's concern and the appointment with the orthopedic surgeon. She brushed it off.

"You know how she gets, she panics about something, like leukemia. The orthopod will tell her Jaime is fine and that will be the end of it." She didn't sound worried at all.

"What if it isn't? What if she talks him into putting rods into Jaime's spine?" Cathy almost laughed at the suggestion.

"He won't, unless he's a total charlatan. Jaime's spine is fine."

He didn't want to tell Cathy that he was having grave concerns about his wife. But the fact that she was trying to drum up a new illness for Jaime that would require excruciating surgery terrified him again. This was deadly serious.

The case studies in the book his mother had given him were endless and horrifying. Some were very extreme, mothers who had killed their children and gone to prison for it. Other cases were harder to discern and more closely resembled the incidents that Jaime had experienced, which had seemed normal or understandable at the time, but no longer did, because of the sheer number of them. His mother had been suspicious of Jaime's injuries for several years. And what if she was right? The thought of it brought tears to his eyes and anguish to his heart. He still loved Zoe, but he was beginning to question how well he knew her or if he knew her at all.

On Tuesday night, when Austin got home, he questioned Zoe about Jaime's appointment with the orthopedic surgeon. He had been reading about mothers with Munchausen by proxy who had caused their children to have serious surgeries, sometimes with death as the result. And Zoe exploring spinal surgery to insert steel rods into his daughter's back had him panicked.

"What did he say?" Austin asked in a strangled voice when he found Zoe in the kitchen.

"He said he wants to see her again in six months. We'll see how it goes and what he thinks then," she said calmly. As far as Austin was concerned, it was a reprieve, and at least he didn't have to confront her about it now, so he nodded and said nothing. The tension between them since Jaime nearly drowned in Florida had been palpable, but in spite of that, he was trying to act as though nothing was wrong, at least until he finished the book his mother had given him, and he had further thoughts on the subject. For the moment he was still confused, or hoped he was. But it was hard to feel close to her when he was so worried. He blamed how distracted he was on problems at work, and she seemed to believe him, and didn't question him about it. She was having problems of her own at the shelter, after the vacation. They kept her busy all week.

He finished reading the book on Munchausen by proxy on Wednesday on his way to work, and called Cathy on her cellphone as soon as he got to his office.

"I know this probably sounds crazy to you, but I'd like to come and see you, confidentially. I don't want Zoe to know about it. I don't want to put you in an awkward position, but there are some things I'm concerned about and want to discuss with you." He didn't mean to sound mysterious but he didn't want to tell her on the phone. He wanted to see her face-to-face.

"Is it about what happened in Florida?" Zoe had already called her and told her her version of the story and that she felt terrible about it, and that Austin was furious with her. "Accidents can happen. You only have to take your eyes off a child

Jaime's age for a split second, and they can wind up at the bottom of a pool and drown."

"She almost did," he said miserably. "But it isn't about that, not entirely. But just for your information, Zoe was talking to a group of women and had her back to the pool. She didn't have her eyes on Jaime, and Jaime was racing around the wet concrete when she slipped, without her floaties on. Zoe had no idea where she was or what she was doing, for a lot longer than a split second. But I want to discuss a broader subject with you, in confidence. I'm sorry if that's awkward for you."

"I can manage it," she said quietly, "if it's important to you." She wanted to help him, and she respected them both.

"I think it is," he said somberly. "Do you suppose you can get your nurses not to say I came in? I know how friendly Zoe is with them. She's always taking them chocolates and gifts, or baking cookies for them." Cathy knew it was true, and the nurses loved Zoe for it.

"I'll handle it." She was glad he had reminded her. She wouldn't have thought of it, but he was right. Her nurses all thought Zoe walked on water and was a saint, the most devoted mother in their practice. They would have done anything for her, and would have mentioned it to her that Austin came in. She knew it would look strange when she asked them not to, but confidentiality required that they respect his wishes, and she would see to it that they did. "Do you want to come in at lunchtime? It's the longest break I have in my schedule today, and it sounds like you want to talk sooner rather than later."

"I do." She was very fond of them both, and hoped that she could put his mind at ease. As far as she was concerned, Zoe was a good wife, a good mother, and a good friend. She wondered if they were having marital problems, although Zoe hadn't mentioned it to her, and she thought she would have. Maybe over the incident in Florida. She could hear on the phone that Austin was upset, and Zoe had told her as much after the accident in Florida and the stitches in Jaime's chin, which Cathy was sorry to hear about. But at least she hadn't drowned and Austin had pulled her out of the pool in time.

He got right to the point when he came to see her. He walked past the nurses and went straight to her office since he knew where it was, and she waved him to a chair after he closed the door so no one would hear them. She had a sandwich on her desk.

"I'm sorry to interrupt your lunch," he said, looking apologetic, "you can eat while we talk if you want."

"I'm fine." She smiled at him, half friend and half physician, and trying to be both. "What's on your mind?"

Before he said anything, he handed her a list

of all of Jaime's injuries, the stitches, the broken arm, the broken wrist, the sprains, the dislocated elbows, the fall off the changing table. The list was long and Cathy read it carefully, and he startled her with what he said next.

"I'm not sure I know who I'm married to. And I'm not sure you do either. That's a long list of injuries for a three-and-a-half-year-old, not to mention the illnesses, the mysterious febrile seizure, apnea, the unnecessary surgery for ear tubes, that she conned me into and lied about, both to me and the doctor. The appendectomy she insisted on, that thank God they didn't do, and you saved the day when you figured out that Jaime had strep in her stomach lining. And now she's chasing an orthopedic surgeon for scoliosis Jaime doesn't have, and Zoe may want rods put in her spine."

"Do you know that for a fact?" Cathy frowned as she asked him.

"Close enough. She's seeing an orthopedic surgeon for scoliosis, and that's what he does. I assume that's what she has in mind." She was moving into the big leagues now, surgeries instead of falls.

"He won't do it to a patient who doesn't need it, if he's a reputable surgeon," she said with conviction.

"For now. He told her to come back in six months. God knows what else she'll come up with by then."

"What are you saying to me, Austin? We both know she's anxious, because she lost her sister to leukemia when they were both so young. It frightens her as a mom. I'm sure she's afraid the same thing could happen to Jaime. She's never said that to me exactly, but it's a normal fear for a ten-year-old who lost her seven-year-old sister."

"She's not ten years old now, and yes, I think losing her sister affected her deeply. She went through years of neglect by her parents, who were too devastated to pay attention to her. In a sense, they abandoned her as a child. They admit it themselves. She grew up with no affection and no help. And now she wants attention by being super-mom, and she can only be that if Jaime is sick. Maybe that's all she knows. I've been reading about Munchausen by proxy, and, Cathy, she's a textbook case."

At first she was too stunned to respond to him, but she could see that he was serious, and she felt she owed it to him to pay attention to what he had to say. He was a reasonable person, and she respected his concerns.

"I don't know much about it, to be honest with you. I'm a pediatrician, not a shrink." She picked up the list of Zoe's injuries for a minute and stared at it, set it down on her desk, and looked at him. "I know the description generally, mothers who make their children sick, set them up in risky situations to get injured, exaggerate symptoms to physicians to make themselves more important, and even cause their children to have unnecessary surgeries."

"Sometimes leading to death," he said somberly.

"The ear tubes weren't serious, but Jaime had general anesthesia when she didn't need to, she'd have survived an appendectomy, and now Zoe's going to an orthopedic surgeon, and God knows what she's telling him. She had Jaime see a neurologist when she got a bump on her head, a gastroenterologist for reflux while she was nursing, and Jaime wore a monitor for a year that drove us all insane. You add that to the accidents, and it's quite a list, and every time, Zoe is the hero, Jaime's savior, except that the only time Jaime gets injured is when she's with her, or because of something Zoe did, like remove the gate I set up, so Jaime fell down the stairs and broke her arm the next day. She was with the nanny that time, but that was the only time. And she put every household poison we had in an unlocked cupboard under the sink, until my mother discovered it, and I put them up high where she couldn't reach them. That doesn't scare you, Cathy? It scares the shit out of me. Or it's starting to.

"Something changed for me in Florida, when I saw her with her back to the pool, while Jaime damn near drowned. Everyone thinks she's supermom, and I did too. Now I think there's something broken so deep inside of her that none of us can see it, but it's there, like a devil hiding in the bushes, waiting to devour my little girl. I don't trust Zoe anymore. She lies to me. And I'm afraid of what will happen to Jaime when she's with her. Every time she takes her out now, I'm afraid Jaime will get hurt." He looked imploringly at Cathy. "I don't know what to do. How do I protect Jaime from her own mother? And do I need to? But, all of a sudden I don't think Zoe is who we think she is. She lies to you too."

Cathy was shocked into silence, and the worst part was that some of what he said made sense. Austin wasn't crazy. He was a sensible, down-to-earth, intelligent person, and she knew he loved Zoe. But his fear for their daughter was clear and sounded rational in some ways.

"Wow, I don't know what to think. Let me go through Jaime's records and try to see them objectively. I want to talk to a psychiatrist I respect. I've never come across Munchausen by proxy in my practice. Probably not a lot of physicians have. I don't think it's impossible, I just want to get an objective opinion from a knowledgeable person to tell me if the puzzle pieces fit together here, or if it's just a series of unfortunate coincidences that look bad but maybe you're wrong. I hope to hell you are," she said, looking emotional.

"I would love to be wrong," he said to her as the intercom buzzed on her desk. She picked up the phone, answered it, looked serious for a minute, thanked one of her nurses for "warning" her, and looked at Austin when she hung up.

"You've got to go now. I'll let you out the back door," she said as she stood up, and seemed anxious and rushed. "Zoe is on her way over with

Jaime. She got bitten in the face by a dog at the park." Austin looked panicked when she said it, and he wanted to stay for Jaime if she was hurt, but he didn't want Zoe to see him here. There was no way he could explain his visit to Cathy, and it would appear suspicious to her. She walked him to the back door of her office, and he followed her. He had parked around the corner, so Zoe wouldn't see his car now when she drove up. "I'll call you after I talk to my psychiatrist friend. Don't jump to any conclusions yet. Sometimes things sound worse than they really are. But I'll admit, it doesn't look great when you shine a light on it. I'll let you know what he thinks. Do I have your permission to share my records with him?" she asked, and Austin nodded. "Now, go," she said, holding the door open for him.

Austin thanked her, gave her a quick hug, and left, and worried about Jaime all the way back to his office. He noticed that Zoe hadn't called him yet. He wondered when she would, so soon after the episode in Florida. It would be humiliating for her that Jaime had gotten hurt again, or maybe she was losing her grip. But she hadn't been a hero when Jaime nearly drowned because her mother wasn't watching her. Maybe she needed another injury to turn it around, so she could save Jaime this time or comfort her. If so, she was a very sick woman, maybe even sicker than he thought. He was grateful that Cathy had listened to him and seemed to take it seriously. Admittedly, the list of Jaime's illnesses and injuries was hard to refute. He had been shocked by them too when he wrote them down.

He wondered what the psychiatrist she knew would tell Cathy. Munchausen by proxy, or factitious disorder imposed on another as it was also called, wasn't something doctors, or even psychiatrists, ran into every day. He was impressed that his mother had spotted it so early, but she was a smart woman and still kept up on her psychology journals, and read voraciously. And he believed now that she was right. What he didn't know was what to do about it, what to say to Zoe, and how to protect Jaime from getting injured again and again, or taken to doctors for illnesses she didn't have. Zoe was reaching out past Cathy now to specialists, like the orthopedic surgeon she had taken Jaime to. The thought of Jaime needlessly having spinal surgery made him feel ill. Their situation was a nightmare, and he didn't know how to wake up.

Cathy was having similar thoughts about everything Austin had said. She loved Zoe, and they had become close friends. She was a wonderful person and remarkable human being, with the work she did, and Cathy had no doubt that she loved Austin and Jaime, yet what Austin said seemed so valid. What if it was true? She didn't know enough about the disorder to know what the remedies were or if it could be treated with therapy. But if what he said was accurate, Jaime wasn't safe with her mother, and Cathy couldn't let their friendship cloud her vision and fail to do what was right for the child. Munchausen by proxy was a form of child abuse, a virulent, insidious kind that was difficult to identify, and harder still to prove. Cathy knew that much about it from the literature she'd read, but she didn't know a single physician who had ever run into it. She hoped Paul Anders had and could shed some light on it, and give her some direction. If Austin was right, they had challenging times ahead. It was all swirling around in her head like a tornado, as she waited for Zoe to show up with Jaime. She hoped the dog bite wasn't bad. She was due to have the stitches in her chin taken out tomorrow. Cathy was going to do it for her, and now she had another injury, so soon after the last one, and also on her face.

The nurse at the front desk buzzed Cathy when they arrived, barely five minutes after Austin had left, and she hurried to the exam room where they were waiting. Jaime was clinging to her mother and looked traumatized, and she had Zoe put Jaime down on the exam table. She was shaking, and Cathy feared at first that the bite was deep, but on closer inspection it didn't look quite so bad.

"Hi, Jaime," Cathy said gently and rubbed her back for a minute, as Zoe looked devastated. It was hard to believe that her fear for her daughter wasn't real. She looked almost as shaken up as Jaime. But Cathy had to focus on Jaime now. "You ran into a big scary dog, huh? Did he chase you and knock you down?"

Jaime shook her head. "No, he was on a leash," she said clearly, as Zoe shook her head.

"No, he wasn't, Jaime," Zoe said firmly, "he was **off** the leash, the leash was in the man's hand." Jaime moved her head from side to side again, disagreeing with her mother.

"Mommy said I could play with him," she volunteered.

"Jaime!" Zoe objected. "I told you to stay away from him."

"What kind of dog was it?" Cathy asked them.

"A German shepherd," Zoe responded.

"He looked like a wolf," Jaime added. "And he had big teeth." All the while they were talking, Cathy was eyeing the wound on her cheek. It wasn't bleeding profusely as Zoe had said her chin had, but the bite was deeper than Cathy liked. She didn't want it to leave a scar on her face. She'd been lucky not to lose an eye, or the dog could have killed her. She turned to Zoe then, trying not to think of everything Austin had told her. She didn't want to make any judgments yet, she didn't know enough and needed further information.

"I'm going to give Jaime a booster for her tetanus shot, just to be on the safe side. Did you get the name of the owner, in case we need to contact him?" Zoe looked blank for a minute and then embarrassed.

"I never thought of it. That was stupid of me, but all I wanted to do was rescue Jaime and get her out of there. The owner called off the dog pretty quickly when I was screaming at him."

"He pulled him back on the leash," Jaime added, and she seemed listless to Cathy.

"He wasn't on a leash," Zoe said forcefully again. "He pulled on his collar when I shouted at him." Zoe was determined to be the hero of the piece, and Cathy felt a chill run up her spine. Her behavior matched what Austin had described, and suddenly she felt sick. Maybe she and Austin had both misjudged Zoe, and the ghosts of her past tragedies had wounded her more deeply than either of them had thought. It was the only explanation Cathy could think of for what Austin had proposed. And more than anything, she wanted none of it to be true. Could they have misjudged Zoe so severely? But what if they had? It couldn't be.

"At least we know he had an owner, and he wasn't a stray dog," Cathy said as she took the tetanus booster out of a drawer, and Jaime cringed when she saw the shot. Zoe held her and it was quick, and afterward Cathy smiled at Jaime and told her how brave she was. "I'm going to send you to a very nice doctor, and I think you're going to like her. She's from Hawaii. I went to medical school with her, and she's only a few blocks away." She turned to Zoe then. "She needs a plastic surgeon. I don't want to stitch her up and have it leave a scar. Since it's on her face, I think it's better. She can take the stitches out of Jaime's chin while you're there. One stop shopping." She wrote down the address of Jane Yamaguchi in SoHo, and handed it to Zoe. "I'll call her and tell her you're on your way." She kissed the top of Jaime's head and hugged Zoe, and they left a few minutes later as all of Cathy's nurses waved at them.

Cathy walked back to her office to call the plastic surgeon, told her what she knew about the dog bite, and said she'd given her a tetanus booster, to be on the safe side. But the dog appeared to be a pet, presumably was licensed, so hopefully rabies wasn't a concern. And then she asked her to take some stitches out of Jaime's chin.

"What is this kid, a prizefighter? She's got stitches in her chin, and just got a dog bite on her cheek?"

"A run of bad luck," Cathy explained to her. "She had a swimming pool accident in Florida ten days ago, and got bitten by a dog today."

"Poor kid. How bad is it?"

"I think it looks worse than it is. But I'd rather have you do it, instead of me, since it's on her face."

"Happy to be of service. How've you been by the way? We should have dinner together one of these days."

"I'd love it, call me."

"I will. And thanks for the referral. I'm going

to throw some business your way shortly too. I'm adopting a baby in Hawaii, using a surrogate. It's due in two months. A little boy." She sounded happy and excited and Cathy was pleased for her. She had always wanted kids, even in medical school.

"Congratulations! That's terrific!"

"Yes, it is. I decided to stop waiting for Mr. Right, and when the right guy comes along, he'll love us both."

"Good for you, Jane."

"My parents are a little upset about it, traditional Hawaiians and very conservative, but they'll get used to it. The sperm donor is Hawaiian, he's an old friend, so they'll relax about it eventually. I'm flying out to Honolulu for the birth. I'll bring the baby in to see you as soon as we get back. It'll be a big change in my life." She sounded thrilled. They were all coming to their own conclusions about turning forty, but Cathy wasn't ready for any major decisions yet.

She called Austin after she spoke to Jane, to tell him about Jaime. She wasn't sure if Zoe had called him yet, and he sounded tense when he answered.

"I just saw Jaime, it's not a deep bite, and I think it will stitch up cleanly. I sent them to a plastic surgeon, I'd feel better about having her do it, and I gave Jaime a tetanus booster. And the plastic surgeon is going to take out the stitches in her chin."

"She's been through the wars. Is she very upset?"

"She was at first. She'll be okay." She hesitated

for a minute, and then decided to tell him the disturbing piece she had noticed when they were in her office. "I think I should tell you that Jaime says the dog was on a leash and Zoe said she could play with it, and then he snapped at her. Zoe says the dog was off leash and she told Jaime to stay away from him. We've got two very different stories. But there was an owner so he wasn't a stray dog, which is good news. He's probably had all his shots and is licensed. Let's hope so."

"What kind of dog was it? Did she say?" Austin sounded jangled and Cathy felt sorry for him. He had a lot to worry about.

"A German shepherd."

"Oh my God, how can you let a three-and-a-half-year-old play with a dog that size? Did she get the owner's name?"

"No, she didn't," Cathy said quietly. So they couldn't corroborate the stories and see who was telling the truth, or even trace the dog and owner. Cathy had a sinking feeling that Jaime was being honest and Zoe was lying to her, which meant that she had encouraged Jaime to play with a dog that looked fierce and was on a leash. But even on a leash, a shepherd could be dangerous, and had been for her. Cathy didn't like the story, and it made what Austin feared seem even more real.

As soon as she hung up, she called Paul Anders expecting to leave him a message, instead he picked up himself. He was between patients and was surprised to hear from her. They hadn't spoken in about a year.

"I have a problem and I need some advice." She got right to the point. They were both busy and her next patient was due in any minute, and his probably was too. "Can I come by and talk to you?"

"Is it serious? Are you in a rush?"

"Serious, yes. In a rush, not so sure. When do you have time?"

"Are you free tonight? I'm going to L.A. tomorrow for a psychiatric convention. I could do it after my last patient. Seven o'clock work for you?"

"Perfect."

"Come to my office. We can have a glass of wine while we talk."

"Sounds great. Thank you, Paul," she said warmly, grateful for the quick response.

"Any time." They had dated a few times, but she liked him better as a friend. He was smart and serious and direct to deal with. She knew she'd get the straight scoop from him about Munchausen by proxy and whether or not Zoe sounded like she fit the bill.

Her next patient was waiting for her by then, and she went to do a six-month checkup, and tried to put Austin, Zoe, and Jaime out of her mind for a few hours, at least until she met up with Paul that night. Until then, she had to be an efficient pediatrician and think about her other patients.

She hoped Jaime had done all right with Jane. She was in good hands.

She smiled at the young mother as she walked into the exam room and a six-month-old baby girl grinned at her, and reminded Cathy how much she loved her job. This was just what she needed today, she thought as she picked up the baby and smiled at the mom. Except for situations like Jaime's, it was a happy line of work.

Chapter 14

Cathy's last patient left at five-thirty, and she had an hour and a half to kill before she met with Paul Anders. She didn't want to go to her apartment, and decided to stay at the office and read carefully through Jaime's records, and see how they seemed objectively, knowing Austin's concerns.

She started at the beginning, with all of Zoe's nursing difficulties and fears about the baby, cracked nipples, Jaime falling asleep at the breast after a few minutes, her fear that Jaime wasn't getting enough milk, that she was a picky eater, might have a gastric obstruction which she obviously didn't, projectile vomiting which she didn't have either, claims at every visit that she had colic, with no real evidence of it. The beginning hadn't been smooth, but none of it was serious. They were nervous first-time parents. And then three weeks in, the apnea incident when Jaime had stopped breathing, an incident that had never been repeated. Zoe had insisted on seeing a pediatric gastroenterologist for testing, and he had found Jaime to be normal. She saw a note from the doctor then, which Cathy had forgotten in the meantime, that Zoe had inquired about a gastric tube, which he had told her was inappropriate and unnecessary. And all along Jaime was gaining weight, and seemed to be thriving in spite of her mother's nervousness.

Then there was her first injury when she rolled off the changing table at four months. Nasty bump on the head, but no concussion. Zoe had insisted on seeing a neurologist. Everything else was normal. And then the broken arm and stitches in her lip when she fell down the stairs, and later a fall in the bathtub. Cathy had made a note in the chart that Zoe had a lot of theories about no feeding schedules, no bedtime, respecting the baby's freedom, no gates when she started walking. They hadn't been friends yet, but she remembered how much she liked Austin and Zoe, how earnest they were, and how devoted Zoe was to her baby.

There was a note in the chart that she sat up all night every night with the baby, holding her upright, to avoid another apnea incident. Their anxiety screamed off the chart, but so did Zoe's dedication. And all the other incidents were listed as she flipped through the pages. The broken wrist when she fell off the big girl swing. The flu and reported febrile seizure at home, and they had admitted her to the hospital for a night, and the fever had gone down by morning. Both dislocated elbows. It was all there, and as Austin said, the list of her injuries was long.

What struck Cathy was that Jaime was a healthy child who bounced back from every injury and incident. There were many notes in the chart, a lot of them about minor injuries, and Zoe's concerns about the baby. She had called in frequently about teething problems for the better part of a year. And the more recent incidents were all listed too. Cathy had forgotten how many there were, many more than she normally saw, but somehow she hadn't strung them all together because she knew what good parents they were, and there had never been a question in her mind about child abuse. But looking at it now, she could see that Jaime had been injured too often, and if she hadn't known the parents so well, she might have questioned it. What came across was that Jaime's mother was neurotic and overanxious and constantly concerned about her daughter's health.

She saw the results of the leukemia testing, which she had done just to indulge her. She and Zoe were good friends by then. Jaime had been in their office far more than most of their patients. Jaime had had the usual coughs and colds and flus during her first year of school, and also the ear infection that led to her getting ear tubes without consulting Cathy about it. She had a lengthy history for what was essentially a healthy child. She had nursed for fourteen months, and was allergic to amoxicillin, none of which was unusual. None of her illnesses were serious, but the list of physical injuries was more extreme. If anything, Zoe came across as overzealous in the chart, and Cathy had made a side note early on: "uber mom." And they had had long discussions about whether or not vaccines were dangerous and caused autism, but Zoe had finally given in and Jaime was up to date on all her shots. Her conclusion when she finished reading Jaime's records was that she was too close to Austin and Zoe to see it objectively. She made a copy of the file, and put it in an envelope for Paul. Then she walked the ten blocks to his office, and arrived right on time.

She pressed the buzzer, and he let her in. He looked like a professor or a shrink. He was wearing a tweed jacket, cowboy boots, and jeans. He wore his light brown hair longer than most of the men she knew, and he had a beard. She knew he was somewhere in his late forties but didn't know exactly where. She followed him up the stairs to his office, and he opened the promised bottle of wine.

She took a seat in the comfortable chair across from his and he handed her the glass of wine, and she noticed a box of tissues on the table next to her. She handed him the manila envelope with Jaime's chart in it.

"So what brings you here, my friend?" She saw

him looking at her legs and pretended not to notice. She knew he had been divorced twice and was something of a ladies' man, which was one of the things about him that had put her off, but she liked him as a friend, and respected him as a shrink. And she had the blond, blue-eyed, wholesome kind of girl-next-door looks that appealed to him, and a great figure. But she was there as a doctor, not a date.

"A three-and-a-half-year-old patient. I read her chart again before I came over, to see if anything stuck out, or I missed anything. She's a bright, happy, normal, active kid. She gets banged up a lot, and has had a lot of minor accidents. Nothing terrifying that suggested child abuse to me, and I know the parents. But she's had her share of injuries, probably more than her share. Broken wrist, broken arm at a year old, stitches, a bump on the head but no concussion, ten days ago she slipped while running at a pool, cut her chin open, fell into the deep end, and went down like a rock. Her father noticed and got to her just in time. She had twelve stitches in her chin. Today, she got bitten in the face by a German shepherd. It's a long list. One minor surgery for ear tubes, and almost an appendectomy. Her mother lost a sister to leukemia as a child, so she's nervous. At her request, I tested my patient for leukemia, negative of course. Now she's seeing an orthopedic surgeon, wondering if the child has scoliosis—she doesn't."

"Shit, it sounds like a lot to me. Stitches twice in ten days?" He looked skeptical.

"Two in a row is unusual, even for her."

"So what are you trying to figure out. Child abuse?"

"No. More intricate than that. To cut to the chase, my patient's father thinks his wife may have Munchausen by proxy. His mother suggested it, she's a licensed, non-practicing psychologist."

Paul rolled his eyes at that. "God save me from my non-practicing colleagues, who have too much time to think. It's an interesting diagnosis, though. What do you think about it?"

"I have no idea. I've never dealt with it. That's why I wanted to talk to you. And the child's mother runs one of the most respected abused-children's shelters in the city, and had two years of medical school. The parents are highly educated, intelligent, nice people, and they're crazy about their child. But I have to admit, the kid has gotten hurt a lot. When I try to look at it objectively, I see it too."

"And you don't think she's abusing the kid in a more traditional sense, and the child is protecting her, as most abused children do?"

"Definitely not," Cathy said as she took a sip of the wine and set it down on the table next to her.

"Interesting case. I have dealt with Munchausen by proxy. It's a bitch to prove. The people who have it are usually smart and educated, a lot of them have medical training, as the mother does in this case. They lie like dogs and they do it brilliantly, and it's very hard to pin anything on them and prove it. It all looks accidental, except for the excessive surgeries. The mother may be moving into that phase, if she's taking her to an orthopedic surgeon.

"The ignorant ones usually kill their kids in more obvious, clumsy ways and wind up in prison for murder. But the children of the smart ones die too, if they go too far. It's all about the parent getting attention from having a sick kid, either sympathy or they play super-mom, and everyone talks about what great mothers they are, except that they're either making the kid sick, or putting them in situations where they'll get hurt. Off the top of my head, just from what you've told me, I think it's a possibility. Is it a sure thing? It almost never is. And most typically, their victims are under six, because they can't communicate what's happening to them. They don't understand it anyway, so they make lousy witnesses. What is unusual is that most of the fathers of these kids never speak up. They either don't understand what's going on, or they don't want to make waves, so they just lie low and pretend they don't see it. Your patient's father is atypical."

"He says he's terrified for his child. He doesn't trust his wife anymore. He says she lies to him."

"If she has MBP, or factitious disorder imposed on another, you can be damn sure she does. And if you try to pin something on her, she'll lie more. And everyone will say what a fantastic mother she is. They make sure that everyone knows that about them. They're the best mothers in the world, except that they're injuring or killing their kids."

"Is that what they want? To kill the child?"

"I honestly don't know. I think sometimes they just go too far, and become too dangerous and it gets out of hand, or maybe they just can't stop. But some of the victims die, there's no question of that."

"How do you stop them? Therapy?"

He smiled wryly at that. "Thank you for your faith in my chosen field. No, therapy has no effect on them. They're like pedophiles, you can't stop them or cure them. You have to remove the child, in order to save its life, and their quality of life. You know what your role is in this, don't you?"

"No, I don't. That's why I'm here."

"If you really believe the mother has Munchausen by proxy, you have to report her to the authorities, in other words, Child Protective Services. It's your responsibility. You have to write the report and turn her in. It's confidential, of course, and if you don't have an airtight case, she'll wiggle out of it. Most of them do, with righteous indignation. If it keeps happening, they may be able to nail her eventually. But it's not easy, so you have to be fairly sure."

"And if I'm not?"

"Then you don't have a case, and the kid keeps breaking bones and having unneeded surgeries, and hopefully grows up and gets away, or she dies. It's been a fairly taboo subject for all these years. Essentially, these kids are child abuse victims, to an extreme degree, and it's often done in a very sophisticated way, by a mother who everyone tells the authorities is a star. I've only had one patient who was an MBP victim as a child. He was in pretty bad shape mentally, and eventually committed suicide. It was a sad case. They go after the elderly too, their geriatric parents who can't defend themselves. They die pretty quickly. Kids are sturdier and more resilient. It's an ugly business. I hope for your patient's sake that you're wrong about this. But at least she has her father on her team. It sounds like he's alert and watching what's going on."

"He is now. But he doesn't know how to stop her and keep the child safe."

"He can't do either one. If she has MBP, he's got to get the kid away from her, as soon as possible. Whatever he does, she's going to keep creating situations where the child gets hurt, or sick."

"My God, it's awful." Cathy looked upset, thinking of Jaime with the dog bite on her cheek. She'd had an email from Jane at the end of the day that everything had gone well, and they'd taken care of her chin too. She promised there would be no scar on her cheek, which was why Cathy had sent them there. She had total faith in Jane.

"I'll look at her file tonight, before I leave for L.A. tomorrow, and I'll call you in the morning before my flight. What you do after that is up to you. You may have to wait awhile and gather more evidence against her. But while you do, the child is at risk. And if this woman runs a child abuse shelter, you're going to have a hell of a time nailing her. She'll smell like a rose in court. What does her father do?"

"He's a child advocacy lawyer, and he does a lot of pro bono work for her."

"It's too bad if this turns out to be true. They sound like good people."

"They are, which makes this that much harder to believe."

"Just know that if she has MBP, she's not a good person, whatever she looks like, or whatever her reputation is. She could kill her kid." He couldn't have put it more bluntly, and Cathy was glad she had come to talk to him. He knew a lot about MBP and made the situation very clear. It was equally obvious that Cathy was in a terrible position, and had to report it if she believed it was true. She would have to do so for Jaime's sake, which was her responsibility here, as Jaime's primary physician, and a licensed doctor in the state of New York. "I'll give you my honest opinion in the morning, as best I can. With MBP, you almost never know for sure, unless you find her with a knife in the kid's back. But they're a lot more subtle than that as a rule. You have to go with your gut. You read about these cases in the papers, but not very often." They talked about his trip to L.A. after that, and her busy practice, and they promised to have dinner when he got back. It was eight-thirty when she finally left. He had given her a lot to think about. She didn't call Austin that night. She had nothing to tell him yet, except the general information Paul had shared with her, but Austin already knew it from the book his mother had given him. And if she called him, Zoe would be there. Cathy had to wait to hear from Paul anyway.

Paul called her the next morning at eight A.M., from the airport, before his flight to L.A.

"I read the file last night. If you want my personal opinion, I think you have an almost classic case of Munchausen by proxy on your hands. She fits the bill in a number of ways, just judging by the child's injuries, and the assortment of specialists she's been to. But the evidence you've got is pretty benign in a practical sense. Falling down stairs as a toddler, resulting in a broken arm, slipping off a swing, broken wrist. Running at a pool and falling in, after she slices her chin open. Rolling off a changing table. She's gotten injured, but it's cleverly done. It's a lot of what appears to be small stuff. It's not so small if you look at the volume of it, but there's no obvious violence. She hasn't poisoned her, or pushed her down the stairs. She wasn't even at home for the stair incident, but she set it up. She unscrewed and removed the gate Jaime's father had installed. I don't think he could win a case with what he has. Even Child Protective Services couldn't pull it off. She's too smart, and they might try to accuse the father, which would be worse. What if they gave custody to her? She's the superstar mom in all this, whom everyone sees adoringly, according to what you told me last night."

"What do you think we should do?"

"He may have to wait for more concrete proof. Jaime will inevitably get hurt again. And he'll have to watch his wife like a hawk, while appearing not to. It's not fair, but I think it may be too soon. And medically, you can keep an eye on her. Don't let her go to some quack who'd operate on the kid."

"I can't stop her." Cathy sounded disappointed. They had gotten the confirmation Austin wanted, but no weapons to use against her.

"Keep me posted on this. It's an interesting case."

"It's more than that," Cathy said emotionally, "she's a sweet, innocent kid in the clutches of a monster if what you and Austin believe is true."

"I'm sure she is. I'd be happy to testify if they ever want me to. I make a great expert witness, I've done it before."

"I'll tell Austin," she said, and Paul had to catch his flight.

"See you when I get back."

"Thank you for reading the file and the good advice."

"It's not what he wants to hear, about moving forward to stop her. But I agree with his mother. I think it's fairly certain that the child's mother has Munchausen by proxy. That's something at least."

"Have a good time in California."

"I'll call when I get back."

She hung up and waited until nine-thirty to call Austin at his office. She repeated everything Paul had said, verbatim, as she remembered it and from notes she had jotted down when she talked to him.

"Talk about good and bad news," Austin said, sounding depressed. "He agrees with my mother's diagnosis, and my suspicions, and we can't do a damn thing about it."

"Yet. Or you can if you want to, we can report it at any time."

"But we can't prove the case. And he's right, Jaime's injuries were all minor, even if there were a lot of them. I guess we have to do what he said. Watch and wait." The prospect was even more painful now, because being with Zoe was becoming intolerable. He felt as though aliens had stolen the woman he'd fallen in love with and left someone else in her place. She had seemed so sweet and pure and earnest when they'd met. Her extreme anxiety and neurotic behavior had only surfaced after Jaime was born. And their relationship had never been the same again.

He didn't feel the way about her he had before, but they lived under the same roof every day, and shared a bed. He didn't know how he was going to pull it off, but he knew he had to for Jaime's sake. It was all for Jaime now. He was determined to give her a good life and keep her safe. He owed her at least that. He wished he could take Fiona into his confidence, ask her to watch Jaime more closely, but he couldn't tell anyone, except his mother, who had seen it first. She was a smart woman, and his ally. Zoe no longer was. Overnight, she had become his enemy. She was trying to hurt his child, their child, in silent sneaky ways. It was like a poison gas that had filled their home when he wasn't looking.

He thanked Cathy before he hung up, and then sat thinking about his daughter. She deserved a better life than this, a mother who was trying to kill her, or might do so by accident if she went too far in her bid for attention as the star mother of a sick or injured child. He wondered if it was Zoe's unconscious revenge for all that she had suffered, or if she was too broken inside to care about their daughter and protect her.

He put his head down on his desk and cried, as he thought about it. He had to be strong for Jaime. He was all she could rely on.

He thought about his wife as he got up to go to a meeting. He thought about how much he had loved her, and now it was all slipping away on a tidal wave of fear for his daughter and an overwhelming sense of loss. And then he suddenly realized he hadn't lost Zoe. He couldn't. He had never known her.

Chapter 15

Austin did everything he could to maintain a sense of normalcy at home, after Cathy had told him what Paul Anders had said. He tried to be hypervigilant and anticipate any possible accident Jaime could have, while appearing not to. He was warm and friendly with Zoe. It took every ounce of energy to seem relaxed when he wasn't and not let her see the anger and fear boiling inside him, knowing that Jaime was at risk anytime she was with her mother, or her safety could be manipulated at a distance, if Zoe set up some dangerous situation for Jaime at home while she was at work. Anything was possible. He realized that now. He spoke to his mother about it, and no one else. He didn't want to burden Cathy with their situation, but he knew that she would warn him if Zoe showed up with some medical situation she created. It was all he could do for now. And nothing untoward had happened since he'd realized what was going on. The lack of incident almost lulled him into thinking that they were wrong, but that was exactly what Zoe wanted, his mother reminded him, for Austin to let down his guard. Maybe she sensed that he was watching her or Jaime. In essence he had to outsmart her, which was no small task.

Her father and Pam came to town for one of their visits, and they had them to dinner at the apartment. Brad had come up with a new line of children's books that were more modern and high tech than Ollie, and they were doing well. He had a magic touch in the world of children's books. Pam was thinking about retiring. They wanted to travel now that their children had grown up. Zoe never saw her half-siblings, and scarcely knew them. She preferred it that way.

Jaime still had the bandage on her cheek from the dog bite when they visited, and Brad ranted and raved about people who let their dogs run around off leash, particularly big ones. Pam said nothing, and for a fraction of an instant her eyes met Austin's, and he wondered if she knew, but he wouldn't have dared say anything to her, in case she said something to Zoe's father and he told Zoe what Austin suspected.

Secrecy was part of his life now and essential to Jaime's well-being. But Pam was an alert, observant woman, and he had the sense that she knew that something was wrong. Zoe told them how brave Jaime had been with the dog bite, and Austin said that Zoe had been the hero, she had saved Jaime from a fierce German shepherd that might have killed her. She'd screamed at the owner and fought off the dog, and Zoe glowed when he spoke up. It would have been confirmation of his suspicions, but he no longer needed it. He was sure now. He had read a second book on Munchausen by proxy, which was even more detailed than the first, and more frightening, and he kept it in his office, and then sent it to Cathy in a confidential envelope, without comment. She had been doing some reading in medical journals too, and was heartbroken by what she knew was facing Jaime, and Austin, when he finally confronted it.

"Take care of yourself and your girls," was all Pam said to Austin when they left town. Zoe had given them a tour of the shelter and the recent changes they'd made. It was easy to see how adored she was when they walked around the facilities. Pam was active in volunteer work in child abuse too, and always expressed a particular interest in the shelter. Zoe had recently won an award for her outstanding work in the field, with an article about her in **The New York Times.** It was one of the high points in her career.

Paul Anders had read it with interest and called Cathy, and commented on it when he reminded her of their promise to have dinner. Austin had signed a more formal release by then, which allowed Cathy to share Jaime's files with Paul.

"She's quite a woman, isn't she?" he said about Zoe. "That may feed her ego for a while. Anything new on that front?"

"I haven't seen Zoe since the dog bite incident the day I saw you. But no news is good news, I guess." She knew Zoe had been busy and she'd called to congratulate her on the award when she read about it. All she'd said was that Jaime's cheek was healing nicely, and you could hardly see the scar under her chin. Cathy didn't know if that was good or bad, if she needed visible signs of Jaime's accidents, or if the fact that they'd happened was enough to satisfy her. The whole situation made Cathy feel sick.

They invited her to dinner, and Cathy went to see how Jaime was doing. She looked fine, and only had to wear a small Steri-Strip on her cheek now, and Austin said again when Jaime was out of earshot that Zoe had saved her from being severely mauled. He was playing the game now, and did it well. Cathy sensed no argument between them, and she wondered whether he had been lulled into fooling himself or was a great actor. Zoe said she had a man she wanted to introduce Cathy to. He was a new member of the board, and Austin disagreed. He said that he was boring, and had never been married at fifty-four, which he thought was a bad sign and probably meant he was phobic about permanent relationships. He was an important investment banker on Wall Street, and was involved in numerous charitable causes, particularly those involving children, and Cathy said it would be interesting to meet him, just so Zoe felt appreciated. In reality, she felt the same way as Austin about men who had never been married at his age, and didn't care if she met him or not.

Cathy had dinner with Paul Anders, as they'd promised, and talked about Jaime and Munchausen by proxy the entire time. He was a treasure trove of information. Cathy read everything she could about it now, as did Austin. He was seeing his mother for lunch more frequently than he had in years. He could speak openly to her, which was a relief.

"Sometimes I think I imagined the whole thing, and I wonder if I'm crazy. She's so perfect, so brilliant at everything she does. Her work at her shelter, the outward appearances of motherhood, being a good wife. How could someone like that want to hurt a child?"

"It's the 'too good to be true' syndrome. I never trust that," Constance said at one of their lunches at Da'Giulio. "She wants you to believe that and see her as perfect. She needs everyone to think that about her, but there's someone very different behind the mask. The act is convincing, that's why people with Munchausen by proxy are so hard to identify." He had come to hate the words.

He didn't tell his mother but sometimes he

realized he still loved Zoe, and felt guilty for sharing his fears with others, like Cathy. What if he was wrong about her, and the incidents really were accidents? There was a seed of doubt in his mind, but it never grew beyond that, when he read more about the disorder, and saw again how perfectly the criteria matched up to his wife. But his heart ached when he saw her in a tender moment with Jaime, or how happy Jaime was with her, and how much she and Zoe loved each other. It was a kind of passion, and they left him out at times.

Cathy felt that way too, and also had doubts occasionally, and wondered if they'd gotten riled up, and panicked for nothing. As time passed, the previous incidents seemed less ominous and their menacing quality began to fade. She and Zoe had spent a particularly nice Saturday together, shopping uptown at Bergdorf's when Austin liberated Zoe by taking Jaime to Central Park, and they met up for tea afterward at the Plaza. Zoe told Jaime all about Eloise, the mischief she got up to, and how much Zoe had loved her as a little girl. She pointed out a portrait of her in the lobby, with her pug dog and turtle, and Jaime loved seeing it. Zoe promised to get her the book. She really was the perfect mom, or so it appeared.

Austin, Zoe, and Jaime had brunch at a restaurant with an outdoor terrace in SoHo the following weekend. It was the first really warm spring day, and they were relaxing in the sunshine, as Jaime finished the donut she'd had for dessert. It was one of their specialties, and the restaurant was known for them. Jaime got flushed after she ate it, and Zoe put more sunscreen on her, thinking she was getting burned. Austin was drinking a cappuccino and struggling with the **New York Times** crossword puzzle when Jaime started to choke and gasp for air. She wasn't eating at the moment, so there was nothing in her throat, and no Heimlich necessary. But she couldn't stop wheezing and coughing, and she looked panicked as she glanced at her mother.

"I can't breathe, Mommy," she whispered. Her face was red and swelling, and Austin put down the paper with a look of panic.

"What happened?"

"I don't know." Zoe looked terrified too. "She just started choking and gasping for air," and then suddenly Jaime stopped talking, she was wheezing, and they could see that she couldn't get enough air. Zoe called 911 on her cellphone, and her hands were shaking, as she held it and told the 911 operator her name, location, and what was happening. They said they would be there in five minutes as a man came over from the next table and said he was a doctor.

"I think she's having an allergic reaction, an anaphylactic reaction." Austin was holding her, and Jaime looked wild-eyed. She couldn't breathe.

"All she had was oatmeal and a donut, and some banana. She's had bananas before, and she eats oatmeal almost every day."

"Is she allergic to honey? The donuts are honey-glazed." It said so on the menu. The doctor was taking her pulse and it was racing, and he was watching her closely. He could tell that her airway was closing. She was dying in front of their eyes, it was a severe reaction, and Austin was silently wondering if Zoe had poisoned her.

"She's never had honey," Zoe said frantically. "I read somewhere that they shouldn't have it till they're four or five." They could hear a siren approaching, and seconds later, the paramedics rushed onto the terrace and spotted them immediately. The doctor told them what he thought.

"Do you have adrenaline, an EpiPen?" he asked them, and one of them nodded, as the other paramedic questioned Austin and picked Jaime up. "You're going to need it in a minute, or even now," the doctor said, and as he did, Jaime went limp in the paramedic's arms and passed out as they rushed her to the ambulance. Austin threw two fifty-dollar bills on the table, and he and Zoe rushed after the paramedics, as he muttered a hasty thank-you over his shoulder to the doctor.

Austin and Zoe climbed into the ambulance with one of the paramedics, and they took off with the other one driving. The paramedic put an oxygen mask on Jaime and an IV in her arm with expert speed, and had a defibrillator near at hand.

"She's having an anaphylactic reaction, probably to something she ate," he said and fired questions at them about Jaime's health and allergies. He never took his eyes off her. She was deathly pale, and her heartbeat was getting weak. He gave her a shot of adrenaline, and she opened her eyes for an instant and then lost consciousness again. Almost as a reflex, Austin called Cathy, got her immediately, and told her what was going on.

"What hospital are you going to?" she asked him and he asked the paramedic.

"NYU," he said, focusing only on Jaime. Austin told Cathy what was happening.

"I'll be right there," she cut him off, and they were at the hospital by then. The paramedics rushed her into the familiar emergency room that they hadn't seen in a while, and nothing had changed. They took her in through the ambulance entrance, and shouted to the nearest nurse that she was coding. She hit an alarm button, and half a dozen doctors and nurses came running, and changed the bag on the IV pole to something else. Austin heard the words "Benadryl," "prednisone," and others he didn't know through a haze. They had Jaime in an exam room by then and her clothes off, with a defibrillator poised if her heart stopped. They expected it to and were prepared, as her parents looked on in horror and the paramedics watched. She was so tiny on the adult table with so many doctors and nurses around her and frantic measures. Zoe was gulping sobs and clutching Austin, and he was crying too. They gave her another shot, and Jaime opened her eyes and looked at them and started to cry, which was a good sign. She could breathe again and wasn't choking. She was scared more than anything and didn't know what was going on. As the panic receded, Austin was filled with terror again, wondering if Zoe had orchestrated it. It brought back everything he had recently learned, and all his most virulent fears.

Cathy arrived at that moment in workout clothes with wet hair, and glanced at Austin and Zoe. "Sorry, I'm a mess. I was at a spinning class." She spoke to the doctors then, and explained that she was Jaime's pediatrician. They filled her in on what had happened and what they had administered. It was clear to Cathy and all the medical personnel that Jaime had almost died. But the adrenaline, cortisone, antihistamine, and other medications they had given her had brought her back. She told Austin and Zoe that Jaime would be all right now, but she'd have to stay in the hospital for several hours, and she might have some minor residual allergic reaction for several days.

Austin and Zoe kissed Jaime then, and she told them she couldn't breathe at the restaurant. "We know." Zoe smiled at her. "That's why we're here."

"Mommy called 911 for you," Austin said, remembering to give her the credit she craved if she was MBP. But did Mommy poison her? It was the only question in his head now, as everything he'd read rushed back into his mind. It didn't seem possible that a donut could have given her such a severe reaction that almost killed her.

The code blue team left the room with the paramedics, and a nurse and an ER doctor stayed with Jaime, talking to her.

"We have to take her to an allergist ASAP," Zoe said to Cathy, and she nodded.

"I use a great one," Cathy reassured her. "I'll get her in tomorrow." They asked Austin to register her, and Cathy went with him, while Zoe stayed with Jaime in the exam room.

"Oh my God," Austin said, after they were halfway down the hall, and looked at Cathy. He was sheet white. "What was that? What did she give her and when?" He was back to believing Zoe had MBP, without a doubt.

"Nothing. That was real. A severe anaphylactic allergic reaction," Cathy reassured him. She was certain of it.

"What makes you think so?" He looked confused, as they stopped to talk for a minute. There was no rush now.

"Because I'm a doctor, and that's what it looks like. Jaime has never had honey, and apparently the donuts were honey glazed. Zoe told me. The only way she did this is if she knew about the honey allergy, but she couldn't have. She's always told me she won't let Zoe have honey. She read that it's dangerous and possibly toxic under the age of five. She may also be allergic to bees. We'll test for it. You'll have to carry an EpiPen for her from now on," Cathy said seriously.

"For once she was right."

"Not really, a reaction that severe is unusual. You see it in nut allergies and shellfish. Apparently, Jaime has a very severe allergy to honey. It's good to know. I have no doubt about it, Austin. It was real this time. She couldn't manipulate **this** unless she knew about the honey allergy in advance. Even victims of people with MBP have real accidents and illnesses sometimes. This wasn't Zoe, I'd stake my license on it."

"I thought she had poisoned her," he said, still shaken by what he'd seen.

"We can run some tests, but I think the only chemicals we'll find in her system are the meds they just gave her."

"Will you run the tests?" he asked, and she nodded. He felt supremely guilty for what he had thought. But the truth was that he didn't trust his wife, with good reason. But apparently, Zoe had nothing to do with what had just happened, which in some ways was a relief.

Cathy ordered the tests after they registered Jaime, and she explained to the attending physician that she wanted to be sure she hadn't ingested any chemicals or medications at home when no one was looking, or if it was a straight allergic reaction. The attending said it was thorough of her, but they both agreed that it was probably entirely an anaphylactic reaction. Cathy wanted to be sure.

The tests came back a few hours later, and were clear. The only things in her system were the drugs they had given her at NYU. Austin looked at Cathy guiltily when she told him. He didn't know what to think anymore. And the attending spelled it out clearly to them before they released her at six o'clock.

"She had a near fatal allergic reaction to something she ate at brunch today. Dr. Clark is going to send you to an allergist tomorrow so you can figure out what. Until then, she needs to stay away from what she ate, banana, oatmeal, honey. You'll need to carry an EpiPen for her in the future. I'm giving you a prescription for one, the children's dosage. You should have it with you for her at all times. Allergic reactions usually get worse every time. She started out with a bang here, the next time we may not get as lucky. Learn to use the EpiPen, you may have to in a hurry, and you don't want to be fumbling with the instructions or trying to figure it out. You can get a practice model, and test it on an orange. She's very lucky you called 911 so quickly. They saved her life, and so did you." Zoe glowed when he said it, and Austin nodded. For once, it was true, and she hadn't caused the problem in the first place. Her innocence in this case left him feeling grateful but confused. "Sometimes people become allergic to foods they had no allergy to before. That can change anytime, so you need to check out everything she ate. And if it's honey she's allergic to, you'll need to be careful. There's honey in baked goods and in many other foods. People use it to cook, even on vegetables sometimes. Read the labels on everything you suspect might have honey in it. It'll spare you another episode like this." They both nodded, shaken and impressed by what had happened. They left the hospital with Jaime a while later. She was groggy from the Benadryl they had given her. Cathy had prescribed a children's dose for the next few days, until the allergens were truly out of her system. They were to start it after they saw the allergist the next day, so they didn't confuse his tests. After that, Cathy said Jaime would sleep for the next few days from the antihistamine.

All three of them were subdued when they left the hospital. Jaime from the drugs, and Zoe and Austin from what had almost happened. Jaime had nearly died from a donut. It had been one of the most frightening moments of their lives as parents. They sat in the kitchen after they put Jaime to bed, and neither of them said a word. They were lost in their own thoughts, with the image of Jaime unconscious in the ambulance, dying, engraved forever on their minds.

Cathy called Paul Anders at home that night and told him what had happened, since he was following Jaime's case. Talking to him was comforting. It was an unnerving case, with their worries about MBP.

"We ran some extra blood tests, and there was nothing in her system except what she ate and the meds they gave her in the ER. Austin was afraid Zoe had poisoned her, but she's clean on this one without a doubt. It was a straight anaphylactic reaction. And I don't think Zoe had anything to do with it. Jaime had never had honey before, because her mother thinks it's dangerous, and has been diligent about avoiding it for her. It turns out that she was right, for Jaime anyway. I think Austin was shocked that it was a real accident this time, and nothing had been engineered. I have to admit, I'm relieved. She came very close to dying. I can't even imagine what that would look like if her mother had killed her. None of us would ever have forgiven ourselves for not moving sooner. This was a freebie."

"Don't celebrate too soon," he said in a serious voice.

"You think she did it?" Cathy was stunned. She couldn't see how in the circumstances.

"No, I don't. I agree with you. Victims of a Munchausen by proxy mother can have an innocent allergic reaction, or real unprovoked illness too. And I agree with your diagnosis and analysis of the situation on this one. But you're overlooking something major."

"What?" She couldn't see what it might be.

"The bad news is that Zoe has just been handed a lethal weapon, a major vulnerability in Jaime. She nearly died from a honey glazed donut today. An allergy that severe is a loaded gun in her mother's hands. It seems like there's honey in damn near everything these days, bread, cookies, cakes, all kinds of prepared foods to varying degrees. We're not talking about a rare poison. We're talking about a common substance that's harder to avoid than to find. Anytime Zoe wants to kill her daughter, all she has to do now is give her something with honey in it, and then claim she didn't know, or lose her EpiPen, or God knows how she'd orchestrate it. Jaime has an Achilles' heel now the size of Yankee Stadium, an allergy to a substance so benign that Zoe will almost certainly get off scot-free if she kills her, unless someone sees her pouring honey down Jaime's throat with the kid tied to a chair."

"Shit. I hadn't thought of that. I was just so glad that it wasn't her fault this time."

"Don't be fooled by her outward demeanor, Cathy. You know better than that," he said wisely.

"The evidence against her is already strong. It may not hold up in court, but we're all convinced of the truth, and her innocence today in this one incident doesn't change that. She's guilty of all the rest, and we know it, almost for sure. But this allergic reaction today is what could kill Jaime. Her life is even more at risk from now on, because of a simple thing like a severe allergy to honey."

"So what am I supposed to do now?" She sounded near tears, and she knew that what he said was true. What would be easier than killing someone with honey, and it wouldn't take much, judging by today.

"I don't think you have any choice anymore. I wouldn't even ask Austin. You can't. He's probably as confused as you are. She's his wife. But you're their doctor, Jaime's doctor. This is a tragedy waiting to happen. You have to report what you know from the past three and a half years to Child Protective Services now. Cathy, you have to. There's no other choice. With the compounding element of a severe allergy which could kill her, to a substance so readily available, they have to open an investigation. I was willing for all of you to wait until now. I'm not anymore. The honey allergy could be a death sentence for Jaime in her mother's hands. Write your report tonight, and call CPS tomorrow. You can't wait any longer."

Cathy was silent for a long moment as she

thought about it, and much to her chagrin, she knew he was right. And just as Austin did, she felt like a traitor to her friend. She was going to write the report, and call Child Protective Services, as Paul said she should. But she wasn't going to tell Austin yet. He didn't need to know.

Chapter 16

Dan Knoll had come to work at Child Protective Services through a circuitous route. Homeless and abandoned on the streets of Chicago at seven, by parents he couldn't even remember, a father who died in prison, a mother who dealt drugs until her boyfriend killed her, he had grown up in foster care. He had been shuffled from one family to the next, badly treated and sometimes beaten. He had never worked out at any of the families where he'd been sent by the state. They said he was difficult, noncompliant, surly, oppositional, but mostly he was scared. He was a big kid, tall with broad shoulders and red hair, six foot four at twelve, and six-six at fourteen, so no one had figured out that anger was his camouflage to keep people from seeing that he was afraid. His friends and enemies called him Big Red. A football coach at one of the schools he went to had taken him under his wing, gave him a job when he left foster care and let him live with him and his family, and trained him. By a series of fortuitous circumstances that seemed more like miracles when he looked back on them, he had gotten into professional football, thanks to Coach Fitzgerald, and played for the Detroit Lions for three years. He was an offensive lineman, and had a bright future until a game against the New England Patriots in Boston ended all of that for him. He destroyed his knee and no amount of surgery could put him back in NFL football.

He played around with drugs for a while, drank too much, spent his money, and felt sorry for himself until Pat Fitzgerald grabbed him by the scruff of the neck, brought him home, threatened to kick his ass, and told him he had two choices. He could either be a bum for the rest of his life and maybe wind up like his parents, or be a respectable human being and do some good in the world. He told him to clean up, get a job, figure out what he wanted to do now that he was an adult. He lived with Pat and his family, worked at a gas station, and at night studied to be a social worker. It took a long time, but he got the degree. He moved to New York, got a job with Child Protective Services at thirty, and he had been there for ten years, handling cases of kids who were just like him when he was their age. He liked working with the bad boys best. It was such a victory when he could do something for them to help turn them around. That was

Pat's legacy to him. Dan wanted to give back what he'd been given. He wasn't married, but had had a series of long-term girlfriends. He was "serially monogamous," as the term went, and unattached at the moment. He had a heavy caseload and the department was understaffed and overworked, and he was usually at his desk at night working till all hours, writing reports to catch up.

The ultimate punishments for him were teenage girls. They were much harder to figure out, bitchier and more vicious than boys the same age. But he took what was assigned to him. His boss was a sixty-year-old African American woman, Yvette, who was smarter than anyone he knew. Dan was in charge of investigations of children whom observers suspected were being abused. It was thankless work, but he liked it. He liked discovering the truth and saving a kid from bad people. He felt like Superman when he did.

"I've got a new case for you," Yvette said as she came by his office on Tuesday morning and dropped the file on his desk. "Came in yesterday. The initial reporter is the child's pediatrician."

"Child abuse?" He hated child abusers with a passion and removed the victims from dangerous circumstances and bad parents whenever he could. He had saved a lot of lives by doing so.

"More or less," Yvette said cryptically. "In a convoluted way, if what they say is true." They both knew that, given the opportunity, most of the people they dealt with were liars. Yvette had been in the field for twenty years before they assigned her to run the office. She'd been Dan's boss since he'd been there.

"What does that mean, 'convoluted child abuse'? Is that like virtual child abuse? They do it online?"

"Don't be a smartass, read the report. She called yesterday. It's confidential as to who called it in. The report is very comprehensive."

"Is it red flagged? I don't have time to read it till later. I have to see three kids today, and talk to the neighbor of a kid who was being beaten every night until they called the cops. She's in a shelter pending a custody hearing." He dealt with the heavy-duty cases.

"There's no flag on it yet, but you should read it. It's unpredictable and could get hot fast."

"Great." Yvette went back to her office, and he attacked the stack of files on his desk. He had interviews to do on each of them. The days were never long enough for him and he often finished work at ten P.M. He had no one to go home to right now anyway, although he hoped that would change. He'd been alone for a year, which was a long time for him. He was a good-looking man and some women loved his "gentle giant" appeal. But he hadn't met a woman who mattered to him, and seemed worth the effort, in a long time.

He made notes on three files, and the orange file Yvette had left with him kept gnawing at him, begging him to open it. He put the others aside, and opened the file. Cathy's neat, concise report on her letterhead looked up at him. She had sent it in hard copy and email. Yvette had said she'd forward the email to him too. Her identity was confidential to anyone except the department, particularly to the parents.

Cathy had listed all the incidents chronologically, and they filled a whole page, much to his amazement. He scanned through them quickly, all events that could be accidental, or engineered by a clever abuser. She included a brief profile of both parents, and he whistled. They sounded fancy to him, and certainly educated. The mother ran a shelter he knew well, but that didn't impress him. He'd had two supposedly respectable physicians with apartments on Park Avenue nearly beat their children to death and lose custody. Fancy meant nothing to him. People were people and some of them were very sick. Those were the ones he was looking for, to put them away, and rescue their kids.

Cathy had explained that both the father and the paternal grandmother suspected that the mother of the child in the report suffered from Munchausen by proxy, and were afraid she would continue to injure the child and put her at risk. She said that a psychiatrist she had consulted, who had not met the family or the child, agreed with them, based on the evidence, and had urged her to report the family and situation to CPS. He could read between the lines that she had done so reluctantly, but sincerely felt that the child was in danger. Her phone numbers and email address, and the address of her office were all included if they wished to interview her.

The report was respectful, smart, not hysterical, and as factual as it could be, based on assumptions and guesswork and hypotheses. But there was nothing hypothetical about the injuries the child had sustained. There were too many of them to be entirely accidental. Dan would have been suspicious immediately if someone at the hospital had brought it to his attention. Some medical workers did, but many didn't. They were supposed to be mandated reporters, but most of the time they were too busy to add up the evidence. They tried to get doctors and nurses to always report suspected child abuse, and many people were afraid to or didn't want to get involved. With a three-and-a-half-year-old in this case, Dan didn't want to let it slide. A child that age couldn't defend herself, particularly not against a clever mother who hid what she did. He wouldn't have suggested Munchausen by proxy on his own, but he had read about it, and was fascinated by the disorder. It was his first case of its kind.

He picked up his cellphone and called Cathy's office number. He gave the receptionist his name but not who he worked for, and Cathy was about to refuse the call when she suddenly wondered if it was someone from CPS being discreet. The woman she'd spoken to the day before had told her that an investigator would call her.

"Yes? Dr. Clark," she said officially when she picked up.

"Hello, Doctor. I'm Dan Knoll, CPS. I think you know why I'm calling. I have to interview someone in your area early this afternoon. Could I have a few minutes of your time after that?"

"Of course." She was impressed that he had called so quickly.

"It would usually take me a little longer to get to you, but the subject is young in this case. I don't like to let those cases sit around. Thank you for reporting it. Interesting situation. Will five o'clock work for you?"

"That's perfect. My last patient is just a measles, mumps, and rubella vaccine, so it should be quick."

"I can wait," he said in a smooth, even voice. She couldn't tell how old he was, but he sounded intelligent, and interested. She could only imagine the shitstorm that would happen when he interviewed Zoe. She would go insane. The world's #1 supermom, interrogated by CPS.

When Zoe took Jaime to the allergist Cathy had recommended, he did a number of scratch tests on

Jaime's arms and back. They had to wait in a room for an hour, watching to see what would react to the substances they'd applied, and come up in red blotches and welts. He was an older man and was wonderful with Jaime. He spoke to her with a red clown nose on him the entire time and she couldn't stop laughing, great big belly laughs, and he asked her innocently why she was laughing at him, and she pointed at the red nose. When he came back into the room for the second time to check on her, he wore a clown wig to go with it, and she laughed even harder, and Zoe laughed too. It was a blessed relief from the shock of Jaime nearly dying two days before. He made it an easy stress-free visit for them.

The result of his skin tests showed that she was allergic to asparagus and eggplant, which weren't part of her diet. She'd never eaten either, they were easy to identify, they wouldn't be a problem. She had minor allergies to some pollens, a slight allergy to dust, which he said everyone had. She was allergic to cats and not dogs. And Cathy had relayed her amoxicillin allergy to him. But her allergy to honey was off the charts. And she was as allergic to bees as she was to honey. Either of those allergies could prove fatal, and both were in the anaphylactic range. Her parents would have to carry a double EpiPen Jr for Jaime, and so did the nanny, in case she ever got stung by a bee, at the playground or elsewhere. All of the other allergies were to a lesser degree which might make her sneeze or give her a rash or hives. But bees or honey would close her throat or stop her heart, and adrenaline, steroids, and a powerful antihistamine had to be administered immediately. As the doctor at the hospital had said, the allergist told Zoe that honey was tricky because it was in so many packaged foods and couldn't always be detected. She would have to ask the question or read the label every time. But other than that, he found Jaime sound, and she said goodbye to "Dr. Clown" when they left and blew him a kiss.

"Come back and visit me sometime," he said as he waved at her. He and his nurse agreed she was an adorable child. He took his clown nose off after she left.

The doctor reported his findings to Cathy, which she relayed to Zoe and Austin as soon as Zoe and Jaime left his office. The only real news was about asparagus and eggplant. But he had confirmed how lethal honey and bees could be to Jaime. Cathy's heart sank when she heard it, remembering what Paul had said about the honey allergy being so severe it was a loaded gun in Zoe's hands, if she really was MBP. She could always claim afterward that she didn't know there was honey in something Jaime ate, and it would be believable because so many commercial products had honey in them, even in small amounts. It posed a major threat to Jaime, especially in her mother's hands. Austin realized it too.

When Dan Knoll came to Cathy's office, he looked like a bull in a china shop as he sat perched on a couch next to the little chairs for children in her waiting room, and the low table with toys on it. The nurse led him to her office, after he heard a baby scream and a mother leave with a crying infant. The MMR shot, he assumed.

She stood up at her desk when he walked in, and extended a hand to shake his. She was startled by his size, he dwarfed her office the moment he walked in. He had a pleasant face and kind eyes, and there was nothing ominous about him. But he looked like he could take care of himself on a dark night, which was accurate. He was a black belt in karate, which his mentor thought would be good discipline for him. He still went to classes twice a week, to teach now, and sometimes he took some of the boys whose cases he handled with him. They were duly impressed. He was fast despite his size, and even more powerful than he looked. He let them try but none of them could get him to the ground. He always told them that you had to be smart and patient, not just strong, to get somewhere in life.

"Thank you for reporting the case, Doctor. Why did you wait until now? Did you ever suspect there might be child abuse involved here, in a classic sense?"

"Never," she said honestly. "I know the parents. They are the most devoted parents in my practice, attentive, loving, responsible. Everybody loves them. I never thought of child abuse, and still don't in the 'classic sense.'"

"You don't think the child's protecting her parents?"

"Not at all. And I thought the accidents she's sustained were just that, unlucky mishaps that could happen to any one-, two-, or three-year-old. Toddlers can get in a real mess sometimes and get badly injured."

"It didn't strike you as odd that she got injured so often?" There was accusation in his eyes, and Cathy looked regretful and shook her head.

"I don't think I realized how long the list was on a day-to-day basis. I do triage. I deal with situations every day. I find solutions and fix them, and move on to the next one. I don't keep a tally in my head. I realize now that I should have."

"You're not alone in that, Doctor. I was just asking." He seemed to be gentle, and forgiving of her, but not Jaime's parents. "When did you begin to suspect Munchausen by proxy?"

"I didn't. There was an incident in Florida when they were on vacation, and Jaime was running on the wet surface next to the pool at their hotel. She slipped, fell into the deep end and nearly drowned, and cut her chin badly on the way into the pool. Her mother wasn't watching her, and was talking to people with her back to the pool. Jaime's father arrived on the scene in the nick of time, jumped in, and saved her."

"No lifeguard?" He looked surprised.

"Apparently he was helping an elderly person and wasn't watching either. That's how tragedies happen. When they got back from Florida, Jaime's father came to see me. His mother is a psychologist and had suspected MBP for some time but not told him until after the pool incident. He agrees with her, and wanted to know what I thought. It hadn't occurred to me until then. I've never encountered it in my practice. I consulted a psychiatrist I know, and he concurred with the father and grandmother. He convinced me to report it to CPS. I felt disloyal doing it, but I felt I had to."

"Disloyal to whom? Not the child."

"No, I reported it to protect the child. I'm very fond of her mother. I always thought she was a good mother."

"And now?" He looked at her directly and Cathy didn't flinch.

"I think there's a problem. A serious one, and they may be right. It breaks my heart to say it, but it sounds more than possible, even likely." She tried to be as honest with him as she could be. She had made her report factual, but she was fleshing it out now.

"I agree with you," he said simply. "Have there been any accidents or injuries since the pool incident?" he asked her.

"She got bitten in the face by a German shepherd ten days later, which required suturing by a plastic surgeon. Nothing since then, other than a severe allergic reaction to a substance she'd never eaten before. I think that was entirely innocent."

He nodded. "It won't be if there's a repeat, however. What was it?"

"Honey." He made a note on a pad.

"That's dangerous because it's so common."

"I know," she said sadly.

"Where do you see this going? Where would you like to see it go, for the child?" It was the toughest question of all and she hesitated, not sure what to say.

"I honestly don't know. Jaime loves her mother. Everyone does. My nurses think she's the best mother in our practice."

"That's not unusual in Munchausen by proxy, in fact, it's typical," he said coolly. "Most of them look like the best parents in the world. They're cagey and cunning and smart, and you can't always see how they do it, but the child gets hurt or dies. We have to avoid that outcome for Jaime."

"That's why I reported it. I don't know what I'd like to see for them. I've been told counseling isn't effective."

"It runs deeper than that. A lot deeper. People

with MBP are very sick. Ultimately, we'll have to protect Jaime from her, if her father and grandmother's suspicions are correct." Cathy nodded.

"Zoe being removed from her life would be a tremendous loss to Jaime, and could mark her forever," Cathy said sadly.

"So would getting killed by her mother," he said bluntly. Cathy didn't know what to answer. "The decision may happen by itself, if she steps too far over the line. She could wind up in prison, or give up custody of her own accord in lieu of prosecution. We just don't want it to get out of hand. That's our goal. We're Jaime's advocates, and I think you are too." Cathy nodded, desolate for them all. What he outlined was so painful and so extreme, but he saw hard cases every day and made hard decisions for the well-being of children in jeopardy. It was just tragic that Jaime was one of them. Cathy had never expected that to happen when she'd met them.

He stood up then and thanked her for her time, and she handed him her card with her cellphone number on it. "Call me anytime. I want to help if I can."

"Thank you." He would have liked to call her for reasons beyond their investigation, but he would never do that. She was a beautiful woman, and a nice person, and shared his love of children. He hadn't met anyone like her in a long time. "Honorable" was the word that came to mind, and she thought the same thing about him. She had been very impressed by how dignified the investigation was, as he conducted it. It wasn't a witch hunt, it was a search for the truth for the benefit of the child.

It was six-thirty when he left. Her nurses had already gone home by then. He said he was going to interview the father and grandmother next, to get their impressions and hear why they thought Zoe was MBP. He was going to interview Fiona, Zoe herself, and all the physicians she'd consulted for Jaime, to get their views of the situation too. And there were a number of them. Cathy knew that when he interviewed Zoe she would hit the roof. She was the director of a shelter for abused children, how could she be accused of abusing her own child? It might even cost her her job if it got out. But if their fears about her were true, it was right to question her. And if they were wrong, hopefully they would discover that too.

Before she left her office, Cathy knew what she had to do. Austin had no idea what was coming at him, that she had reported it to CPS, and she felt she owed him a warning now.

She called him in his office and hoped he was still there. He worked late frequently, and she was relieved when he picked up.

"Hi, how are you?" Cathy asked, sympathetic.

"Managing," he said, sounding tired.

"I called you to make a confession."

"That sounds interesting." He smiled as he said

it. She was a faithful friend and he was grateful for her wisdom, expertise, and support. They were lucky to have her as a doctor, and a friend.

"After the allergic reaction, I spoke to Paul Anders and he said I had no choice, and I agree with him. The honey allergy gives Zoe too dangerous a weapon to leave this dormant any longer. I called CPS on Monday and made a report. An investigator just came to see me in my office. I think you and your mother are next. They're taking it seriously, but he was a smart, sensible guy, and he's not going crazy with it. I was very impressed."

"Thanks for the warning, Cathy. I understand. I think you did the right thing. I felt guilty for what I thought about the honey attack, but it doesn't change the rest. I'm still on the fence, but leaning heavily toward MBP." He sounded almost matter of fact about it, but she knew how profoundly upset he was. Their whole life was on the line, their marriage, and Jaime's life, in an even more real sense. "When are they going to talk to Zoe? Do you know?"

"I don't. I assume they would talk to her last, so as not to tip her off before that. But that's just me talking. I don't know how they work. It may not be as methodical as that."

"She'll go nuts." Cathy agreed with that. "It strikes at everything she cares about, and how she wants to be perceived as the best mother in the world. Her ego is going to take a heavy hit," and so was their marriage. Cathy had thought of that too, and so had he. "I guess we'll just deal with it when it happens."

"Anything you say is confidential, so you can be honest with him. You should be," Cathy urged him.

"I intend to be. Now that it's in their hands, we all have to be honest. Zoe too, if she's capable of it, or willing to be." It was a sad statement to make about his wife. "Thank you for telling me. I'll expect to hear from him sometime soon."

"His name is Dan Knoll. He just left my office before I called you."

"Talk to you soon," he said in a tired voice.

Her cellphone rang as soon as they hung up. It was Dan Knoll from CPS.

"I forgot to ask you one question. How solid do you think their marriage is? Is there trouble there?"

"There wasn't when I met them, or until recently. I'm not sure now. They're not splitting up or anything, but he was furious about the last couple of incidents, especially the one at the pool, and he blamed her for it. She doesn't do well with that. I think things are chillier than they used to be, but he's not threatening to leave her over it. I think he realizes that if she's really MBP and she's orchestrating these incidents, he can't stay with her, and it's going to hit their marriage like a bomb."

"I just wondered. Thank you. Have a great night."

"Thanks, Dan. I will. You too." She liked his approach, and he smiled as he hung up.

Chapter 17

Dan Knoll interviewed Austin in his office two days later, and was candid with him. He got a clearer picture of Austin's fears about his wife, but he told him that people with MBP were the cleverest child abusers in the world, and proving a solid case against them was damn near impossible in most instances.

"Have you thought of just divorcing her and suing for sole custody?"

"I don't think I'd win that either. And I don't want to. What if she didn't manipulate these accidents, and she's not guilty? She's my wife and Jaime's mother and I love her, even if I don't trust her. Maybe she's just not vigilant enough." Dan thought Austin's loyalty was misplaced but he didn't say so. He felt sorry for him. The poor guy looked tortured about his child, and had dark circles under his eyes. He told Dan every single detail he could remember, and Dan thanked him and promised to be in touch.

The following day he went to see Constance Roberts, who was intelligent, clear, lucid, well-informed, and convincing. There was no doubt in Dan's mind that Zoe had Munchausen by proxy by the time he had seen Cathy, Austin, and Connie, and he'd believed it from the beginning. But the question was how to prove it or catch her at it. She was too cunning to be obvious about it or get caught easily, like most people with MBP.

He decided to wait before interviewing Fiona, in case she said something to Zoe, and the following week, he met with all the physicians Jaime had seen in her lifetime. Austin had given him the list. The gastroenterologist for her apnea as a baby, the neurologist after the fall off the changing table, the ENT she had lied to, to get the ear tubes put in, and more recently the allergist, the orthopedic surgeon about possible scoliosis, both plastic surgeons, and the ER doctor and surgeon Zoe had tried to push into an appendectomy. Austin didn't remember their names, but the hospital had a record of them, and both orthopedists who had set Jaime's arm and wrist in casts. It was a long list, and by the end of it, Dan was more worried than before. The ones that alarmed him the most were the gastroenterologist she had asked about an abdominal feeding tube when Jaime was five weeks old, and the ENT she had lied to, to get ear tubes inserted surgically, claiming Jaime had recurring ear infections when she'd only had two. The back surgeon admitted that Zoe had inquired about steel rods in Jaime's spine and claimed she suffered from severe backaches, which both Austin and Cathy said wasn't true. But the back surgeon was no fool.

"She seemed neurotic to me, and very insistent. We get patients with mothers like that. They want surgery for their kids, they want to feel important. They lead boring lives, and they want something major to happen. I never touch them, unless the children genuinely have a severe problem. I either tell them it's unnecessary, or refer them to someone else. No one needs patients like that. Guaranteed you'll end up in a malpractice suit or wind up with a nut job on your hands. Plastic surgeons see a lot of them too. They're lawsuits waiting to happen. In my line of work, most people beg to avoid surgery. With people like that, they want you to operate on them or their children. It's crazy, but most of them stick out like a sore thumb. She's supposed to come back in six months, which is just a stalling tactic. I plan to send her on her way then. I avoid patients like her like the plague." Dan shared what the orthopedist had said with Cathy, and she sounded shocked that Zoe had asked for rods for Jaime and claimed she had backaches, which was a flat-out lie. But it all confirmed what they feared.

"The sad thing," Dan told her, "is that less reputable doctors, or less alert ones, will perform surgeries they shouldn't, that's how a lot of these kids die, from surgical procedures they never needed. The doctors either believed the mothers who were lying, or didn't know what they were doing. The worst case is a woman who talked a doctor into a gastric tube for her infant, and then moved all over the country and left it in. She used it to pour salt into her five-year-old's abdomen and killed him. She's serving life in prison, and her little boy is dead. We don't want something like that to happen to Jaime."

"Her father wouldn't let it, and neither would I," she said firmly to Dan. "He stepped in when she wanted an appendectomy for Jaime, and they called in a surgeon and he flatly refused after he saw a normal sonogram."

Dan saw Fiona and was cautious with her. He didn't ask her any leading questions, or to confirm anything they were worried about. He said that the meeting was entirely confidential and he preferred she not tell her employers about it. All she said was that Zoe was a wonderful woman, an outstanding employer, and an adoring mother, and Austin was a kind, loving father, and he let it go at that. She was not going to tell him anything of value. And that afternoon, he showed up at Zoe's office. Her assistant asked if he had an appointment, and he politely said he didn't. But his sheer bulk and size were daunting, as well as the agency he worked for, and he handed her his card and asked if Mrs. Roberts would see him briefly. She took it in and handed it to Zoe, who was having an insanely busy day.

"Oh shit. I guess I have to see him. It must be about one of our custody cases. I don't want to screw it up for them. I can skip lunch and give him half an hour. Send him in."

She was wearing a white blouse with a red sweater over her shoulders, and black jeans. Her shining dark hair hung below her shoulders, and she smiled and stood up when he walked in. He was struck by how pretty she was, and how young and personable she looked. She instantly tried to put him at ease.

"Which of our cases are you here for?" she asked him pleasantly with a warm smile, and offered him coffee, which he declined. "I think we have half a dozen going at the moment." He smiled back at her, but he was guarded and didn't make the mistake of believing that they were friends.

"This is a confidential, closed investigation, Mrs. Roberts, which is why I didn't mention it to your assistant. It comes from the medical sector, from one of the physicians or hospitals you've seen in the past three years. It's an investigation of you and your husband. Your daughter has had a number of minor injuries, and past a certain point, they are required to notify us." Zoe looked horrified and narrowed her eyes at him. He knew just what to say so that she didn't feel directly accused or at fault. He made it sound entirely routine, and had protected Cathy's identity.

"Which doctor was it?"

"My superiors don't tell me that. It's confidential, and so is our investigation. You've seen quite a number of physicians apparently as well, it could have been any one of them."

"She's a very active child, she fell a lot as a toddler, she was very unsteady on her feet. And she had severe gastric problems as an infant, and apnea. We had to use a monitor for a year so she didn't stop breathing and die in her sleep. I sat up with her every night," she said angrily, furious that she had been reported, but not wanting him to see it. But her eyes looked like blue fire, and her mouth was set in a hard line. The charming smile was gone.

He was careful not to mention the recent pool incident, or the dog bite, because she would have known it came from Cathy and he protected his sources. He didn't mention having seen her husband a week before.

"Has your daughter had any surgeries or stitches?" he asked, following a list of questions.

"Only one surgery, if you can call it that. She had ear tubes put in for recurring earaches, and a stitch in her lip when she fell down the stairs when she started walking. We had a gate up, but someone left it open." He nodded and made a note with a bland face, well aware that she had already lied to him. She had taken the gate down herself, according to

Austin, so there was none, and she didn't mention the stitches in Florida because they were in another state and she figured he wouldn't know, or the dog bite, because it was done in the surgeon's office, and she was a friend of Cathy's and she was sure he wasn't aware of it. And she wouldn't suspect Cathy of reporting her in a million years.

"Any major illnesses? We understand she's missed quite a bit of school."

"Kids catch everything the first year and she just started preschool. She's had the usual colds and flu, nothing major."

"Hospital records show that she was admitted for a febrile seizure."

"She never had another one," Zoe said in a clipped tone.

"Broken bones?"

"Two. A wrist and an arm." She was trapped on that one.

"And two dislocated elbows?"

She could barely contain herself when he asked her. "What are you suggesting? That my husband and I are child abusers? This is outrageous. She's a normal child who falls down and gets hurt from time to time. I run the most respected shelter for abused children in the city. You don't actually think I beat my child?"

"Good Lord, no," he said, looking dumb for a minute. "These are all standard questions. And I know the work you do. I've worked with some of your clients. Every agency in the city admires your agency and uses you as a role model for theirs." Her ruffled feathers smoothed down a little after that. "I didn't even think we should be following up on this, but CPS can't make exceptions, or some of the real abusers would slip through our nets, so occasionally we wind up investigating respectable people. It's all routine, and then that's it. Your little girl must be a bit of a tomboy," he said, smiling at her.

"Very much so," she said, smiling back, but he could see that she would have liked to strangle him and throw him out of her office, but she was too smart for that. And he had couched it well. She looked at her watch then. "How much longer will this take? I have a meeting with the head of foster care."

"Just a few minutes. Mrs. Roberts, would you say your child is in good health?"

"Of course. She has regular checkups and her shots are up to date."

"Do you trust your nanny and think she's responsible?"

"Yes, I do." She looked bored by then and annoyed, but she had definitely lied to him about several things, which he found more interesting than what she'd said.

"Has your daughter had any recent injuries? Significant falls, broken bones, stitches, anything that required medical attention by a doctor or in a hospital?"

"None." She lied again, about Jaime's chin in Florida, and the dog bite.

"I'm happy to hear it," he said as he stood up. "Thank you for your time. We'll just file this for now."

"I assume the file will be closed after this. Or are you going to continue counting doctors' visits until she goes to college?" She was trying to intimidate him and it didn't work. He looked her squarely in the eye when he answered.

"You know how CPS works. Once a report is made and we investigate it, the file stays open for a year. We check in now and then if we think it's necessary, which is unlikely in your case. But we're obliged by law to keep the case open for a year. You deal with CPS all the time, so you know that."

"That applies to us too?" She almost shrieked at him.

"It applies to everyone. If we made exceptions, we'd be all over the press for favoritism, or saying that money talks. You know what the media do with that."

"I can't believe this. Have you seen my husband yet?"

"No, I haven't. I plan to, but I haven't had time and I wanted to make you aware of it first." She nodded and walked him to the door.

"Thank you for your visit," she said with clenched teeth, and she almost slammed the door behind him and would have liked to. She called Austin five minutes later after she tried to calm down, but Dan Knoll beat her to it, and he was talking to Austin when she called.

"I just saw your wife," Dan warned him. "She's not too happy with me. I told her I haven't seen you yet, and I wanted to give you a heads-up. I told her this is just routine when a child gets injured as often as Jaime has, and is treated at a hospital. I told her that either a physician or the hospital reported it, as they are obliged to. She couldn't say much to that. She also lied to me about several things. She said you had a gate when Jaime fell. She said Jaime has had no recent injuries. She's only had stitches once, not three times, and she didn't tell me about the pool accident in Florida or the dog bite. I think she figured I'd have no record of either one. Let's agree now on when you say you saw me. How about late this afternoon?"

"That's fine, I'll be in the office."

"I asked her questions about childhood diseases, vaccinations, missed school, very benign stuff. You can say that I asked you the same questions as a matter of record."

"Thank you. You may save my marriage yet." Dan wasn't sure that was a good idea. She was a liar, which confirmed what he thought of her.

"She asked me how long the case would stay

open, and I told her we keep our files open for a year and then we close them, which is true. We want to make sure everything is solid and a child is in a stable situation. I said there are no exceptions to the one-year rule, and she was livid. And since she adheres to the rules at the shelter, she could hardly object to doing it at home. She was very unhappy about it." She had called Austin four times while he was on the phone with Dan, so he could tell that she was pissed.

"Thanks for the warning." He called Zoe back then and she sounded crazed.

"Can you goddamn believe it? Someone reported us to CPS because of Jaime's hospital visits. Are they crazy? What kind of parents do they think we are? How could they do such a thing?"

"What did you tell them?" Austin asked, immediately tense.

"The truth of course, within reason. They don't have to know everything, Austin. The same investigator is going to come and see you. Don't tell him anything he doesn't already know. Don't volunteer anything."

"Like what?" He played dumb.

"They don't have to know about the pool in Florida, it's in another state. And I didn't mention the dog bite, we didn't go to the hospital for that. We don't want to look like child abusers, for God's sake, or have them in and out of our house every ten minutes for the next year. This is ridiculous.

And I could lose my job over it, if it winds up in the press."

"I thought those things were confidential," Austin said innocently.

"They're supposed to be, but who knows. And I told him we had gates up when Jaime fell down the stairs and broke her arm."

"We did have a gate up," he said quietly. "You took it down."

"Are you on my side or not?" she snapped at him. "We're in this together, you know. If they accuse me of child abuse, they'll accuse you too."

"There's nothing to accuse us of, Zoe. We're not child abusers. And you're the darling of the nonprofit world for rescuing children. It will all calm down," but he sounded dead as he said it. She wanted him to lie for her, and she sounded frightened to him. Of what? What else was there? What didn't he know?

Dan had told Cathy that the orthopedic surgeon had admitted that Zoe wanted rods put in Jaime's back, but he hadn't told Austin. The case was growing and Austin felt better about it. There wasn't enough yet to prove that Zoe was purposely endangering their child's life, but there was enough to make a serious case for Munchausen by proxy, even if some of Jaime's injuries had been mild. But it was still child abuse in the eyes of the state. She didn't have to be paralyzed or brain dead for them to make a case. Child endangerment was a felony too. And Dan's goal now was to protect Jaime and keep Zoe away from her in the future, and get full custody for Austin. Their marriage would be the inevitable casualty, and Austin understood that too. But he couldn't stay married to a woman who was harming his child and might kill her one day. The **Titanic** was going down, it just hadn't sunk yet.

Austin listened as Zoe continued to instruct him about what not to say. Essentially, she was telling him to lie.

"Don't blow it!" she told him before they hung up. She had no idea that in his eyes, she already had. He had told the truth, which was dangerous for her. She couldn't afford for anyone to be honest. Not Cathy, or him, or even Jaime, like the discrepancy in the story about the dog. He believed Jaime, and so did Dan Knoll.

Austin called Cathy after he and Zoe hung up. She could hear the minute she answered that he was depressed, and who wouldn't be. Everything was on the line, their marriage, possibly her job, and their child's life. What else was there? And somewhere in his heart of hearts, Austin kept hoping that they were wrong, but he knew in his head and his gut that they weren't. Their whole life was about to go out the window. And what if they were both charged with child abuse, because he hadn't reported her sooner? He wondered if that could happen, and hadn't dared ask Dan. He felt cowardly now for not dealing with it earlier. He had been so blind for so long.

"Dan Knoll interviewed Zoe today," he told Cathy.

"How did she take it?"

"Badly, of course. And she lied to him."

"I thought she would." She didn't sound surprised, and her loyalties were clear. They were with Jaime, and Zoe was no longer a true friend, if she had been purposely injuring her child for three and a half years. Zoe had lost Cathy's support when she made her decision and turned her in to CPS. She was ready to stand by it. It was harder for Austin, he had more to lose and at times still felt torn, between love and disbelief, and wanting to grab Jaime and run, and save her from her mother. But he was still terrified they were wrong and doing Zoe a terrible injustice. He would never forgive himself if that was the case. But even less if she killed Jaime. That was unthinkable.

"He told her he hadn't seen me yet, and I went along with it. So I guess I'm a liar too."

"You have no choice," she said gently, "you have to protect Jaime. If you don't, something bad could happen."

"Bad things have already happened. A lot of them," he said grimly.

"I know it sounds crazy, but I think it will turn out okay in the end."

"For who?"

"For Jaime, for starters. If Zoe is doing what we think, she has to be stopped. For everyone's sake. If what we believe is true, her demons are running her life. She needs help." He sighed, listening to her. He didn't know where to turn anymore or what to believe.

"I wish I could just grab Jaime and run away," he said sadly.

"And how would you explain that to Jaime?"

"How will I explain it if her mother goes to jail? This is more than just a custody battle in the making, Cathy. There will be felony charges, if they can prove any of it."

"I know," and she had started it, but she didn't feel guilty anymore. She had done the right thing. She had no doubt.

Things calmed down for a few weeks after that. Dan Knoll's interviews were over, and he was writing his report. He wanted to think about it carefully and make the right recommendation, and he didn't know what that was yet. Possibly to wait until they had stronger evidence to bring criminal charges against Zoe. But he didn't want Jaime at risk in the meantime, until the next injury. He had consulted a psychiatrist about it too, and done extensive reading about Munchausen by proxy. He felt like an authority on it now. They all did.

Austin was still having lunch with his mother once a week. She asked what was happening with the investigation and he said he didn't know, which was true. Cathy didn't know anything either. He checked in with her every few days.

Zoe had calmed down after Dan Knoll's visit. She was still incensed about it, but since they'd heard nothing further, she assumed everything was in order and the file would be in a holding pattern now for the next year. And she was satisfied with what Austin had reported he'd said to Dan Knoll. She was warmer again after that, but Austin didn't trust her anymore, ever, for a single second, especially with their daughter. And Zoe was such a convincing liar, who knew what was true?

Zoe came home early from work one Friday afternoon after Jaime got out of school at two. She let Fiona leave early, and took Jaime with her to buy some groceries. She was in a good mood, and Jaime loved spending time with her. It felt like a special treat when her mom came home early from work, and they could have mother-daughter time alone. Zoe promised her they would buy colored sprinkles for a surprise.

When they came home from the grocery store, Zoe smiled at her.

"I have the surprise for you! Let's have a party!" Zoe said and clapped her hands.

"With balloons and cake?" Jaime's eyes lit up instantly.

"How about cake, no balloons?"

"Okay!" As Jaime watched, her mother pulled out a see-through box from a supermarket bag with a pink frosted cake in it. She'd picked it up on the way home and Fiona hadn't seen it before she left. She took off the label and tossed it into the garbage, crushed the plastic lid and shoved it way down to the bottom of the trash, and took out pink paper plates left over from Jaime's last birthday. She even had pink candles and strawberry ice cream. "It's a pink party!" Jaime said, clapping her hands, and out of the corner of her eye, she saw her mother put something on the counter. It was her EpiPen, which Zoe had in her purse. Zoe carried one all the time now, and so did Fiona. "What's that, Mommy?"

"Just some medicine Dr. Clown gave us. He was funny, wasn't he?"

"I liked him."

"Me too." Zoe put the cake on a round plate, cut two slices, and put sprinkles on them. She lit the candles on Jaime's for her to blow out, which she did with a giggle and blew her mom a kiss. "I love parties with you, Mommy," she said happily as the buzzer from downstairs rang, and Zoe looked annoyed. She answered the intercom. It was Cathy.

"What are you doing here?" Zoe asked into the speaker.

"I took the afternoon off. I thought I'd drop by

to say hi to Jaime. Are you playing hooky too? Can I come up?"

"Invite her to the party, Mommy!" Jaime was excited. This was fun.

"It's just our party. A mother-daughter party. Let's save the cake till later," she whispered and buzzed Cathy up. She was about to put the cake away when Cathy rang the doorbell. Zoe put the whole cake into a cupboard, and then opened the door and hugged her. She turned around and saw that Jaime had taken a big bite of one of the slices with a plastic fork. "Don't eat that!" she said sharply to Jaime, but she was already halfway through the slice Zoe had cut for her.

"Why not?" Cathy looked confused, as Jaime started to choke. Cathy thought it was stuck in her throat but her face turned bright red and her eyes rolled up in her head, as she fell off the stool she'd been sitting on, and Zoe caught her as she fell, grabbed the EpiPen off the counter, and pulled off the cap, as Cathy understood what had happened and grabbed it from her. "Oh my God, what did you do?" She jabbed the adrenaline shot into Jaime's thigh, and felt her pulse immediately. It was racing and then stopped as she started giving her CPR, and shouted at Zoe. "Call 911! Now! Tell them she's code blue. And we need a defibrillator!"

Zoe called them and pushed the paper plates into the garbage, as she watched her friend try to revive Jaime. Her heart had stopped, and Cathy was maintaining her heartbeat artificially with the CPR, pressing on her heart rhythmically and blowing into her mouth alternately. She could keep her going until the paramedics got there, and longer if she had to, but technically, Jaime was dead. Her heart wouldn't beat on its own. What Cathy was doing was keeping her heart beating and oxygen flowing to Jaime's brain. The EpiPen hadn't been strong enough to save her.

The paramedics arrived less than five minutes later, and Zoe let them into the apartment looking terrified.

"My daughter is having an allergic reaction. I don't know what happened." They rushed past her and saw Cathy giving Jaime CPR. Her heart began beating on its own then, but the rhythm was irregular. They applied the defibrillator, shocked Jaime's heart to regulate it, then felt her pulse, and they nodded at Cathy.

"She needs epinephrine stat," she told them. "I'm her pediatrician. We need Benadryl and cortisone. She's had one dose from an EpiPen, she needs more."

"We have them downstairs," they said as they put Jaime on the gurney, and hurried to the door. Her heart was beating, but Cathy knew it might stop again. The allergic reaction had been faster and worse this time.

"Are you coming?" she asked, looking hard at Zoe, who nodded, grabbed her purse, and rushed to the door. She didn't dare stay. The two women got in the elevator with Jaime and the paramedics, and they were in the ambulance a minute later, with the siren shrieking as they headed to NYU. They rushed her into the ambulance entrance, and the code blue team came running and worked on her. Zoe was standing in the doorway of the exam room, sobbing, as she watched them fight for her daughter's life for the second time. Cathy hung back just long enough to send two texts. She sent the same one to Austin and Dan Knoll. "NYU ER Jaime. Come now." And on Dan's she added, "Bring cops." And then she joined the code blue team to watch them fight to bring Jaime back to a normal state. She was in a coma, but they were working frantically as Zoe stood staring at her.

"What happened?" she kept saying again and again, and Cathy turned to her with fury in her eyes.

"You know goddamn well what happened. I saw the cake you threw away, and the EpiPen was waiting on the counter. How were you going to explain it if she died from a cake with honey in it that you gave her? You're a fool, Zoe, and you tried to kill her." As she said it, Zoe's eyes turned into those of a devil as she fixed her gaze on Cathy and looked like she wanted to kill her too.

"I was going to save her. I was all ready for it. I didn't know what was in the cake. It had no label on it. I was going to give her the shot and **save** her." She was screaming at Cathy, inches from her face. **"You ruined everything."** Her voice was an evil growl that Cathy didn't even recognize as the woman she knew, let alone her friend. Zoe wasn't her friend anymore. She was a monster.

"You couldn't save her. Her allergy is too severe. Do you see what it takes? And she's not out of the woods yet." They were intubating her as Cathy said it and she had tears in her eyes. She had the feeling she was watching Jaime die. It was entirely possible, even likely. Zoe's plan to play savior had backfired, and she was a murderess instead.

Austin showed up a few minutes later, wild eyed and panting. He had run the last five blocks when his cab got stuck in traffic.

"What happened? Where is she?" he asked both women and then saw his child on the table with the team working on her, intubated and comatose but still breathing.

"She had another allergic reaction," Cathy said soberly.

"How?" He looked at Zoe, unable to understand, as Dan came down the hall with long strides, with two policemen behind him. "What's going on?" he asked Cathy.

She tried to give him the fast version and Austin was listening. Zoe looked like she was about to bolt and run but she didn't dare with the policemen standing there.

"I dropped by unannounced for a visit. Zoe and

Jaime were there, about to have a party. There were two slices of cake on plates on the table. Jaime's EpiPen was on the counter, ready to go. While Zoe let me in, Jaime took a big bite of the cake. She was choking and couldn't breathe almost immediately, her airway closed and her heart stopped. I gave her the shot, Zoe called 911, and I gave Jaime CPR till they got there. And now, here we are again." She looked at Austin. "If you check your garbage and your kitchen, the two slices of cake are in the trash, and I assume the cake is there somewhere, loaded with honey, and pink icing so Jaime would be sure to eat it. I'm sure Zoe was going to claim she didn't know what was in the cake. She just told me she was going to **save** her and I ruined everything. But she tried to kill her first. She thought the EpiPen would do it, and bring her back. I told her before it would be worse next time, apparently, she didn't believe me. Jaime's allergy is too severe. She's in a coma now," she said for Dan's benefit, as Austin stood there crying and looked with horror at his wife.

"How could you do it? How could you, Zoe? And you thought you'd get away with it. You're insane!" He reached out to grab her with fury in his eyes, as Dan stepped forward with one of the two policemen and blocked him before the scene could get uglier than it already was. They were standing in a little alcove, but a few people had noticed the police arriving and heard the commotion outside the exam room when Zoe screamed at Cathy, and Austin shouted at his wife. A few of the nurses were staring at them.

"You're under arrest," one of the policemen said to Zoe in a firm voice, "for attempted murder," as Austin stared at her. The policeman read her her rights, and snapped handcuffs on her as Austin looked at her and his rage melted into despair.

"What if she dies, Zoe?" he said in a choked voice.

"You'll survive it," she said harshly. "I did when Rose died. So did my parents. And Jaime wouldn't have died. I would have revived her myself if Cathy hadn't showed up and spoiled it."

"You couldn't have," Cathy said coldly, as the efforts to save Jaime's life continued in the exam room.

"Call me before you go back to the apartment," Dan said to Austin and Cathy, as the police led Zoe away to put her in the squad car outside to take her to jail. She walked down the hall with her head held high and an icy, angry look on her face. She looked crazy and like a person Austin didn't even know. Her plan to show off by "saving" Jaime had gone awry and she had tried to kill their child. Austin stared after her with a mixture of sorrow, hatred, and disbelief. "The police have to go in before you do, and collect evidence. It's a crime scene," Dan explained and Austin nodded. He wasn't going to leave Jaime at the hospital until she was either safe again or dead.

Dan left them alone then, and Austin and Cathy waited until the medical team was satisfied that Jaime was stable, and then they let them go in to see her. She still appeared to be in a coma, but was actually heavily sedated. They had pumped her stomach too to get rid of the honey cake.

Cathy and Austin sat with her, Cathy offered to leave and he asked her not to. He didn't want to be alone.

"You saved her life. Thank God you dropped by," Austin said in a whisper.

"I don't know why I did. I just wanted to say hi. The hand of fate, or of God. Something." She wiped tears off her cheeks, and they sat looking at Jaime, so tiny on the bed, but she was breathing on her own.

Jaime opened her eyes finally at midnight, and looked sleepy but she recognized them both. Cathy hadn't left yet. She and Austin had sat in silence side by side all night, watching Jaime. Dan Knoll had called repeatedly to see how she was. And Austin had called his parents and told them what happened. They both cried for what he and Jaime had gone through. Constance wasn't surprised.

"Where's Mommy?" Jaime asked them. "We were going to have a party. Mommy bought me a pink cake. And then Cathy came, and I had some, and I think I fell asleep."

"I know, baby," Austin said, and didn't answer her question about Zoe. He didn't want to lie or tell the truth. How did you tell a three-and-a-half-year-old that her mother tried to kill her and was in jail?

"Try and sleep some more," Cathy said softly, and stroked her hair. Jaime drifted off again, and they left the room for a few minutes to talk. "What are you going to tell her?" she asked him and he shook his head.

"I have no idea. I don't even know what to tell myself yet. What are they going to do to Zoe?" He looked overwhelmed by everything that had happened.

"They may put her in a psych hospital for an evaluation, to see if she's competent to stand trial. I don't know much about it."

"Neither do I," he said grimly. But they knew Jaime was going to survive now. She was no longer at risk. The danger was over, but so was life as she knew it. Cathy wondered if she would ever see her mother again, or if she would even remember her, if she lost her at three and a half. She had a long life ahead of her, and a father who loved her and would keep her safe from now on.

Dan Knoll came back in the morning with a detective and two policemen. Cathy had gone home the night before, and Austin had spent the night in a chair in Jaime's room and looked it.

They had to go to the apartment with Austin to collect the evidence, and Cathy agreed to meet them there since she had seen what had happened, and the cake, and could identify it. Jaime was still dozing when they left, and Austin told the nurse they'd be back soon.

Austin unlocked the door to the apartment on Charles Street with his keys, and the police walked in. Zoe had taken hers with her in her purse when she was arrested. Cathy looked around as they walked in. It was the same scene they had left eighteen hours before, with Jaime dying. The EpiPen was on the floor after Cathy had used it. One of the two policemen picked it up and placed it in a plastic bag as evidence, and Cathy pointed to the garbage. They lifted the bag out and set it on the floor, cut it up one side, and spread it out. The two slices of cake with the pink icing were there, on the pink paper plates. They put them in a separate plastic bag to send to the lab, and they were all sure what they'd find. Then they dug through what was below it, and found the see-through plastic lid from the supermarket cake box, with no label on it. The paper label was also in the garbage with the list of ingredients on it, with honey right there. The label had been torn off the box and crumpled. The whole story and the convicting evidence were there. They put the lid and label in separate bags, and took the paper party plates and candles too. They found the rest of the cake in a cupboard where Zoe had put it hastily when Cathy rang the bell.

Dan commented that Zoe had no way of getting

acquitted with what she had done, what Cathy had seen, and the evidence that the police had just collected. And if they deemed her competent to stand trial, she was going away for a long time, hopefully for life.

In one fell swoop, Jaime had lost her mother, and Austin his wife. The police spent an hour in the apartment, looking around, photographing some things, but all they needed was the cake, and the list of ingredients on the label from the box. The crux of the matter and proof of Zoe's crime was there.

They all walked out together, and Cathy left them once they were outside. The detective said they would meet with her later to get a statement. She hugged Austin then, and he went back to the hospital where Jaime was eating lunch. She asked him the same question again the moment he walked in.

"Where's Mommy?"

"She had to go to California to see Grampa Brad," was all he could come up with to account for her disappearance. It would explain her absence for a while.

"Is he sick?"

"A little, but he'll be fine." And so was she. Jaime was recovering, and they said he could take her home in a few hours.

"When is she coming back?" Jaime asked, looking worried.

"I don't know," he said quietly. All he knew and was infinitely grateful for was that Jaime was alive. Cathy had saved her life. And he didn't have to protect Jaime from her mother anymore. She was safe at last.

Chapter 18

The next days were a blur for Austin with everything he had to do. He called Brad and Pam, out of respect for them, before he left the hospital. He told them what had happened and that Jaime was going to be okay. Brad cried like a child when Austin told him, trying to understand what had gone wrong. He told Austin he was going to hire a lawyer for Zoe.

"It's nothing against you. It's just what I have to do for my little girl," Brad said. Austin told him where she was, in jail, pending a hearing in thirty days to determine if she was competent to stand trial. Zoe would be sent to a psychiatric hospital in the meantime for evaluation and kept in a locked ward. Her crime was so heinous, trying to kill her own child, that it raised the question of whether she was sane or not. She didn't look it when they'd taken her away. No further hearings were going to happen, and she wouldn't be arraigned until the psychiatric evaluation came back to the court in thirty days. If they decided she was unable to stand trial, she would be committed to a hospital for the criminally insane.

After Austin talked to Brad, Pam got on the phone. She spoke gently to Austin, imagining what he and Jaime had been through.

"I always suspected there was something wrong with her, even when she was a little girl," she said quietly. "I've been telling Brad that for years. We tried to reach out to her, but I think her mom didn't want her to come to see us. There's always been a piece of Zoe missing," she said sadly. "This is going to be very hard on her dad," and on all of them.

"Come and see Jaime if you come to New York. But not right now. I told Jaime that her mom had to go to California to visit you. I said Brad was sick, but not too sick. I'm not sure what else to say to her to account for her mother's disappearance." The truth was too ugly to tell. It was hard enough for the adults to try and understand, let alone a child her age, not yet four.

After he spoke to his own parents, he had messages from his brothers. They wanted to know what they could do to help. They offered to take Jaime, but he wanted to be with her, and keep her at the apartment with him. It was where they both belonged.

He asked Fiona to come in to help him, and explained the situation to her too. She was so shocked she burst into tears. "Imagine if Jaime had died," she said in a choked voice. And she felt sorry for Zoe too. It was impossible to understand someone so sick that they would risk killing their own child to try to "rescue" them, and pretend to be a hero, not the murderer that she almost was. The whole idea was desperate and sick, and twisted beyond belief. It was exactly what Paul Anders had described to Cathy, that usually when women with Munchausen by proxy killed their children, it was because their plan had gotten out of hand. Zoe had thought she could impress everyone and save Jaime in a spectacular way with the epinephrine shot, but there was no way she could have. Jaime's allergy was too severe, even more than Zoe understood.

Cathy had called Paul Anders that morning and told him what had happened. None of it surprised him, but he was sorry for Austin and his child.

They'd already heard that the story was going to be in the press the next day, probably on the front page. Austin was sure that no one at the non-profit would believe it. Not Zoe the saint and fabulous mother, it just couldn't be. She had fooled so many people, even her husband for a long time. Austin felt gullible and foolish and guilty now for not reporting her to CPS sooner, but he hadn't been sure. It seemed so unreal for so long, and at times she was so loving with Jaime that he thought his fears were wrong. In this case, there was a high price to being right.

Cathy called to check on them as soon as they got home. Austin had just given Jaime lunch, and Fiona was due in any minute.

"How are you two doing?" she asked in a tone of concern.

"We're okay," he said, still sounding shell-shocked. "I have to figure out where to go from here, and what to tell Jaime eventually. I can't tell her that her mother is in California forever. Maybe she could write to her from wherever she is." Or maybe it would be better to let go now. He didn't want curiosity gnawing at Jaime later, but he also knew that he could never allow Zoe back into their life. She didn't belong there. It was a privilege someone would have to earn now to come into their home. It wasn't a casual thing, open to anyone who drifted through or wanted to visit. It was a sacred trust people had to deserve. He needed to protect himself and Jaime, so nothing like it ever happened again, and he was sure it never would. He had been blind when he'd married Zoe, and the cracks deep within her had never shown until after Jaime was born, and then everything inside her began to crack and break apart. He saw that now.

He called Zoe's mother too, which was harder than calling Brad. She was a more withdrawn woman, and parts of her were dead, just as parts of Zoe were broken and had been since her sister died. Beth had never been able to give Zoe what she needed, embrace Jaime or reach out to Austin, and now he had to tell her that her other daughter was lost forever. Beth sounded sad but not surprised.

"I always knew something like this would happen one day. I saw it, but I didn't know how to stop it. It was like a train coming at her. There's nothing you can do for her, Austin, there never was. Don't torture yourself. Take care of yourself and have a good life, whatever that is to you."

"I had a good life with Zoe," he said, crying again. "It just fell apart."

"You didn't have the life you thought you did, nor the woman. And it didn't fall apart. Zoe did. Remember that. You're going to be fine and so is Jaime, whatever happens now." He had the feeling that she was saying goodbye, and he and Jaime wouldn't be hearing from her again. Beth couldn't be close to anyone, not even her own daughter, or granddaughter. He wondered if she ever could, even before she lost Rose. Maybe she was colder than Zoe had remembered, since she was so young. Brad had made his mistakes, but he was basically a warm person and he loved his daughter. Austin was sure he would stand behind her now, even if she went to prison. Austin sensed that Brad would do everything he could to get her committed to a hospital instead. It was where she belonged. Austin knew it too.

It was strange. He felt as though he were suddenly widowed, and Zoe and their marriage had died when she had almost killed Jaime. Jaime had survived but nothing else had. Zoe had taken it all down with her, and in an odd way, he felt as though his prison walls had come down. He had been trapped with a woman he didn't trust, even if he loved her. He had been blind for too long.

Dan Knoll and the detective who had gone to Austin's apartment met Cathy at her office that afternoon to take her statement about what had happened the previous day. She told them precisely and simply, about when she'd decided to drop by, coming up to the apartment, seeing Zoe and Jaime, and Jaime having already eaten several bites of a slice of the cake, and how quickly she had reacted, and everything Cathy had done to revive her.

They asked her if she thought what Zoe did was intentional, and she said yes, to a certain extent.

"I think she wanted to make her sick, but not kill her. She wanted to do some kind of spectacular gesture to show Jaime and everyone that she could 'save' her. She was going to pretend she didn't know there was honey in the cake, but of course she did. It was listed on the label she tore off and threw away. She thought she'd get away with it and no one would know she had bought a cake with honey in it. It was a naïve and delusional way to prove she was super-mom and play hero.

"I had told her, and so had the allergist, that allergies of this kind get exponentially worse every time there is an exposure, and even we might not be able to save Jaime next time. I don't think she believed that and she wanted to try it, maybe to show off. It was a sick form of reasoning, and she was willing to risk Jaime's life to do it. I don't think she specifically set out to kill her, but she was willing to take the chance. There's a subtle difference there. I don't believe she wanted a dead child. She wanted one she could rescue and revive against all odds, maybe because she hadn't been able to save her sister as a child, and she was trying to make it come out differently this time. Her pathology made her willing to take the risk. If she'd been alone in the apartment yesterday with Jaime, Jaime would be dead today. I have no doubt of that." Dan nodded as he recorded her. They were going to bring a transcript back for her to sign.

"Is there anything else you remember, Doctor?"

"No, I don't think so. Everything happened very fast, Jaime was unconscious within minutes after I got there, and the paramedics came minutes after that."

"How long do you think you did CPR on her before they arrived?"

"Five or six minutes maybe, seven at most, but

probably more like five. Jaime's heart stopped as soon as she lost consciousness, I kept her going with CPR, but she was technically dead, with no pulse, except what I gave her artificially with the resuscitation."

"Thank you." The detective turned the recorder off and nodded at Dan. He left a few minutes later and said he'd wait for Dan outside. Dan had told the detective before they met with Cathy that he wanted to see her alone for a few minutes at the end.

"I just wanted to thank you for all your cooperation during my investigation. You were incredibly helpful with all the information about Munchausen by proxy. I learned a lot." He smiled at her.

"So did I," she said sadly. "I lost a friend yesterday," she admitted to him.

"You lost her a long time ago, if she ever really was a friend. It's hard to say, but I think you were just a pawn in her game. She was too sick to have friends." It struck Cathy that they all spoke of Zoe as though she was dead, and Austin did too. In some ways, she was. She was just a shell of a body with a twisted mind and no heart.

"I wanted to tell you something else too," he said, hesitating, but he didn't know when he'd see her again, except in court. "I don't usually cross any lines, but I was tempted to this time. You're a remarkable person, and I've met with you in an official capacity. I didn't want to screw that up, but I was hoping to call you when this is all over. That's never happened to me before." She looked embarrassed but touched by what he said. She liked him too, but she wasn't sure she liked him that way. She hadn't thought of it before. "But I realized something yesterday. You're an honorable woman, which I knew before, and I don't think you or Austin Roberts would have betrayed his wife, no matter how twisted and dangerous she was. My guess is that it never even occurred to you. You're both genuinely nice people. I wanted to give you a call, but you already have a family, Cathy, and I don't think you even know it." She looked at him in surprise, unsure what he meant. She didn't ask and he didn't pursue it.

"Let's have lunch sometime when this is all over, after the court case, however that turns out. I know she was your friend, but she tried to kill a child. She belongs in prison, and I doubt they'll let her plead insanity. She knew what she was doing every step of the way. She willingly and knowingly risked Jaime's life. I hope they make her stand trial. She deserves it." It made her heart ache to think about it, but she was angry at Zoe too.

He left a minute later, and she thought about what he'd said, trying to sort it out. It sounded like he had wanted to date her, but decided that it was inappropriate. He was a good guy, and she would like to be friends with him, the way she was with Paul Anders.

She went home after that and tried to unwind after the anguish of the past two days. She thought of Austin and Jaime, but decided they needed time alone together. They'd both been through so much. They all had. She shuddered every time she thought about what might have happened if she hadn't dropped in on Zoe and been there to save Jaime's life.

Chapter 19

The morning of the sanity hearing, Austin dropped Jaime off at school, as he did every day now, not just some of the time. He made breakfast before they left. He burned the pancakes sometimes, but managed the rest okay.

Jaime had turned four, and she'd had a birthday party without her mother, which was sad in theory, but mostly different. She still thought Zoe was in California, and Austin was trying to find ways to tell her the truth. School was getting out soon, and she wanted to go to Santa Barbara to visit her mother. She didn't know that Brad and Pam were in town for Zoe's hearing. The time wasn't right for them to see her anyway. Brad was deeply involved with the lawyer he'd hired for his daughter, and they were optimistic about getting Zoe committed to a psychiatric hospital long term in lieu of prison. The press had covered the story for weeks.

It was shocking to read in the papers and hear on TV. A pillar of the community had tried to kill her child.

Austin hadn't heard from or seen Zoe since she was arrested. He wanted to write her a letter but hadn't yet. He was still adjusting to everything that had happened, trying to understand it, and taking care of Jaime every day when Fiona left.

Austin had arranged to meet his parents and both his brothers just inside the courthouse, and they looked somber as they filed in, reporters crowding around them. Austin and his family sat in the row behind the prosecutor's table, the assistant district attorney was already there with an assistant with a stack of papers on his desk. Cathy arrived a few minutes later, touched Austin's shoulder, and sat behind them, and Dan Knoll slid into a chair next to her.

Austin had already seen a lawyer about a divorce and sole custody. They were going to request termination of Zoe's parental rights, and the lawyer said there would be no problem doing that, but he wanted to wait until after the hearing, and possibly the trial, or until after she pled guilty if she did. He said she'd be a fool to go to trial, given the solid evidence against her, and Cathy as an eyewitness who had seen the whole thing.

Brad and Pam were seated across the aisle behind the defense attorney he had hired for Zoe, and Brad looked old and pale, as Pam sat next to him, holding his hand. Austin acknowledged him, and Brad nodded, but it didn't feel like the right time to go over to him. The tension was too high for all of them as they waited for the judge to step up to the bench.

He arrived a few minutes later, and asked the defense if they had anything to say.

"We're waiting for your ruling on the competency of my client, Your Honor. My client will be here in a moment. She's in custody. We'd like to set bail. Her parents are here. She's not a flight risk." The judge nodded and didn't comment, as Austin realized that Beth hadn't come. She just couldn't do it. She couldn't be there for anyone, not even her only child.

Zoe had called Beth once from jail, and her mother had been harsh with her and pointed out to Zoe that she had lost her child, and Zoe had tried to kill hers. Zoe wanted no contact with her after that.

They brought Zoe in, wearing black slacks and a white blouse. She looked faintly rumpled, her hair was neat, and she had on running shoes. They had her in handcuffs and leg shackles which they removed as she walked into court. Austin was watching her closely and wanted to see some sign of torment or remorse, but she looked calm and controlled, and looked at Austin as though she'd never seen him before. As she whispered to her lawyer, her father touched her shoulder, and Zoe turned and smiled at him. She looked calm, normal, and sane as she did.

The judge asked the state-appointed psychiatrist to take the stand then, which he did, and the bailiff swore him in. A female sheriff stood near Zoe in case she tried to make a run for it. The scene was sobering, and Cathy felt slightly dizzy as she watched.

The assistant district attorney rose from the prosecution table, and approached the expert witness, and asked him to state his credentials. It was a long list of schools and associations, which satisfied the court. And then the judge asked him simply if he felt that Zoe Morgan Roberts was competent to stand trial for the attempted murder of her daughter.

"Yes, I do, Your Honor," he said in a strong clear voice. "We've evaluated the defendant for the past thirty days in a locked psychiatric ward. Three competent psychiatrists have seen her daily, and we all concur. She understands the crime she's accused of, she's fully conscious of what she did. She was fully aware of her daughter's potentially fatal allergy at the time. We could find no reason for her not to stand trial. She is competent to stand trial and face the charges. She understands the gravity of the crime."

"Thank you, Doctor," the judge dismissed him, and addressed both attorneys. "The defendant will be held without bail until the trial. The arraignment is set for a week from tomorrow. There is no more heinous crime than the murder or attempted murder of a child, and even worse, one's own. The defendant will remain in custody." He rapped his gavel hard and left the bench as Zoe stood up and the deputy put the handcuffs and shackles back on. Zoe was expressionless as her father cried, and the lawyer spoke to him in a whisper. Austin stared at Zoe before they led her away. He was in the seat on the aisle, and their eyes met as she stood there.

"I love her more than you ever will," she said coldly, and then let the deputy lead her back to jail with hobbling steps from the leg irons. Even Cathy had tears running down her face. The scene was surreal. Austin left the courtroom with swift strides as the others followed, and they gathered at the top of the courthouse steps. Austin told the reporters he had no comment, then walked down to the sidewalk in silence, as they trailed behind him. It had been a powerful scene.

The Roberts family stood in a tight cluster together, not speaking, but they were satisfied with the result, and Austin hugged Brad and Pam as they walked past to a town car waiting for them at the curb. Neither Brad nor Austin said anything. They didn't need to. They had both lived through their own particular hell, and it wasn't over yet. They still had the trial to get through if she didn't plead guilty. And Brad would have a daughter in prison for the rest of his life. She had injured them all.

Dan left quietly, and Cathy wasn't sure whether to speak to Austin or not, and stayed off to the side, as he spoke to his family for a minute. The outcome had been what they all wanted. Austin was satisfied, but it was a hollow victory. They had hard times ahead. Not just the trial, but the years after. Jaime would grow up without a mother, and one day know that her mother had tried to kill her. It would be a heavy burden to carry, and a mystery she could never solve, as to why. She had seen the dark side of life and of love before she was four years old.

Austin looked past his family then, and saw Cathy. He smiled but his eyes didn't. She had lost a friend, he a wife, and Jaime a mother. Heavy losses.

"Thank you for coming. Do you want to ride with me?" he asked her. The others were talking, and she nodded. He hailed a cab, and he waved at his family, as Cathy slid in, and he got in next to her. He gave the driver the address of Cathy's office. He was going to drop her off and go to work. Somehow life had to start again and become normal.

She could see unshed tears in his eyes as he looked at her and took her hand, and held it. They didn't speak all the way to her office. The one thing they all knew was that whatever happened, Jaime would be safe now. It was all that mattered. Cathy and Austin knew it too, and as they held hands, she remembered what Dan had said to her, that she already had a family and didn't even know it. Austin smiled at her. They had come a long way together, and still had far to go, but they were no longer alone.

About the Author

DANIELLE STEEL has been hailed as one of the world's most popular authors, with almost a billion copies of her novels sold. Her many international bestsellers include **Lost and Found, Blessing in Disguise, Silent Night, Turning Point, Beauchamp Hall, In His Father's Footsteps, The Good Fight, The Cast, Accidental Heroes, Fall from Grace,** and other highly acclaimed novels. She is also the author of **His Bright Light,** the story of her son Nick Traina's life and death; **A Gift of Hope,** a memoir of her work with the homeless; **Pure Joy,** about the dogs she and her family have loved; and the children's books **Pretty Minnie in Paris** and **Pretty Minnie in Hollywood.**

Daniellesteel.com
Facebook.com/DanielleSteelOfficial
Twitter: @daniellesteel